THE SECOND
KOTHAR THE BARBARIAN
MEGAPACK®

This volume collects the last 2 books of the Kothar sword & sorcery series. Included are:

Kothar and the Conjurer's Curse

Kothar and the Wizard Slayer

THE SECOND
KOTHAR THE BARBARIAN MEGAPACK®

GARDNER F. FOX

WILDSIDE PRESS

CONTENTS

KOTHAR AND THE CONJURER'S CURSE 7

KOTHAR AND THE WIZARD SLAYER 101

KOTHAR AND THE CONJURER'S CURSE

CHAPTER ONE

The rider on the grey horse was a mere midge on the vast sea of sand between the city of Kor and Alkarion. The big warhorse walked slowly and with effort, kicking up puffs of sand with its hooves. Like its rider in the mailed shirt, it was worn with exhaustion and its mouth was swollen with thirst.

The man in the high-peaked saddle turned often to stare behind at the dancing sand demons that crept after him, their red eyes glistening with a hunger for human blood that chilled the spine. These were the *yemli,* the spirits of the desert which were dreaded even by the Mongrol horsemen who sometimes rode this way to raid in Phalkar to the north or Makkadonia to the east.

No other than those dreaded Mongrol horsemen and this rider out of the Haunted Lands dared use this corner of the sandy wastes. Bleached skeletons of men and animals along this trackless trail to far Alkarion told of other men at other times who had traveled these pathless sands, and of what had befallen them.

The rider twisted his sword across the high pommel of his saddle, ready to be drawn from its scabbard. His huge hand, tanned by tropic suns and polar winds to the color of soft leather, closed down on the hilt that held a huge red jewel.

He was a giant in stature with a mane of golden hair hanging to his shoulders. Over a cotton hacqueton he wore a shirt of chainmail forged by the artisans of Abathor, great workers in iron and armor. A bearskin kilt hid his upper thighs, heavy with rolling muscles, while leather war boots encased his feet. His eyes stared out from under golden brows, blazing blue with barbaric fury and a sense of utter helplessness.

"By Dwallka and his War-Hammer!" Kothar snarled.

He was tempted to step down off Greyling and test the power of his great blade, Frostfire, against those sand demons. He was not afraid of anything human, but this evidence of witchcraft and sorcery put a coldness down his spine. To his surprise, the *yemli* had kept their distance, but day by day they grew greater in number.

Kothar stood in the leather stirrups and sent his gaze left and right. Aye! They were there on the horizon, like drifting swirls of sand, coming ever nearer. To east and west and south they ringed him in, giving him only the north to know the hoofbeats of his horse.

"As the sheepdog herds his flock," Kothar rumbled.

His hand swung the reins, turning his warhorse northward. He would delay the inevitable for a little while; the love for life beat fiercely in his deep chest. To the north was Phalkar and Alkarion, and while he had hoped to make for Makkadonia and war in that vast land, he would be satisfied with the taverns of Alkarion—and life.

His throat was raw, swollen. Thirst was a kind of madness in him. His tongue was twice its normal size, and his lips were blistered and stinging. The sun was a ball of fire overhead, baking the sands beneath. When Greyling stumbled, he came down out of the saddle and walked beside him, gripping the reins with one hand, his sword hilt with the other.

Twice he fell and picked himself up. The sand devils waited closer than they had been, but not so close as to give him the opportunity to use his sword on them. In something of a stupor he staggered on and on.

Toward sunset he saw the palm trees and made out the glint of dying sunlight on water. The sand demons were herding him toward that oasis. Kothar rasped a curse in his throat and walked where the *yemli* wanted him to walk.

Many times had the barbarian scanned the few parchment maps that showed this section of the Dying Desert. None of those scrolls had ever shown an oasis. From Niemm almost to Alkarion this sandy sea was an eternity of barren emptiness where men died because there was no way to maintain life upon it.

His eyes made out a seated figure on a flat rock, close beside a pool of water that appeared more real at every step. Thanks to Dwallka! Water! These *were* trees above the head of a man who sat there looking at him. Waiting.

It was unreal. It was a fragment out of a daymare, a wish grown to reality. An oasis where no oasis should be; water, where only sand existed; a man without horse or caravan, sitting calmly and staring back at him. He was dreaming all of this, most certainly. The *yemli* had stolen his wits before they destroyed his body.

Yet dream or no—He stumbled the last few feet, ignoring the man, and fell face down in the water. It closed about his head and he felt coolness and soothing moisture. Beside him Greyling dipped a muzzle daintily to drink.

Kothar pulled back out of the water and knelt, crouched over, filling his palms with the liquid sweeter than any wine. He drank sparingly, he did not feast as his parched flesh bade him feast. Enough for now to drink a little and bathe his sunbaked face and lips.

He got to his feet and pulled Greyling from the water. "Easy now, easy now," he said, turning to look at the seated man.

The man inclined his head. "Greetings to Kothar the barbarian."

"Who offers greetings?"

"Merdoramon the magician."

He was a short, plump man clad in an ankle-length silken robe, under which he wore a kalisiris belted with silver balls. A pointed cidaris protected his balding head. His face was as round as a happy child's, beardless and plump from good foods and excellent wines.

"A magician," Kothar shrugged.

He knelt again and drank even deeper, easing his tensed muscles and parched membranes. As he turned from the water, reaching for the leather wineskin that had held water until two days ago, he saw Merdoramon whisk a large kerchief off a platter of meat and bread. There was a flagon of wine within hand reach of the platter.

"Come eat with me, barbarian," invited the magician.

Kothar filled the water skin and hung it on the high-peaked saddle.

"Oats for your horse," said Merdoramon.

A second kerchief covered a canvas bag that was filled with oats. Kothar nodded his thanks and fitted the bag over the horse's head. Then he swung about and strode toward the plump man.

"The price for this food, magician?"

Merdoramon smiled genially as he waved a soft, plump hand. "Eat, eat. We shall discuss price and payment when your belly is filled…and by the way, look yonder."

The desert was empty of the sand demons.

"You sent them," nodded Kothar biting deep, "to bring me here. Very well. I accept it as a grim jest. I am grateful."

Merdoramon said slowly, "I have watched you, Kothar—needing a brave man to carry something for me north into Phalkar. I summoned up the sand demons to fetch you, that I might make my offer."

Broad shoulders shrugged. "I am a sellsword, and have no employment at the moment. What is it I am to carry?"

A plump hand reached into a purse hanging at the belt of silver balls. It lifted out a cube of transparent, yellow amber in which was imprisoned a tongue of blue fire. The fire was alive, burning in some dimensional world at which Kothar could only guess.

"An amulet of awesome powers, barbarian. It must be delivered to Themas Herklar, who is regent in the land of Phalkar."

"A simple matter," Kothar muttered, finishing the last of the food and stretching out a big hand for the wine flagon.

"Not so simple, not so simple," demurred Merdoramon, shaking his head gravely. "The regent has two sorcerers beside him day and night who protect him from other evil influences." The mage chuckled, "They even protect him from good influences, such as this amulet."

"Why are you sending it to him?"

"Because he asked for it. This amulet will protect him from the acts of sorcerers, no matter how evil. Themas Herklar dreads those magicians whose black arts he has used to raise himself to the supreme rulership of Phalkar. They have done wicked things for him, and now Themas Herklar suspects they intend to become king regent in his place."

"Why pick me to carry it?"

Merdoramon chuckled. "I watched as you fought the demon-queen of Kor, man from Cumberia. I have seen and admired your courage, your resourcefulness. You will need all your courage and wits to bring the amulet to Themas Herklar. It is not an easy task I set you."

Kothar stared at the plump man. "You have hired me, Merdoramon. I will be worthy of the hire—but what is that hire? How do you intend to pay me?"

"With your life, Kothar. Deliver the amulet and you shall live. Fail, and you shall die."

The barbarian showed his teeth in a mirthless smile. "Poor pay for a warrior. A man must eat to live and I have few coins in my beltbag."

"Oh, that!" The magician reached once more to his ball-girdle and freed the velvet almoner he carried. He tossed it across the sand at the barbarian who caught it deftly. "Take it. There is no treasure in it such as Afgorkon forbids you to possess while you bear the sword Frostfire, just enough to enable you to eat and drink and mayhap buy a wench or two on the road to Alkarion."

Kothar felt the hardness of the golden dinars inside the purple velvet. They made a satisfactory weight in his palm. This might be no treasure to Merdoramon, but it was a treasure of sorts to a man who sometimes did not know whether he would eat or not when the sun went down. He hefted the bag in his hand and nodded his thanks as he tucked it into the worn leather purse hanging at his swordbelt.

"I will deliver the amulet," he growled.

He turned away, unsaddled Greyling and drew his saddle blanket to the ground, where it would serve to cover him as he slept. The oats bag was empty and the warhorse nuzzled his arm in gratitude. Kothar slapped its grey shoulder and rumbled laughter.

"We are employed again, Greyling. We shall eat well, for a little while, once more."

He turned from the horse, staring about the oasis. The magician was gone, faded out as if he had never existed. Kothar shrugged, seeing no footmarks in the sand but his own and those of his warhorse. The magician had come here by magic and had departed in the same manner.

Kothar lay down and drew the saddle blanket up over his big body. It grew cold on the desert of nights, and the blanket would keep him warm against the cool winds. He slept deeply, but with a hand near the hilt of Frostfire. He did not anticipate attack, but he was always ready for it.

The morning sunlight made a golden pallor on the pool as Kothar went to sip deeply, moments after he opened his eyes. He was surprised to find the oasis remained; he was positive Merdoramon had conjured it up to serve his needs. There were two kerchiefs covering another platter of food and a bag of oats, such as there had been last night.

Kothar dined on the flat stone where the mage had sat. He scanned the desert for signs of the *yemli*, but apparently they were gone as was Merdoramon himself. He drank half the flagon of fresh wine. Merdoramon took good care of his hirelings.

An hour's ride from the oasis, Kothar turned in the saddle to stare back at it. There was only a stretch of empty waste. Where the palm trees had been, where the pool of water had reflected back the morning sunlight, there was dry desert sand. Kothar put his hand to his beltbag, felt the outline of the amber cube that held the blue fire. This, at least, was reality.

Greyling walked on toward Alkarion.

* * * *

Kothar heard a scream as he came into Sfanol.

He reined up his warhorse, leaning his rump against the high cantle to rest his legs, looking down the dusty street that divided the houses and the taverns of this little town. The cobblestones were empty of all life.

Between the edge of the Dying Desert and the great city of Alkarion, there are a number of small villages such as Sfanol, each with public hostelries to service the caravans that travel the southerly routes into Makkadonia and Sybaros. Their few houses seem almost to lean with the wind, bent with years and the usage of unremembered generations, and their tavern signs creak when they sway on chains rusted with the weight of time.

Kothar drew a deep breath. Surely he had not imagined that scream! It had come ripping through the silence, as a girl will scream when attacked.

"Aiiieeee! Have mercy! I am not guilty…"

Kothar growled. He heard the jeers of men and the cruel laughter of women. He toed the horse forward; its hooves made dull thuds on the cobbled street.

Man and rider came around a wooden building into the town square. A fountain gurgled water, and at one side a tall pole had been erected. Against the pole was tied the body of a young woman, little more than a girl, with loose brown hair half veiling a face contorted in fear and abysmal terror.

Men and women were piling underbrush and small logs about the girl's bare feet, carrying them from a nearby wagon. The girl was sobbing, her head down, her long brown hair drooped below her breasts. Her brown dress was half rent from her body and bare skin glinted in the light, revealing swelling, rounded breasts and slim bare legs.

Suddenly her head lifted. Her terror and fright were less than the stark fury of her anger. Boldly, she screamed, "Beasts of hell! Torturers! You know Zoqquanor was a good man. He fed you when—"

A man stepped forward and smashed her mouth. Her head banged into the wooden pole. She strained at her bonds as her blazing eyes raked the faces of the men and women who had paused to listen.

"He fed you when the caravans came not! He caused water to flow in the fountain when it ran dry! He shared his wealth with you in times of need! Yet you—!"

Again the hand clipped her cheek. The burly man who swung it turned to the men and women. "She lies! She is a familiar of the sorcerer! She deserves to die as we have killed Zoqquanor. Burn her as we burned her master, and good times will come again to Sfanol!"

Other voices agreed.

"Burn the witch!"

"We must not suffer her to live!"

"Slay Zoqquanor, slay Stefanya!"

Kothar scowled and lifted his great blade free of its scabbard. His quick wits saw these men plotted to burn the girl alive for what reason he knew not. The townspeople were all piling underbrush at the stake, it was true, but they moved in fear of the shouting men. Nervous, frightened, the townsfolk were under the control of their leaders.

Kothar growled, "Leave the girl be!"

The girl lifted her head, shaking it to free her eyes of her tumbled hair. Her mouth hung open. She breathed faster, and Kothar saw hope dawn in her brown eyes before he glanced at the five men who were turning toward him and putting hands on their swordhilts.

"The girl dies!" one of the men growled. "She is a sorcerers familiar. She served Zoqquanor the wizard."

"I know nothing of Zoqquanor, but the girl goes free!" Kothar snarled. His eyes ran over her sweet shapeliness disclosed by her torn garment, and he grinned. "It would be a waste of wenchhood to burn her."

The five men moved forward, separating slightly, drawing their swords. They planned to attack him from five sides at once. He had fought with such men before, many times since his earliest years in Grondel when men had come out of the sea mists with swords and axes to loot and raven. He felt no fear of their kind, only contempt.

Yet their steel could cut, and he shouted to Greyling. The warhorse surged forward. To left and right Kothar laid his sword and two men went down with cloven skulls erupting blood and brains.

The grey warhorse reared high.

Kothar met a sword swing with the flat of his blade. The steel sprang and sang a metallic war cry. Kothar, turning the edge, driving it downward through flesh and blood into the shoulder of a third man.

As he pulled his steel free, he saw that the other two men were backing away from him, glancing at one another. The fight was gone out of them, having seen how easily this huge man in the mail shirt had slain their companions. They turned their backs and ran.

Kothar dismounted, knelt to clean Frostfire on a garment one of the dead men had worn. All around him the men and women stared, never moving, watching him with emotionless eyes. Their hands still retained bundles of underbrush and twigs to place before the girl tied to the pole, but they merely held them, waiting.

Kothar stood upright. He growled, "The girl goes free!"

A woman said, "We do not want her kind in Sfanol."

"I shall take her with me to Alkarion."

A townsman nodded. "So be it. Take her, then."

The barbarian stepped to the wooden pole, slashed twice with his swords edge. The girl crumpled, her knees giving way as she slid down the pole. The Cumberian moved with the swiftness of a wild animal; his arm encircled her middle and he raised her, holding her upright.

She lifted her face and looked at him. To his surprise, she was even prettier than he had thought when his eyes had first studied her. A straight nose, tipped slightly upward, a mouth like a rich red fruit, a dimpled chin and wide forehead with bright brown eyes glaring back at him—this was Stefanya.

"You heard them. You ride with me, girl."

She did not move for a moment, but her eyes were alive as they ate into his stare with doubt and suspicion. Slowly, she nodded, sighing.

"I ride with you, barbarian. Only take me away from here."

He freed her. She turned and walked to the warhorse. As she walked, she sought to fasten the brown wool tunic about her otherwise naked body. Kothar saw all of her shapely back, faintly tan and smooth, before his eyes halted on a brown splotch to one side of her spine and just above her left buttock.

Then she had the woolen thing fitted more closely about her so that her nakedness was hidden by its folds. She paced to the great warhorse and turned. Her gaze went among the townspeople of Sfanol and showed them her scorn. She could not mount, Kothar saw; her hands held her tunic at front and back, so that it might hide her body.

The barbarian grinned, eying her smooth, dusky flesh. This Stefanya would while away the long hours of the ride to Alkarion. She was a pretty thing with a curved body that showed she was no child. Defiance and outrage glittered in her brown eyes as she faced the people. If she had not needed to hold her garment together, he felt she sure would have hurled herself upon a man or two with clawing fingernails and biting teeth.

He said as he came up to her, "You can ride behind me, girl. And don't worry about those people. They won't harm you."

She spat, "I'm not afraid of them! I was never afraid of them—only of what they meant to do to me. But I shall return—some day! And I shall make them pay for what they did to Zoqquanor."

Kothar lifted easily to the saddle.

He reached down and caught Stefanya by a wrist, hoisting her upward behind him so that she sat with both legs dangling. Instantly, she put both arms about his lean middle and leaned against him so that he felt the impress of her breasts.

"Now they won't see my flesh," she breathed. "Ride, barbarian!"

Kothar smothered a grin and toed the warhorse to a walk and then a canter. He eyed a swinging sign; *Tavern of the Ringing Bell*. They went past it, and the faint breeze carried to his nostrils the smell of nut-brown ale.

He rasped, "I'd hoped to quaff a jack or two of mead, girl. I've been a long time on the desert and water merely quenches thirst, it doesn't put iron into a man's backbone."

"There are other towns between here and Alkarion."

"Aye, but how far?"

She was silent, clinging to him until they came to a fork in the dusty road. Then, when Kothar would have swung the grey northward toward Alkarion, she cried out in remonstrance.

"No! Not that way. To the right!"

"Alkarion lies northward."

"And the great hall where I lived with Zoqquanor is to the east!"

Kothar drew rein. "What do I want with dead Zoqquanor and his great hall? The wizard is dead."

The girl slipped from the horse and dropped to the dusty road. She ignored her torn garment to plant brown fists on her hips and glare up at him.

"Zoqquanor lives!" she snapped. "Otherwise, I'd be dead myself."

Kothar blinked. "Tell me that again, girl."

She walked about in the dust, ignoring the fact that her feet and ankles grew grimy with dirt. She was equally careless of the tunic that was her sole covering so that the barbarian was able to study her flesh with an admiration that might have startled her, had she looked at him.

"There was a spell put on me at birth, Zoqquanor has told me. As long as he lives, I shall live. If he dies, then I shall die."

Kothar scoffed, "A great wizard like that—unable to remove such a spell? Pah, he was no more than a newcomer to necromancy!"

"He is a great magician!" she snapped, turning to scowl blackly up at him.

"Then why didn't he remove the spell?" he jibed.

"Because—Zoqquanor put it on me himself!"

Kothar folded his hands on the tall saddle pommel as he stared down at her. "Now why should he do a thing like that?"

She kicked at the dust with bare toes. "To insure my good behavior— and to prevent my sticking a dagger between his ribs while he slept!"

A bellow of laughter rose from the barbarian as he slapped his thigh with a big hand. "Girl, I like you. By the gods of Thuum, I do. So you'd have killed the magician, would you?"

"Twice over," she nodded angrily. "He treated me like a charwoman, to sweep and clean for him—and sometimes he used me in some of his sorceries." She shuddered at her memories and brushed a hand across her forehead to remove a strand of her long brown hair.

"That is why I must go to him, to put his body somewhere where it will be safe. Nothing must happen to it or I will die. And I have no wish to die, man of the north."

Kothar considered, turning his head to study the forking roads. There were deep forests, here at this cross spot, that extended almost to Alkarion. They went eastward into Makkadonia as well, judging by the maps he had studied. He did not know these roads hereabouts, but he supposed he would not become lost were he to do what Stefanya asked.

"After we dispose of Zoqquanor safely," he growled down at her, "then we will ride on to Alkarion."

She nodded, not looking at him. "Yes. It is a debt I owe you." She turned and her eyes glinted at him, and Kothar could not tell whether there was fleshy promise or lethal glare in their brown depths.

She mounted up behind him and clasped his middle and her soft words in his ear directed him to guide Greyling to the right, along a narrow road between the tall trees. For a mile they moved in silence, with the deep hush of the woods all around them. The road grew small at this point, it was scarcely wide enough for a man to walk, so that twigs and branches slapped their bodies at every step.

They came to the end of the forest in time, and before them spread a vast grasslands. In the distance, smoke was rising from a charred ruin.

"Where Zoqquanor lived," murmured Stefanya.

As they neared that pile of charred timbers and smoke-stained rocks, Kothar saw that at one time this had been a noble dwelling. A roundhouse of grey stone and rock had been built at the back end of the great hall, behind what had been the dais where the dining tables were set. Nothing of this stone building had been destroyed. It loomed above the charred remnants of the great hall as if in defiance of the flames that had come and gone.

Kothar eased the girl to the ground. A moment later he swung down to stand beside her. "There's not much hope of finding a body in this ruin," he pointed out.

"They caught Zoqquanor in the roundhouse. I saw its door burning as they carried me off. I don't know what they did to him, but they didn't kill him. Now let us go and see."

The wooden floor and what was left of the walls still smoldered, powdering underfoot as the barbarian and Stefanya went through the opening where had hung the door into the great hall. Smoke still rose, black and odorous, from the remains. The girl halted and turned her eyes this way and that, remembering the hall as it had been. In her sudden sorrow, she brushed closer to Kothar as if seeking solace from his companionship.

When he put his arm about her shoulders she turned on him, teeth bared and hand up for the slapping. "Not yet, barbarian!" she snarled. "You haven't helped me move Zoqquanor! Until then, don't touch me."

He grinned down at her, rubbing a hand across his cheek where her swinging palm had caught him, "I meant nothing but friendship, girl," he growled. And then he added, "If I wanted you now, I would take you and that would be the end of it."

She faced up to him, straight as a war-arrow, small beside his muscular bulk. Her eyes could read the friendliness in his own; they saw no lust. She shrugged, saying, "I'm sorry. It's just that I've had to fend for myself all my life—Zoqquanor was no help against visiting men-at-arms or an occasional sorcerer. I see every man as I remember them to be."

His big palm clapped her rump, half toppling her off her bare feet. "Then get on with it. I've no desire to spend the night in this ruin. There is evil here. I can't see it—but I sense it."

She nodded and walked ahead of him, placing her feet carefully to avoid a smoldering bit of wood or fallen timber prickly with splinters. Her hips swayed gracefully and she walked as might a courtesan, with flirtation in her every step. Kothar chuckled, following after; the girl was walking temptation to a man, though she did not appear to realize it.

They came to the burned door, half fallen from its iron hinges. With a heave of his hands and mighty shoulders, the barbarian dislodged it and stepped into a small hallway. What remained of a partially burned wooden stairway, that was set into the stone wall with rock dowels, still clung to the western wall of the room. Stefanya brushed past the barbarian, began running up the steps.

She was light compared to his bulk, but even so the burned-out staircase trembled and Kothar was forced to lay a hand on the charred wood to steady it. His eyes followed her slim brown legs up those treads. Then she was hooking a hand on the edge of the upstairs floor and swinging through the opening.

An instant later, she screamed in horror.

CHAPTER TWO

At the same moment, Kothar heard the thumping of heavy feet on the floorboards over his head. They were not the feet of a man, they were too heavy, too ponderous for that. An itch of uneasiness crept along his flesh, making him raise his head and stare hard at the stairwell opening.

"Stefanya? What is it?"

"Shokkoth!" she wailed.

Kothar swung upward. He moved lightly for all his size up those stair treads so that they held his weight, for he rested it an instant only on any step. The charred wood powdered and cracked, but it did not fall, and then his head was at the level of the upper floor.

A living statue stood in the center of this room that had been the necromantic chamber of the wizard Zoqquanor. It was squat and thick, it was of colored stone, it was malignant of feature and gave off a sense of awesome power. As it moved, its stone feet crushed the glass of what had been vials and alembics in this conjuration chamber where Zoqquanor had worked his wizardries. There were pools of acids and unknown liquids spilled upon the floor, as the monstrous statue swung away from an object on a refectory table.

The huge bulk of the living statue had hidden the body of Zoqquanor, Kothar saw as he came up into the room and drew his sword. Stefanya crouched at his right war boot, sobbing softly.

"It is Shokkoth, a demon from some hell that Zoqquanor had summoned up to slay his mortal body before the villagers got to him." She moaned her words, shaking her head back and forth. "Stop him, barbarian—if you would keep me alive!"

Kothar rasped, "Why should the mage order that thing to kill him? It doesn't make sense!"

"The kind of death Shokkoth gives will allow Zoqquanor to go on living, in a sense. After a lapse of time, he will be able to return to his former body, alive and well—though I myself will not!"

The Cumberian hunched his broad, muscular shoulders. He did not like this talk of wizards and demons. It made him uneasy. Yet, he knew that to save the girl, he would do his best to slay this Shokkoth. Frostfire held out before him, he advanced upon the monster being.

He leaped, steel swinging in an arc.

His blade rang on a stone neck, bounced off. Kothar jerked to a stab of pain as his steel met that stone throat. The shock of contact sent a spasm of agony up his sword arm. Shokkoth turned from the comatose body of the sorcerer, aiming a great stone arm at the barbarian.

Kothar ducked and lunged. His swordpoint hit the statue a little above its middle. The blade bent, making a strange singing sound. The being swung its arm again, hit the blade and sent it flying through the air out of Kothar's hand.

The barbarian crouched on bent knees, staring up at this awesome thing on which even the steel of Frostfire had no effect. There was no change in the malign stone face as the body moved toward the barbarian.

Slowly the Cumberian backed away from the oncoming monster. His war boots crunched glass and splashed in puddles of acids and serums. So, too, did the statue's feet as it pursued him slowly but inexorably across the floor of the circular room. Kothar's eyes went this way and that as the barbarian sought for some weapon with which to defeat this demoniac evocation.

He saw nothing that might aid him. Against a rounded wall of the chamber, Stefanya wept and moaned as if in acknowledgment of his helplessness, even as Kothar discovered an iron tripod on which had rested a glass container. His big hands went out, raised and swung the tripod, brought it down across the stone head of the squat statue. The iron bent to that frightful blow, but the thing called Shokkoth merely laughed and jeered in a croaking voice that resembled the language of frogs.

"Foolish mortal! Nothing can harm Shokkoth of the Red Spheres!"

"I shall," Kothar panted, not knowing how.

Even more he retreated before those jarring footsteps that splashed the acids and ground the vials that had contained them into powder. The townspeople who had burned the dwelling of the wizard had ravened here, breaking all they could lay hands on. They had tried to slay the wizard, but some necromantic spell had protected Zoqquanor and left him in that frozen state, not alive and not dead.

As he retreated before the juggernaut, Kothar found himself slipping on more than puddles of acids. He glanced down, saw that grains of sand were mixed in with those liquids. At first he did not understand what it was he was seeing; he went back and back, grateful that the circular room held no corners in which Shokkoth might trap him and close those rock hands about his windpipe.

The statue-being rumbled laughter and planted his feet on either side of the open trapdoor, straddling it like a colossus. Where his stone eyes were, Kothar could see faint white flashes of light, deep inside. The deep, croaking voice mocked him, telling him that Shokkoth might stand here until, weakened by lack of food and water, Kothar must fall, unable to prevent himself from being killed. The barbarian realized this; so, too, did Stefanya.

"What can we do?" she wailed.

Again that sand ground under his war boots as Kothar moved. He growled, "There must be a way!"

He saw Frostfire on the floor, bent to pick it up. Armed once more, but knowing how useless was his steel against the statue, he stood and panted, staring at Shokkoth who looked back at him with flashing white eyes.

Up and down that rock body the barbarian ran his gaze.

And, suddenly—

He started in excitement. Where its feet had been set into those liquid pools, some of the stone had dissolved. The conjuring acids and mixtures of the wizard were potent, filled with sorcerous spells and ultramundane necromancies.

Against cold steel, Shokkoth was invulnerable!

But against those serums on the floor, the rock structure of his body was weak! Kothar bellowed, "Gods of Thuum! There is a way!"

Desperately, his stare went about the room. The villagers had left little in their frightened fury; the room was a shambles of shattered containers and alembics. Yet they must have missed something. Something!

Closets had been built into one wall. Some of those closet doors were open, showing empty shelves. Kothar leaped toward the closed shutters, yanking them wide.

Inside one were curiously shaped retorts and crucibles. Each of these held elixirs and draughts. His big hands went out, grasping at those cruets. He whirled and showed his teeth in a mirthless grin. His right arm went back.

A flagon filled with reddish liquid flew through the air. It hit the face of the statue-being. It shattered, splashing its contents across that rock face, covering forehead, eyes and nose.

For a moment Shokkoth did not react.

Then its stone arms went up, its stone fingers spread apart to cover that marred face. A cry of inhuman agony ripped upward through its stone throat.

"Aaaaaaaggghhh!" Stefanya shrieked happily in answer to that scream.

"Barbarian—you've won! You've destroyed Shokkoth!"

The acids were steaming on that crumbling rock head, little tendrils of grey mist rose upward toward the vaulted roof. The statue shuddered and howled in the terrible agony of lost eyes and nose, and between the interstices of its fingers, Kothar could see where those malefic liquids were eating into its brain. What was left of its mouth opened, releasing an ear-shattering wail of pain.

Shokkoth took two steps forward and fell. The shock of its impact on the wooden floorboards almost tore them loose from their rock moorings. The girl was on her feet now, staring with wide brown eyes. Slowly, she crept across the floor toward Kothar, putting her hand in his big one.

"I never thought anything could harm him. Who are you, that you knew that one simple way?"

The Cumberian grinned. "I'm Kothar out of Grondel Bay to the far north. I'm a sellsword, girl—and you've hired me for a little while."

"I have no money," she breathed.

His grin was disarming. "I'll take my reward when the time comes." His hand clapped her buttock, making her yelp. "Now let's go look at that magician of yours."

Zoqquanor lay mute and white, as if frozen to the frigidity of polar snows. His graying hair was tousled on his large head, his eyelids were closed over big eyeballs. There was a peaceful expression on his face, as if he dreamed of faraway places and pleasant things. He lay on a long refectory table, one which he had used for scores of years to hold crucibles and retorts, but which had been swept clean of everything but his body, which was clad in a simple white chiton.

The barbarian touched Zoqquanor's cold arm, grimacing.

"The man's dead. His chest does not move, and his nostrils give off no sign of breath." Kothar lifted Frostfire, held its bright blade near the magician's nostrils. "You see? No mist on the steel. You've made a mistake, Stefanya."

She shook her head stubbornly. "There's no mistake. He's alive, but in a deep trance brought on by the same conjuration that fetched Shokkoth here. Zoqquanor has told me of the spell a number of times."

Kothar sighed. "Well, if you want his corpse as a companion, I'll indulge your whim but—by the ten red toenails of titian-haired Hastarth!—when he begins to stink, we leave him!"

He put his big hands to the body and heaved upward, lifting it easily to one wide shoulder. Like a log the wizard lay, unmoving, stiff unto death in his rigidity of arm and leg and body. Kothar waved the girl to precede him, which she did after gingerly stepping over what remained of the statue on the floor.

Stefanya had to turn on the stairs and lend a hand to keep the body from touching the sides of the trapdoor as Kothar came down with it. Then, once his war booted feet were planted firmly on the steps, he shouldered the corpse once more.

As they came out into the twilight of the day, with the setting sun no more than a faint redness to the west, Kothar shook his head and grunted. "I don't know how were going to carry this thing. I have one horse."

"We aren't going to leave it," the girl flared.

"I could make a travois."

"Then make one."

"Tomorrow, girl, not now."

Stefanya glowered at him, fists on hips. Her head jerked toward the stone keep out of which they had taken the body of the wizard. "Do you want to stay here this night? Do you want to face other demons whom Zoqquanor may have summoned up to protect him if Shokkoth failed?"

Kothar rubbed his jaw thoughtfully. The girl made sense, of a sort. He stared down at the rigid white body at his feet, wishing he might pour acids over it as he had splashed acids over Shokkoth.

Stefanya swung her hips as she strode back and forth. "We can be well on our way within two hours' time. There is a place I know, not far away, where a forest glade can shelter us and I can cook a meal."

"A meal? You make it sound tempting, girl."

She ran from him toward the burned timbers still projecting upward from the ground. Into the ruin on the great hall she went, toward what used to be the buttery when she and Zoqquanor lived here. She fumbled for a while, throwing things, and then Kothar saw her rise to her feet and run for a small hill with a wooden door set into its slope.

She returned from the hill with her arms filled with meats and round bread loafs, and big wedges of uncut cheese. Her dusky face was flushed triumphantly.

"The springhouse keeps these things fresh. And the townsfolk never thought of it, nor of the food it might hold."

Kothar ran his dagger across one of the cheeses, cutting off a slice for the girl and another for himself. "Eat, then. I've no mind to let my stomach wait two hours for something to digest. It's been a long time for me since breakfast."

He went into the forest and cut two slender saplings, trimmed them of their branches and bade Stefanya find a hide to bind to the poles. Two ends he tied together so that they might hang from Greyling's rump; the other ends would drag, farther apart, on the ground.

When his travois was done, the moon was high in the blue sky and an azure dimness lay upon the world. He swung the body of the magician onto the hide that Stefanya had found in the springhouse and tied it, then swung up into the saddle.

The girl he lifted with his left hand as she swung her right leg up to straddle the croup. Her slender arms came about his middle, holding herself to his bulk.

"Which way, girl?"

"Northward, Kothar, along the forest road."

It was dark in these woods, black with nighttime shadows. The road seemed plain enough, the moonlight showed its narrow ribbon as Greyling plodded patiently with his triple load. The wind through the leaves moaned faintly as if with siren voices as the breezes shared the sweet scents of sleeping flowers and slumbering grasses. The iron horseshoes thudded softly into the dirt and from time to time the walking horse shook its head, making its silver ringbits jingle musically.

Saddle leather creaked beneath his crotch. The warmth of the girl who lay along his back with her arms about his middle and her head resting between his shoulder blades added its inducement to the soft breezes and the dark forests. His eyelids grew heavier as weariness seeped down into his muscles. His head nodded. Soon his chin was resting on his mailed chest and he dozed.

The grey warhorse walked on...

* * * *

An inner sense woke Kothar, made him open his eyes and straighten in the high-peaked saddle. Stefanya still slept, her head a weight on his back. Before them was a vast, wide plain on which high grasses stirred to the wind down from the north, and where a dozen marble columns reared their broken cornices. There were other columns, shattered and half buried in the loam, and beyond them marble blocks, tumbled and eroded by time and rain and wind, telling him that here had been a magnificent structure, once and long ago.

Kothar sighed, remembering what Kylwyrren, who had been court conjurer to Tor Domnus of Urgal, had told him of the age of this, his world. Long eons ago, mankind had gone to the planets surrounding those tiny blue dots in the nighttime heavens called stars, and they had made those planets their many homes.

From time to time a building of those other-men was uncovered in this land of Yarth or half seen beneath the moving salt sea waves, or perhaps buried in the dirt and grasses, as was this marble ruin. Doubtless those men had built it, and left it here as an unwitting testimonial of their existence.

The barbarian shook himself, growling softly. He was becoming a niddering with his poetic fancies! His eyes touched the stars and the moon and he chuckled, realizing how long he and the girl must have slept.

His hand touched the silvery mane of the warhorse. "You've earned your rest, Greyling. We camp here, under the shadows of those columns."

He half turned in the saddle, gathered the limp, sleeping body of the girl into his arms. For an instant he stared down at her, studying her lovely features. She was clad like a gypsy girl in a bit of wool that, being torn, showed the smooth skin of her back and breasts, but there was a kind of nobility about her, despite her crude garb.

Kothar pressed his mouth to her lips. Under his caress her own lips stirred and shared in his caress. She murmured something unintelligible in her slumber and nestled closer to his arms, her head resting on his mailed chest.

"Little gypsy wildcat," he grinned.

Holding her carefully, he got down out of the saddle, spread his cloak on the ground, and wrapped her in it. He unsaddled the horse, let it roam. The travois with the body of the wizard he propped against a broken marble column. Then he rested his spine on a shattered marble block and dozed.

* * * *

The girl woke him, shaking his arm.

"Kothar—look!"

He was awake with the wariness of the barbarian warrior, his hand already on his sword. Her rigid finger caused him to swing his head and stare.

The body of the wizard was glowing with a silver radiance that spread outward like a fine mist into the night. In the silvery mist, the barbarian could make out the bloated, swollen bodies and heads of monstrous dwarfs, hairless and obscene, as they crept toward the frozen body of the sorcerer.

"Dwallka!" rasped Kothar, coming to his feet.

He moved toward the mists, sensing the evil and malefic designs of the hobgobs. They paid him no heed, their bulging blank eyes were fastened on that which was Zoqquanor, and their clawed hands were outstretched as if to shred and rend.

The barbarian bellowed and sprang.

Frostfire glittered as it clove through those silver mists. Little sparkles of brightness ran from point to hilt seconds before the edge buried itself in the skull of one of the bloated beings.

As that dying hobgob shrieked, the others turned their baleful eyes toward the huge barbarian. They chittered and leaped, lifting clawed hands to dig into the blue eyes that glared down at them.

Back and forth went Frostfire, like a scythe in the hands of a seasoned farmer cutting down the grain. Bits of flesh and globs of bluish blood flew here and there at the trained hand of the giant swordsman. There was no time for anything but slaying at this moment, the hobgobs were many and they were filled with a wicked will to slay. Claws scraped on his chainmail and bloodied his legs, bare between the bearskin kilt and the furred tops of his war boots.

These bloated beings hurled themselves upon him with utter disregard for the keen steel that stole their lifeblood, that slaughtered where it touched. Their mewlings rose up about his ears as they fell away from the barbarian to die in agonized convulsions on the ground. Back and forth wove Frostfire as it played a death song on their bodies.

Once Stefanya leaped to catch one of the hobgobs as it would have hurled itself on Kothar's back. Her own nails sank into its flesh as she hurled it to the side, where the point of Frostfire could dip deep between its ribs.

She watched, panting, as the Cumberian finished off the last of the dwarfs with a slashing sidestroke. Her flesh was wet and clammy where the mist touched it, and she seemed gifted with supernal vision, as she saw the body of Zoqquanor lying as he might sleep. There was no frozen quality to his flesh inside the mist, it was as warm and soft as her own.

"Dwallka's War-Hammer!" breathed Kothar, shaking himself, bending to run the steel blade into the clean ground, cleansing it. "What were those things?"

"Imps out of hell," muttered the girl. "I've seen Zoqquanor summon them up before times, to work his evil will."

"He called them up to kill him, you think?"

"As he did Shokkoth to gain new life at another time."

She shivered and lost a little of her inner fire as she pressed closer to the giant youth. "If they had killed Zoqquanor—I would have died." Her brown eyes lifted to his face. "Twice now I owe you my life. Perhaps even three times. Shokkoth would have slain me like those men in the market square of Sfanol."

His arm hugged her to him. "But you're alive and safe, and dawn is breaking in the east. It's time to go on toward Alkarion."

She raised her hands to her tumbled brown hair, pushing it back and away from her eyes as she stared around her. The marble columns and the blocks of what had been a great edifice puzzled her. She turned her glance at the horizon, seeing the vast plain to her right and the distant forest to her left.

"Where are we, Kothar?"

He growled, "On the road to Alkarion."

"No." She shook her head. "I have never seen these ruins before, nor this plain. This is not the way to Alkarion."

He scowled down at her. "We were on the road last night. Unless—" He turned his head toward Greyling, who cropped at the lush grasses close beside the base of a broken pillar. "Unless Greyling wandered off on another path while we slept."

Stefanya moved away, knelt to fumble at the straps of worn saddlebags. She turned her head to look at the barbarian.

"I'm hungry, if you aren't. Make me a fire, Kothar. I've meat to roast. We'll eat before we set out."

The morning sun warmed them and the wind off the plain came laden with sweet odors as they feasted, sitting on a long, marble building block. Kothar watched the girl as she hunted in his gear for a needle and some thread with which to repair her single garment.

When she saw him staring, she smiled. "I must do up this tunic of mine, or else watch it fall apart around me. Already the tears are wider than they were yesterday."

She turned her back to him and bent to lift off her wool tunic. Naked she stood a moment, drawing it off over her head, her long brown hair tumbling free. Once again, the eyes of the barbarian were drawn to the dark blotch on her back, just above her left buttock.

Stefanya sat down in the grass, partially hiding her nudity and bent her face above the needle and thread and the garment she was mending. Her action hid the birthmark as well. Kothar sighed and rose to his feet. It was time to be about his own chores.

Greyling was saddled and the travois holding the rigid body of the wizard Zoqquanor was tied to the saddle stirrups when Stefanya rose, satisfied with her needlework, and draped the tunic about her body. She laughed when Kothar glanced at her and she made him a little bow.

She had cunningly altered the styling of the simple garment, putting diagonal pleats in its skirt as well as widening the low vee of her collar. Her high-held head, the brilliance of her sparkling eyes, told Kothar that she knew she was lovely and wanted to be admired.

"You look prettier," he grunted. "Less the hoyden, almost like a fine town lady out for a romp on a feasting day."

She laughed and ran to him, throwing her arms about his neck and pressing her lips to his. His own arms closed around her, lifting her off the ground.

"I like you, Kothar," she laughed when he let her go. "You're like a big, trained bear. I feel safe with you."

He scratched his golden poll, rumbling, "I'm not sure whether I like being told that. It makes me feel stupid. Maybe I ought to throw you down on the ground and enjoy you before—"

Her laughter rang out. She caught his arm and tried to move him with her bare toes planted in the grass, but his huge bulk did not yield. He grinned down at her.

"Not now, Kothar—not now!" she panted, pushing.

He swept her up with an arm and carried her, mock-struggling, toward his warhorse. "You see how easy it would be for me?" he asked.

She nodded, flushing. "Yes, I know. It was mean of me to tease. Perhaps I should alter the tunic again."

His eyes studied her bare legs and arms and the dip of the woolen bodice. "I like you as you are, a little gypsy spitfire without any modesty. It gives my eyes something nice to look at when the sun glare hurts them."

She thrust out her tongue at him and dodged the palm he aimed at her backside. A camaraderie was developing between them, and as Kothar mounted and then swung her up behind him, she begged him to tell her something of himself.

"I know you come from Grondel Bay," she prattled, hugging his middle with her bare arms, "but what did you do after you went away from home? And what was your home like? Did your mother cry when you left her? What was your mother like? I never had a mother that I remember, did you know that? And your father! Was he a kind man?"

"You race on with questions like trout over the bottom stones in a Cumberian stream. How can I answer them as fast as you ask?"

"Try, Kothar," she teased.

"I was a babe cast ashore on Grondel strand in a small boat," he replied. "I never knew my real mother either, only fair-haired Gudrunna who was wife to Elvard Forkbeard, my adoptive father.

"He was a grim, bluff man—hard and resolute, though kind enough, I suppose. When I was twelve, he put me out in the woods in the mid-winter season with only a bearskin wrapping to keep me warm."

"How horrible!" she gasped.

"It is the way of the northland kings to test a male child for fitness. Oh, they trained us well before they gave us to the wilds. I could shoot a bow with the finest of their archers. I was big for my age. I used a sword with better than average skill, even then, with old Svaim for my teacher. Svaim fought in the southland as a mercenary and for some reason he took a liking to me."

"What happened? In the woods in winter, I mean?"

"I killed three wolves to get at their kill, a baby deer. I cooked my fire and roasted the venison and fed well, girl. I found a fallen log and laired there when it snowed."

He chuckled thickly. "To wander is part of my nature, I guess. Most boys sent into those wilds are happy to come home after a night out in the open. Not me! I had always wanted to search those high hills that bordered my home and to which all youngsters were forbidden to go."

Kothar drew breath, eyes wide as he searched his memory for those moments of exultation, with a bow on his back and a small sword at his side, with his bearskin protecting him from the wind and the fire of discovery in his heart. He felt once more the drifting snow as the mountain winds blew it like white crystals through the upper reaches of the hills. The tang of balsam was in his nostrils. Part of the dead deer hung in a sack of its own hide he had made against its carrying.

Aye, by Dwallka of the War-Hammer! Those had been glorious days, when his boyish strength was still untested and the world was his oyster for the opening.

Something shook his lean waist, bringing him back to the present. He patted Stefanya's arms where they rocked him.

"I went up onto the mountaintops. I looked to the south where there were no snows, and I thought that some day I would go to the southlands and become a great warrior, wealthy with gold and renown. Pah! It was the dream of a child.

"And yet—

"It was on the mountain that I met the priestess."

He could see her before him even now, her long black hair blowing in the wind about her lovely white face, her supple body swaying to those borean blasts, wrapped in the pelt of a gigantic bear. She was standing, watching him with calm grey eyes as he came striding up the rock path where no youngling had ever walked before.

She was the most beautiful woman he had ever seen.

He had gawked at her with his young eyes, and perhaps she read the admiration in them for she laughed suddenly, a rippling torrent of delight, and she held out her hands to him. They were warm, those hands, despite the fact that they were not covered, and when she spoke, her voice made his heart sing.

"Never before has such a youthful warrior come to me. Now what is your name, and where are you from?"

He told her, walking easily beside her, knowing that even at this early age he was almost as tall as she. She listened with head bent slightly so as not to miss a word, and he understood also that she listened with amusement mixed with admiration of a sort.

"So you came where Ursla lives, just because you were curious? It's a deed not many boys your age would attempt."

They were at her dwelling place, a rather large hut of hewn logs with a pointed roof and two stone chimneys at either end. There were fires lighted in those hearths that shed a heady warmth, so that the young Kothar gladly let drop his bearskin wrapping and stamped about the hearth stones until his skin was flushed with throbbing blood.

Ursla said, "You shall dine with me, young one. And we shall drink a toast in southern wines to your courage." Her grey eyes twinkled as she unfastened a brooch from the scarf at her soft white throat. "And this you shall take back with you to show to grumpy Elvard Forkbeard, your foster father, that he may know what a brave young bull he has raised for protection in his old age."

They ate of tender venison and vegetables, seated at an oaken table before one of the fireplaces. Kothar was filled with boyish curiosity.

"I asked as many questions as you do, girl," he chuckled, reliving those moments in the telling. "I wondered who she was, why she lived alone this high in the hills, and why she had no husband. I was very young and stupid in those days."

She had smiled at him tenderly, staring across the emptied food platters at his intent young face. "I am a priestess of the wild, young Kothar. There are many of my kind in the world in these days—hidden in the remote places where men come very seldom. My servitors are the bears that live here in these mountains, and the wild eagles and the hawks. Even the snow rabbits come to me, knowing they are safe from man or beast while in my company."

Kothar marveled, for never had any man spoken of this Ursla to him, though Elvard Forkbeard apparently knew her.

Ursla smiled gently. "Men come to me, too, on occasion." She gestured toward the stall bed built against the wall, hung with curtains against the mountain cold.

"Why do men come?" he had asked in his innocence.

Her laughter rang out, rich and melodious. "If you were not so young, I might show you, boy. You're big for your age, however, and handsome in a craggy sort of way—with all that yellow hair hanging down, and your blue eyes...I wonder...

"Perhaps we shall make attempt, later.

"As for now, know you that there are other priestesses such as I, far to the south of these frozen wilds. Some run with the deer in the forests, some with the wolves. Others to the far south have taken command over the tigers and the lions and worship our god with their aid."

"I would not care to live alone like this," Kothar protested, reaching to grasp the leather tankard that held the last of the warming wine she had poured.

"No, you're a barbarian at heart, despite your ancestry."

"Do you know my ancestry?" he asked eagerly. "Elvard Forkbeard has told me how he found me adrift in a boat, but no more."

"There is no more—as yet. You must find your own destiny, young Kothar. And part of that destiny will be interwoven with a priestess of my own kind, to the south. Aye! You shall go south to sell your sword arm. I see it as I see your face."

"And what else?" he whispered.

"War and battle, girls and women to put their arms about you and fit their bodies to your own. But little treasure, because of a sword you shall carry until—"

Ursla broke off and shook her head, her grey eyes enormous and vaguely troubled. "No more, no more. The moment passes for me. Here, have a little more of this rich wine that you seem to like so much."

Young Kothar drank greedily, for this was a potion that made the home-brewed ales and meads of Elvard Forkbeard's steading seem insipid by comparison. The wine put a flush in his cheeks and a warmth in his belly, making him feel older than his years.

Across the table he stared at her and for the first time he looked at a woman with knowledge of her as a female and himself as a male. She read his stare; she laughed softly, almost under her breath.

"Sa ha! Our boy becomes the man, I think."

She rose to her feet, her grey eyes never leaving his face, and she put her hands to the combs in her thick black hair and removed them. She shook her head, her fingers freeing those rich black strands so that they fell below her middle. Her face seemed to glow with its own beauty and young Kothar felt his heart leap and thud and dance in a feverish excitement he had never known.

As Greyling walked beneath his weight, Kothar sat and dreamed until the girl behind him shook him again.

"Well? Well? Did she? Did she?"

"Some things I keep to myself, girl," he growled.

"She did, she did!"

"Girl, be quiet. She was tender and sweet and kind, and I remember her so. Later, when I went back down the mountain, I found them burying me. Aye, by Dwallka! They'd made a little coffin and they were about to burn it, supposing me dead of a wild animal.

"It is considered a test of manhood, that overnight stay in the high hills. The boy who lives and returns is made ready for the weapon training and service as a warrior. He who fails—there are few who fail, they're a hardy breed at Grondel Bay—is given a good funeral and is assumed to have died like a warrior in battle."

Slyly, Stefanya asked, "And the brooch? Did you show it to Elvard Forkbeard? Did it make him believe what happened to you?"

Kothar grinned hugely, his thick chest quaking with silent laughter. He had come strolling down the hill path, swaggering a little, expecting the happy cries and shouts of his mother and father, sisters and brothers.

Instead, he found the skalli empty, mute and deserted. He ran through the woman's quarters, surely expecting to find Gudrunna and her servant girls knitting or stitching as was their custom in this morning time.

He went outside the hall and shouted, hands to his lips. It was then that he saw the brushpile on the distant headland, and the men and women and children standing there about what he suddenly knew to be his empty bier. He shouted mad laughter to the sky and took off at a run, arriving seconds before Elvard Forkbeard could touch blazing torch to the dry underbrush and twigs.

Gudrunna saw him first, and screamed.

Elvard Forkbeard bellowed oaths and ran to greet him. The others were with them, crowding about and marveling at how well he looked. They chorused questions at him asking him if the trolls had wined and dined him, and why he had stayed away so long, almost a week, when most boys came home next morning, glad that their ordeal was at an end?

He jested with them, telling them he enjoyed his own company and the antics of the big black bears of the hills, whom he had made his friends. Elvard Forkbeard looked a little startled at that, with a few of the other men, the hunters and the warriors, and Kothar grinned when he saw them glance at one another.

They feasted well that night, and Kothar was given the seat of honor, to the right of his adoptive father. Not until later, when the women were gone to sleep, did he bring out the brooch and turn it over and over between his fingers.

"Where did you get that, boy?" rasped Elvard Forkbeard, staring.

"From the woman you call Ursla." Elvard Forkbeard glanced over his shoulder nervously, but Gudrunna had retired with her women. The room was dimly lit by flickering torches which were guttering out, one after the other. They were alone on the high seat as his father reached for the brooch.

"You'll not tell me you spent the days with her?"

"And the nights. Ursla bid me say that you should take me with you in the spring when you go south to raid."

"I'll go see her about that," growled Elvard Forkbeard, tucking the brooch into his belt pouch. He considered his young son, head tilted. Then he showed his teeth in a grin and clapped Kothar's shoulder.

"Well done, boy. I'm proud of you," he roared.

And as they rode northward toward Alkarion, the barbarian told Stefanya of his first raid and of the loot he gathered, and of how his father died from a war-arrow in a city on the Salt Sea coast. Kothar had stood alone on the strand and watched his father's crew head homeward with his body for a burning burial.

He himself chose to remain here in the southern lands.

They rode onward, the man and the girl with her arms locked about him, through the morning and the afternoon. Behind them, the body of Zoqquanor shook and trembled to the rocking of the travois.

They made camp near a rock bluff out of which small, stunted trees grew at an angle. Stefanya told Kothar of her life as a child with the wizard, and of her very earliest remembrance.

"I see a street with cobblestones upon it," she murmured, nestling within his arm that held her sheltered from the night cold. "And a glowing torch that shows a wagon and a horse. I see a face, a very lovely face under a spill of ebony hair. This woman is lifting me, handing me to someone."

Her shoulders shrugged. "After that, I recall nothing.

"My next memories concern Zoqquanor and his great hall with the stone keep attached to it where he did his magics. I was very young then, but he taught me to fetch and carry for him, vials and alembics and athanors. He beat me when I dropped one, so that in time I learned to be very careful with his necromantic properties.

"I played very little in my childhood, though I do remember a rag doll that was precious to me, and to which I would whisper of nights when the candles were out and the covers were up over my head."

She stared into the fireflames dreamily, filled with cooked food and red wine from the skin Kothar carried. "I suppose I thought of Zoqquanor as my father. He taught me from hornbooks to read and write, and he hired women to come and train me in certain courtly ways, as if I were a high-born child who might someday live in a palace.

"At least, this is what I told myself when I gave any thought to it at all. Not until years later did it strike me as strange that the wizard should spend good silver coins on educating me. It made no sense to me then, nor does it now."

When her head rested too heavily into his shoulder, the barbarian knew she was asleep. He lowered her to the saddle blanket and folded it over her. His own bearskin cloak he drew out and wrapped about himself.

For three days, Kothar and the girl wandered slowly toward the north and Alkarion. The Cumberian was in no hurry, as he enjoyed the company of the girl and her happy laughter. They were in a remote corner of Phalkar, that might have been Makkadonia for all he knew, since he was lost and there were no landmarks anywhere that he could recognize. There was no need of money and his horn bow brought down a deer or two and any number of big hares when it came time to feed.

Behind them were the rolling grasslands of the plateau onto which they had wandered after leaving the great hall of Zoqquanor. They came to a series of gorges, deep and rocky dales where nothing grew and only bare, grey rock faced the sun that warmed it. Alkarion was somewhere to the north, but what lay to the east or west he could not say. The hoofbeats of the warhorse and the warm arms of the girl about his middle were enough for the barbarian.

Soon the gorges grew deeper and more numerous, and now the ground was sloping upward under the hooves of the grey warhorse. There were high hills about them, and this road that wound between those hills was littered, here and there, with a rusty weapon fallen from some dead hand, and a horse skull off beneath some bushes, and rotted things tossed aside as if discarded.

"The caravans come this way, or did," the barbarian told the girl. "It may be the northway from Phalkar into Makkadonia and Sybaros. And if it is—"

His hand brought Frostfire about in front of him. "There will be robber barons here who may think the magician we carry is a treasure worth the looting."

"Nothing must happen to him, Kothar!"

"Nothing shall. Be at ease, girl."

It was in midmorning of the fifth day of their traveling that the barbarian saw the three men in link mail sitting their horses athwart the road before them. They held lances in their hands and their faces were split with big grins. There was greed in their eyes when they stared at the sword Kothar owned, and lust when they looked at Stefanya.

One of the men shouted, "Stand and pay tribute to Torkal Moh of Raven Garde, who is lord baron of all this Gyrolois gorge country hereabouts."

A second man raised his lance to throw.

CHAPTER THREE

Alone, Kothar would have charged like a mad tiger at those men, ignoring their lances as if they had been no more than splinters. But there was Stefanya to consider, and the comatose body of the mage. With anger flooding his face redly, biting his lip to smother the challenge that rose inside him, he toed Greyling forward.

His hand was about the hilt of Frostfire, in case soft words proved of no avail. He called, "We are simple travelers on our way to Alkarion."

A big man with thick yellow hair showing under his rounded helmet roared, "Fool! You are far off the track to Alkarion, which is to the west. Now disarm yourself and step down off that horse, which catches my eye."

A man growled, "Take the horse, Xenic! I'm for the sword, myself!"

"Well said, Thadrum. I, Richol, choose the wench!"

Kothar rasped to Stefanya. "Slip down, girl. Run into those hills. I can fight them better without you clinging to my back. After I've killed them I'll come hunting for you."

He heard her sob an instant before her arms fell away, and then she was gone. Kothar saw her running out of the corner of his eye as he urged Greyling forward with a softly spoken word. One of the three armed men had seen Stefanya drop from the warhorse, and shouted his worry that she might escape.

The robber called Richol forgot the barbarian. It was a mistake. His spurs sank into his mount's side. The horse lunged forward, head jerking against the stab of pain at his barrel where the spurs scraped bloody furrows. To reach the girl, he must go past the Cumberian.

Greyling thudded into the smaller horse. At the same instant, the blue steel of Frostfire drove deep into link armor. Kothar stood erect in his stirrups and vented the fury of his rage in his awesome swing. Richol made a gurgling gesture, but no more, as his arms flung wide apart while that blade bit deep through mail and leather into living flesh.

Kothar rasped a curse and yanked on his sword, freeing it from the dead body on the galloping horse. The other two men were coming for him at the gallop.

At the same moment, he heard Stefanya scream.

He whirled in the stirrups and saw a horde of armed horsemen coming at a run down the hill up which Stefanya was scrambling. The girl was turning, trying to evade their rash. At the same time, the two men were almost on top of the barbarian.

Kothar flailed with his sword, beating aside one lancehead.

He threw himself sideways in the saddle, but not fast enough. A lance tip scratched a bloody gouge in his bare thigh, slashing the bearskin kaunake that he wore. The barbarian bellowed in pain. He drove sideways with his blade, catching the lancer between jaw and throat. The head leaped from the body even as a sword crashed down against the plate mail that he wore. The blow rammed him forward onto the high pommel of his saddle.

He raised Frostfire and hewed savagely, seeing only enemy faces, ringed with mail or enclosed by the nose-pieces and combs of a dozen helmets. Frostfire was red with blood that flew in all directions. He slew and slew, until his thickly muscled arm ached with the shock of each succeeding blow. Without the girl to worry about, he might have broken free by charging Greyling through the press. But when he decided that he might do her more good free and began his run, half a dozen swords and axes crashed home on him.

Stunned, bleeding, he swayed like a dead weight in his saddle. Voices shouted and bellowed about him. He saw steel flashing and strove to parry it with his own blade. Something crashed into the back of his head. Another something rammed his belly. Blinded by his sweat and the blood—his or others', he could not tell—he was like the rag doll that had been Stefanya's plaything long ago.

Hands tugged him from the kak. He could not resist them. Men pushed him to the ground and the bloody dirt was like a cradle holding his body. Voices were sounds without direction or intonation.

"Gorthol, lord of gods," breathed someone.

"Fifteen dead and more than that with blood wounds—all from one man!"

"Too bad he isn't one of us. I'd relish a sword-companion like that."

"Stake him out. It's Torkal Moh's command."

"Too bad. He's a man worth saving."

Fingers came and stripped away his kilt and war boots, his leather hacqueton and plate mail. Naked but for a cotton loincloth, Kothar found himself tied down with leather thongs to four deep-driven wooden stakes. He felt the rays of the dying sun, the beginning of the cool wind off the hill slopes.

The sky swam lazily in circles to his open eyes. He became aware of pain, of a hot redness running down his thigh and a calf, a weakness in his middle and a thudding ache at the back of his head. He lay there spread-eagled, unable to move a muscle, so tightly were the thongs that held his wrists and ankles stretched.

A face came into view, appearing out of the sky.

A man with long black hair and clad in a red velvet jupon was bending over him. Black eyes stared down coldly into his own, like the flat orbs of a cockatrice or basilisk.

"Barbarian, I am Torkal Moh."

Kothar would have spat, but his throat was too dry, his tongue too swollen. He could make only a croaking sound which made the thin, red lips above him curve into a smile.

"I leave you here for the rats to eat, barbarian. There are many rats in these gorges. They came in the past because we robber barons made of this caravan road a graveyard of rotting corpses. Aye, the rats fed well—and since they clean the road of carrion, we have never bothered them.

"Once in a while, such as now—I find a whimsy in me to punish a man who displeases me. You killed my men this day and wounded others. You shall regret your temerity. Nathvor!"

A man came running, bearing a large jar.

"Cover him well with those slops off our table and smear in a little honey to make the eating more palatable. I should judge a man with your bulk to last a long time, barbarian.

"While I am enjoying that little girl who was your companion, I shall think of your sufferings. I shall try to last until the dawn in my lovemaking, to match the length of time it will take the rats to eat enough of your body to be fatal."

Footsteps went away.

"Water," bellowed Kothar. "Water for love of whatever gods you worship!" Laughter rose up from half a hundred throats.

"Give him water, someone," called a man.

"No—wait!"

Torkal Moh came striding back, carrying a jar and a waterskin. So that Kothar might see, he poured water into the jar and placed it close to the extended left hand of the barbarian. By reaching and stretching his fingers, the Cumberian could not touch it by the matter of an inch.

The robber baron laughed, watching.

"You shall die, barbarian—with that water jug almost within your grasp. It will make your thirst the more torturesome, knowing that. I am pleased that you called for water. It's a refinement I never thought of."

Around him was the creak of saddle leather and the ring of metal as men mounted into their saddles. He heard Stefanya crying out in pain and he bulged his muscles, testing the leather thongs and the stakes that held him to the ground. They did not yield. Deep in his throat Kothar rasped curses, until he realized that any form of speech only tormented his throat the more.

He lay and watched the shadows gather on the highest rocks about him, and saw the bright blue of the sky change slowly to a deep purple. The sun was going down to the west, somewhere in the Salt Sea. He could hear furtive little rustlings and the muscles tensed in his body. He knew the sound rats made when they were coming through the underbrush.

A big, grey rat ran down onto the road and stared at him. Others joined it, waiting. A few came forward to sniff at his huge body that was coated with refuse and dabs of gravy. He would make a fine meal for the rats of the Gyrolois gorges.

One rat could not wait. It scurried forward, crouching to nibble at his leg. Kothar rumbled anger in his throat and felt the sharp teeth of the rodent. He knew it would not be long before the others, crazed by hunger, would scamper to the side of the more adventuresome rat and also begin feasting.

He turned his head to the left, where three fat rats were advancing on him. Waiting with the patience of a wild animal, he steeled himself to the pain the rat teeth soon would be inflicting. Now the other rats were gathering up their courage. They were coming toward him, big and grey, and their hairless tails were poised swiftly, ready for instant flight.

Teeth bit into him. His blood flowed.

Several of the rats leaped onto his chest and began feasting there on the slops that covered him. A few were already fastening teeth in his flesh and tugging.

The three fat rats were very close, almost within reach of his left hand. It would do no good to grab one of them and squeeze the life from it, the others might run away, but they would be back. It would only be delaying the inevitable.

One of the fat rats came to his fingers, sniffing.

Its fellows were devouring the refuse spilled on him. Their teeth were uncaring if they ate a little of him as they finished off the swill before they settled down to eat the man. This was an old story to these rodents, finding a man pegged out naked for the eating. Kothar supposed that the robber barons gave many travelers to these rats. It was an enjoyable way to get rid of prisoners.

His teeth were sunk into his lower lip as the rats ate on. Now they were tearing his flesh, and the pain was fiery, agonizing.

Still, Kothar watched the grey rat beside him.

It was sniffing at his fingers. Satisfied there was no danger from them, the rodent waddled away. Kothar groaned. The thing had been so close. Not quite satisfied, the beast began to circle suspiciously. Its beady little eyes saw the crock of water. It moved toward it, rearing up and sniffing.

"Gaaaghhhh!"

The sound was an outburst of fury from the bound man. The rat leaped, instinctively pushing against the earthenware jug with its forepaws. The carafe toppled, fell and spilled its water.

Kothar closed iron fingers about the lip of the jar. He lifted it, slammed it against the stone of the road. The container shattered.

He held a piece of broken jug between his fingers. Bending those fingers, he found he could bring the sharpened edge of the crock against the thongs that held his left wrist. Sweating, his great frame quivering from the bitings of the feasting rats, he sawed away.

Back and forth went the sharp jug edge.

Up and down, down and up, he worked steadily.

Then he caught the thong at the right spot and it parted with a snap, freeing his arm. The rats felt his huge hand sweep them from his chest as he swung it. Then he was jabbing the shattered chard at the thong holding his right wrist. The rats were scampering off, chittering among themselves.

In a few seconds Kothar stood up. He stared down at his bleeding, refuse-covered body. He was in pain, but the barbarian warrior was used to pain. It hurt him more to think of the loss of Frostfire and Stefanya and Greyling than to dwell on his bleeding body. He turned his shaggy golden head and stared along the road where the robber barons had gone. First he needed to bathe his body and to find something to shelter his skin against the chill blasts that came over the rock gorges on either side of the caravan road. He was weak and needed to strengthen his body.

He began walking, his bare feet making no sound on the roadbed. The night was black about him; in the distance he heard the faint wail of a wolf on the hunt. His lips curved in a grim smile. Weaponless, he would fall easy prey to a wolf pack.

The night was cold. He felt half frozen, but he was used to cold, having been bred in the frozen north-lands.

Once he lifted his head, nostrils quivering.

An animal can smell water. Kothar was not an animal, but there was much wisdom of the wild in him. Ah, there! Beyond that ridge of rocks he could hear the sound a beast makes as it laps. On horseback or walking in boots, he might never have made out that sound. But being barefoot in the stillness of the night, he could hear it. With the sound came a faint drift of the water smell.

He angled his feet off the road and climbed in among the rocks until he stood on the tallest clump of twisted granite and stared down at a forest world where a small pool made little ripples as a deer nosed at it.

Kothar went down the rocks, leaping from one stone to a boulder and then downward onto the smaller rocks at the base. He ran for the pool. The deer caught his scent; it raised its antlered head and stared an instant, then it was off between the trees at a dead run.

The Cumberian hurled himself into the pool, diving deep. The shock of the cold water was numbing, but it took a little of his pain away and washed him clean of the last bits of refuse. He swam back and forth, luxuriating in the coldness of the pool. Just so had been the northland lakes where he learned to swim.

He came out of the water and stood, a great naked man, on a flat shelf of rock that ran down into the mere. His palms slapped away the water from his flesh. Some of his cuts still bled, but he was invigorated, renewed of his barbaric energies.

"I'll need a weapon," he told himself.

He walked through the woods toward the road.

It was not in his nature to hide or skulk, and he walked boldly with his head high. He paused to listen again and again to the hunting cry of a wolf pack, and it seemed to Kothar that the wolves were a little nearer each time he paused. He growled low in his throat, his right hand opening and closing as it itched to feel the hilt of Frostfire.

Kothar began to trot.

And yet the wolves came closer, closer.

He ran swiftly now, as fast as any deer. Though he was not afraid of the wolves—he feared nothing that lived—it was just as well to show a little caution. He came to a long straightaway of road. In the distance he could see more hills, foliaged with pine and balsam trees. He set off at a trot for that distant forest.

A wolf called, ululating and savage, behind him.

Kothar whirled, stood on tensed legs as a big grey wolf came leaping from the rocky gorges, followed by another and another until there were a score of them bounding along on his trail. The barbarian turned his eyes to the side of the road, hoping to see broken bits of rock with which he might defend himself.

This far along the straightaway there were no rocks, only a rolling slope of grassy meadow stretching away into the distance. He worked his long fingers, knowing he must depend on them to preserve his life. Against two wolves or even three, he might do that, just with his bare hands. Against twenty, the task was hopeless.

Still, he did not run. His teeth showed themselves in a savage snarl, and he crouched, waiting for the onslaught. He would die swiftly beneath the fangs and slavering jaws of wolves. It would not be a slow, agonizing death such as that to which Torkal Moh had condemned him.

The first wolf leaped.

Kothar stabbed with his hands, one for a hairy throat, another for a leg. He caught the beast, swung it yelping downward into the red eyes of two other wolves just beginning their own jump. Then the others were around him.

He felt his forearm tear, a leg knew the slash of razor-sharp fangs. His hands gripped two beasts, choked their lives out in his palms.

"Drop them!" a voice cried.

In complete surprise, Kothar opened his hands.

A woman was standing twenty paces away, staring at him. In response to her softly voiced command, the wolves fell away from him and retreated a dozen feet, there to sit and regard him with salivating hunger.

"Who are you?" Kothar rasped.

The woman made a little gesture with her hand. She wore a wolf pelt over her shapely body, which otherwise was clad in cross-gartered leggings and a linen shirt. The head of a wolf was drawn over her head, part of the hood of her wolfskin cape. Under it, Kothar saw black hair piled on her head and spilling downward to her shoulders. Her eyes were green and faintly slanted, and her mouth was large and appeared purple in the night darkness.

"I am Lupalina, the wolf mistress," she declared proudly.

Kothar blinked, remembering those almost forgotten days when he had shared her mountain cabin with Ursla of the bear folk. He ran his fingers through his shaggy yellow mane.

"You probably saved my life," he muttered. "I'm grateful."

Her eyes brooded on him. "You were caught by Torkal Moh and staked out to be eaten by the rats. How did you get away?"

He told her, observing her graceful body and the spear she carried in one hand. Attached to a belt at her middle was a leather sling and a pouch containing stones to be whirled about her head as ammunition. Kothar wondered if she were good at it.

When he was done, she said, "And this girl you speak of, this Stefanya, she was taken by Torkal Moh to his fortress?"

"With my sword, Frostfire. I go to get them both."

Her eyebrows rose mockingly. "Alone? And naked?"

"I can do it," Kothar snarled. "Besides, they took an amulet from me which I am to deliver to the regent of Phalkar."

Her green eyes flickered in something approaching surprise. "What amulet is that? And why to Themas Herklar?"

His great shoulders lifted in a casual shrug. "The whys and wherefores, I never ask. I've been paid to deliver the amulet and—by Dwallka of the War-Hammer—I mean to do it!"

She considered him, standing hipshot with her spear butt resting on the road. "It may be that I can help you, barbarian. At least, I can tend to those wounds of yours so that you can go healthy into Torkal Mohs stronghold."

"I could use a cloak to keep off the wind."

She laughed, head thrown back. "Well said! Come with me, then—to my lair." She turned and whistled up her wolves.

Kothar ran with her across the grassy meadows to one side of the road and through the forest, until they came to a sod hut. A lamp showed yellow through a greased-paper window and from the small chimney, smoke came fluttering.

She opened the wooden door, beckoning him inside. "It is not the sort of place I would choose as a dwelling, but it serves me well enough—while I plan my vengeance."

Kothar strode to the fireplace and stood there, letting the warmth of the flames seep through his flesh. The woman crossed the bare dirt floor to a small wooden chest, threw back the lid. From the garments piled inside, she turned her stare to the barbarian.

"You're big," she commented. "I don't know if I have anything to fit you. Still…here—try these breeks and this cross-gartering, and here's a shirt that may not button on that chest of yours. For greater warmth—this wolfskin cloak."

He dressed before the hearth while Lupalina busied herself beside him, putting meat and vegetables and water into an iron cauldron that she hung on a swinging crane and pushed over the hottest part of the fire. She made bread and placed the loaves inside a baking tin on the brickwork.

Lupalina smiled at him. "There's wine. Fine red Massimia from Makkadonia. I'll pour you a goblet."

They ate at a wooden table before the hearth. The wolf-woman was filled with questions which Kothar answered as best he could, between mouthfuls of the stew and bread. He spoke of Zoqquanor and how the robber barons had dumped his comatose body in a rocky gorge, of pretty Stefanya who believed that if the old magician died, she would also die.

The woman shook her long black hair, freed of the wolf-head covering and glinting brightly in the fire-flames.

"She may be right. Zoqquanor is a great mage, and it would be like him to doom the girl." She hesitated, rolling a bit of bread between her fingertips.

"This Stefanya you mention—has she a birthmark?"

The barbarian stared at her. "Low on her back, just above her buttock."

Her thin black brows rose upward. "You've seen it? You two must have become quite intimate on the road."

He growled, "When I saved her from the mob in Sfanol, they'd all but ripped the clothes from her back."

Her green eyes were narrowed in thought so that her eyelashes were ebon feathers half hiding her curious stare. "I am interested in seeing this girl, Stefanya. I may know of her—from long ago."

She would not answer any of his questions, but merely smiled enigmatically. She promised that on the morrow they would go together to the stone fortress which Torkal Moh used as a base for his raids and forays into Phalkar and Makkadonia.

"You are east of Alkarion by about a hundred miles," she went on, rising and gathering up the wooden platters, empty now of the stew and bread. "If you can recover Stefanya and that sword of yours, with your amulet, I will show you the way to the city ruled by Themas Herklar."

She brought him a bear hide and a blanket. "Sleep before the fire, Kothar. I will be in my bunk bed."

He told himself he would slumber like one of the vampires of Abathor, which are reputed to come forth from their grave-beds only when the smell of fresh blood allures them to the feasting. His eyelids closed, and he dreamed he was in the northland once again, meeting Ursla on the high crags and speaking of Lupalina to her. The bear-woman urged him to reveal to Lupalina that she, Ursla, was a protectress of his in those northern wilds.

In the morning Kothar spoke of Ursla and the wolf-woman listened, nodding her head from time to time.

She was combing her thick black hair as Kothar spoke to her, and braiding it on either side of her head so that the braids fell down almost to her hips.

"I was not always a woman who lived with wolves," she said when he was done. "Years ago, I lived in Alkarion itself." She smiled at his start of surprise. "Aye! In Alkarion of the marble streets, where I was friend and confidante of Themas Herklar."

She paused, frowning.

She went on, "There were two wizards in Alkarion, fellows of mine in the magic we made in the service of the regent." Her green eyes danced as she studied his face. "Yes, yes. I am a sorceress as well as a priestess of the wild things, Kothar. But I no longer practice my necromancies because if I did so, the wizards Thalkalides and Elviriom would know I yet live—they now think me dead."

"If they knew you were alive?"

She put down her comb and swung about to face him. "They would kill me—whom they know as Samandra—to prevent my telling what I know. Thalkalides and Elviriom are very ambitious men. They scheme to rule all Phalkar—after they depose the regent, Themas Herklar."

Kothar grinned coldly. "Then I'd best be off to find Torkal Moh and win back that protective amulet. It seems this regent could use a little help against those sorcerers."

Lupalina threw back her thick black braids as her oval face, tanned by the sun and the winds of this vast moor where she ran with her wolves, broke into a faint smile. For a moment, her green eyes seemed to dream. "I shall go with you, then. For I have a score to pay Thalkalides and Elviriom, and it comes to me that through you I may repay that debt."

She moved gracefully to a wooden rack where she kept her weapons and took down three light throwing spears. About her slim middle she fastened a long dagger, with a curiously wrought handle in the shape of a serpent entwined about the haft, beside her sling and the pouch of stones.

"We shall attack Raven Garde this day," she murmured.

Kothar grinned, "By Dwallka! I like your spirit—if not your wisdom. You—me—and a handful of wolves? What kind of fortress is this Raven Garde?"

"Strong, Kothar. Its stone walls tower to three times the height of a very tall man. It has one gate that is always barred." She bit her lip, frowning. "You may be right. Raven Garde may be too strong for us."

"Then we won't attempt it," he laughed.

Her green eyes showed her puzzlement. Then they blazed with scorn, and she would have opened her mouth to protest when the barbarian lifted a hand.

"Oh, I mean to attack the place. But in my own way."

He buckled his swordbelt about his middle, chuckling at the manner in which his garments all but split in response to the heavy muscles rolling beneath his tanned hide. His body longed for the weight of his mail shirt and leather hacqueton, his upper thighs for the warmth of his bearskin kaunake. He shrugged and heard a seam of the linen shirt tear.

"The sooner I find my own garments, the sooner I'll be at ease. A good fight would leave me all but naked, I think."

Her laughter came with him through the door, and in the morning sunlight she whistled up her wolves who came trotting from the edge of the forest, feral eyes gleaming and red tongues lolling. They were big brutes, grey and bulky, and their fangs were like small ivory swords set in their great jaws.

"They will make good allies," grunted the Cumberian.

He set off at a trot, with the woman elbow to elbow with him and the wolves romping all about them. Kothar lead the pack to the edge of the road and then along it, until the wolf-woman stretched out her hand and caught him by the arm.

"Tell me your plan, barbarian. I will not throw my pack against the stone walls of Raven Garde."

"You need not. This is the only road to Torkal Mohs fortress. Sooner or later, a band of robber barons will come riding. We shall attack them, stripped of the safety of their high walls."

She nodded, showing her teeth in a pleased smile. "Ah! Then you and I, in their garb, will enter the gate. We shall slay and be slain."

"I have no desire to die, Lupalina. I mean to live and reach Alkarion. But in that disguise, I can come within sword-swing of Torkal Moh. This will be enough."

As the sun rose higher into the sky, they took up their positions behind rocks and trees, the wolves sitting silent, sheltered by the underbrush. They were hidden from view of the wall walks of the outlaw fortress, yet they commanded a view of the road for several miles.

The hours dragged, as legend says Time must drag in the haunted halls of Ombremol, where the gods hold congress beneath a starless sky. Twice the wolf-woman was on the verge of giving up, twice Kothar beat her down with words and promises.

"There will be loot in Raven Garde. Gold for your arms and silver combs for that black hair of yours," he breathed. "And magical vials and alembics too, mayhap, by which you can practice your sorceries. Think of Elviriom and Thalkalides and be patient."

The sound came first, a low hum that became the weeping of women and the hopeless groans of men, along the road from the south. A dust cloud appeared on the horizon, and with it the clank of armor and the thudding of horses' hooves. The barbarian straightened his back, leaning against the tree bole behind which he was crouched.

"They come," Lupalina breathed beside him.

"And in great numbers! But why are they moaning so? And who are the women who weep?"

The woman shook her head, her right hand moving its fingers up and down the serpent haft of her long dagger. "We shall know soon enough. They come closer."

Six men in link-mail armor rode big warhorses that clomped slowly along the dusty highway, maintaining this slow pace because a score of men-at-arms in mail shirts and metal caps, trailing lances and with swords hanging at their hips, brought up the rear. Between the horsemen and the men-at-arms were twoscore men and women in chains, with another three-score children wailing and walking beside them.

Lupalina growled in her throat, like a wolf.

"I know those men, those women. They come from a village between here and Thankarol called Tomillur. Those men are peasants, farmers. They pose no threat to the robber barons."

Her forehead wrinkled. "Though now I think on it, I do recall some story of how the serfs have banded together to drive off Torkal Moh's men who come seeking their pretty wives and daughters to take back to Raven Garde for their high revels. And sometimes they take a man as well—for a sacrifice of some sort, it has been whispered.

"I suppose Torkal Moh sent these men out to destroy Tomillur and teach the other peasants a lesson." Her green eyes slid sideways at the big barbarian who towered above her. "Well? Do we still attack? The odds are desperate."

He made no answer other than the angry rumble in his throat. His hand brought out his borrowed sword. "Order your wolves to attack when they see me leap for those horsemen."

Thin eyebrows lifted. "One—against six?"

"Three will be dead before they know what's happening."

"It will be a pleasure to watch you fight, I assure you."

They lowered behind the tree bole and the rock that hid them, and the wolves crouched even lower so that their hairy bellies scraped the soil. On came the little cavalcade, and now Kothar blessed the men and women who cried and moaned for that keening deafened the ears of the men-at-arms to the faint rustlings of bush and twig alongside the road. Beneath him, his thick thighs gathered for the leap; his blue eyes blazed with the lust of battle; his breathing was deep, silent.

Kothar lunged. He made no battle cry, he had no wind to spare for this refinement. He was off the ground and the fingers of his left hand went around the throat of the horseman nearest him even as he leaned across him and smote with his sword edge at the second man, catching him between neck and shoulder with his blade.

The man in his fist raised hands to rear away the iron fingers that choked his windpipe. Kothar yanked free his blade and toppled the man from the saddle, landing atop the struggling robber soldier with his sword blade at his throat. The barbarian tensed his muscles and the sword went through flesh and cartilage.

Instantly, the barbarian was up, flinging himself beneath the barrel of a riderless horse and striking up ward with the point. Into the belly of a third man it went. That man died while Kothar was leaping to parry a slashing blade and driving his steel into a startled face.

The two remaining horsemen were fighting maddened mounts by this time, for there was the smell of wolves all about. The savage beasts dove for the throats of the startled men-at-arms who were too taken by surprise to bring their lances into play. They were down and writhing in the dust, bleeding out their lives as the gaunt grey shapes of their attackers whirled to finish off any man left standing.

One man would have fled to give the alarm at Raven Garde, but Kothar caught him with a big hand and yanked him backward from the saddle. His bloody sword spitted him from backbone to navel with one savage swing.

The barbarian whirled to face the last horseman.

A voice called sweetly, "Leave one, barbarian—to me!"

He saw the wolf-woman at the edge of the road, right arm coming forward, hurling her long dagger. There was a wink of steel and the thin blade drove deep into the throat of the man who was still fighting his panicked horse.

The fight was over, and the men and women in chains were silent, staring at the half-naked man whose clothes flapped about him, with the bloody sword in his hand, and at the woman who walked among the gaunt wolves, quieting them. There was terror in their stares, and a few of them shuffled backward as if they would turn to flee.

Kothar moved toward them. "Who bears the keys to your chains?" he asked. He stooped above a fallen horseman at their direction, lifted an iron key and went among the peasants, setting them free.

A man growled, "Why did you do this?"

Another muttered, "Torkal Moh will burn you alive for it."

"We are going to kill Torkal Moh, you and I," grinned the Cumberian, clapping the serf on a shoulder.

They drew away from him as if he were mad.

One of the women whispered, "Torkal Moh lives in a great fortress. Nobody would dare attack it."

Kothar threw back his head and sniffed. "I smell blood, the blood of dead outlaws. What will Torkal Moh do, think you, when he finds these men of his slain on the high road he considers to be his own?"

"He will come for us again!"

"Aye, by the gods of Thuum! So to prevent that—we shall go to him. Now, now! No need for panic. Four of you men and Lupalina there shall go disguised as horsemen—in the armor of these six we have slain. You others—you men who can use swords—will put on the caps and mail shirts of the dead men-at-arms!"

They began to understand him, and they drew together in dismay, looking from one face to the other. The barbarian read their timidity and would have snarled his scorn, but the wolf-woman was beside him, a hand on his forearm and a smile on her lips.

"It is the only way," she explained gently to the frightened people. "You women who were to be his lemans, the playthings of his men—will you fight for your honor? You men—some of whom are marked for sacrifice to whatever evil god it is that Torkal Moh worships—will surely fight to meet a clean death?"

Their panic gave way to doubt and from doubt their faces changed to a kind of sullen resignation. The men nodded slowly and swung their eyes to the dead bodies sprawled on the roadbed.

"Some of you will stay in your chains," the barbarian said, "so that it will appear we have captives to offer Torkal Moh. The chains will not be fastened securely. You men will snatch up swords when they fall from the robbers' hands and aid in the attack. And remember—you're fighting for your families!"

It took only moments to strip the dead and don their armor. The wolf-woman rode beside Kothar at the head of their little troop, swaying easily to the walking horse; Kothar noticed that she still had her throwing spears in her hand, but that she had added a swordbelt and sword to her armament.

At the bend in the road they saw Raven Garde.

CHAPTER FOUR

A mutter rose and swelled behind him as the peasants saw that pile of stone and rock and the armed men who were mere winks of sunlight on steel caps as they patrolled the sidewalks. Their feet began to drag and their murmurs of sullen dismay broke out into cries of fear.

Kothar turned, putting a hand on the cantle and sweeping them with his glare. "Fools! They've seen you now. It's either go forward to fight—or have them sally out and capture you."

"My wolves are in the bushes, Kothar. Once the fight begins, they'll join us."

"And if any man flinches—have them pull him down," the barbarian snarled. He felt pity for these peasants, but he knew the robber barons. They respected only force and stronger sword arms than their own.

They were thirty men and one woman marching into the stronghold of the fiercest robber baron between the border and Alkarion. There must be a hundred men-at-arms inside Raven Garde, tough fighting-men, every last one. Kothar wished only for one thing: Frostfire. He would have felt more secure with its hilt between his fingers.

The men pacing guard duty on the sidewalks paid no attention to these dusty travelers. They saw the armor of the riders, the weary walking of the men-at-arms. They heard the keening of the women who were chained together. There was no reason to be suspicious. Only a madman would dare Raven Garde with so few swords at his back.

Through the wooden gate they passed without incident, on to an inner courtyard paved with worn, ancient cobblestones. Their horses' hooves struck sparks on the stone, and then they were drawing rein.

The barbarian ran his gaze across stone walls and stairways leading up to solars. The fortress had been built around a square tower that was part of the keep, on which was carved the image of a saurian face of black basalt, stamped with all the lusts and desires known to the race of men. The eyes glinted as though they knew a life of their own. Where the sunlight caught them, for a moment Kothar thought he saw an entity staring down at him; in a moment, that life spark was gone and he saw only the bulging eyes.

He swung a leg over his saddle cantle.

In answer to that signal the disguised peasants gripped their lances and ran at the soldiers lounging in the shadow of the armory, wearing only cotton shirts and breeks. They were unarmed. The lance-heads went into their middles and they died squirming on the cold steel, impaled against the wooden framework of the building.

Two men from the sidewalk shouted.

The wolf-woman was slipping a round stone the size of an egg into her sling-cup. Around her head she whirled those leather thongs, releasing one at the apex of its circling. The stone flew true, thudding into the forehead of a soldier lifting his bow.

Again the sling twirled; a second man died.

Kothar was flinging open the armory door. A dozen men inside the dirt-floored room, polishing armor and sharpening their swords and daggers, gaped at him with bulging eyes. He was across the space that separated them, his sword cleaving the air an instant before burying itself in warm flesh. He ravened like a madman, for of all those who had ridden into Raven Garde he alone was battle-wise enough to understand that not one of this small army of brigands must be left alive to carry on their grim trade.

His blade dipped and darted. He slew coldly, without regret or compassion; to the barbarian, this was a task that must be done. And when he eased the point of his borrowed sword to the ground, so that the drops of blood fell redly to the dirt floor and were absorbed, the muscles in his sword arm ached.

He whirled and sprang for the open door.

His eyes touched his little force, seeing that the peasants disguised as men-at-arms were giving a good account of themselves. They fought like men paid to bring death to other men, and he supposed that, to them, freedom from the tyranny of Torkal Moh was as great a price as anyone had ever paid for mercenaries.

The wolf-woman was running with her beasts along the sidewalks, pulling down any who still lived behind the merlons. The peasants were overtaking a few fleeing men-at-arms and running them through with cold steel.

Then a door swung open from the keep.

Torkal Moh stood there, an amazed look on his face and a sword in his right hand. Kothar grunted when he saw the sword was not his Frostfire. He ran out into the sunlight and let the robber baron look at him.

Torkal Moh opened his eyes wide. "You! By the dweller in the pool—I thought your bones picked clean by this time!"

Kothar ran for the stone steps. Torkal Moh took one look at him, whirled and ran back through the doorway. An instant later the door slammed shut and the barbarian heard the snick of a bolt being shot home.

He paused only to scoop up a war-axe from the fingers of a dead mercenary. He shifted the axe to his right hand, placing the sword back into its scabbard as he took the steps three at a time.

On the stone landing, he swung the axe, drove its edge deep into the door. His huge hand wrenched it free; again he struck; again; again. A voice from inside the chamber shouted at him.

An arrow whizzed through an opening the axe blade had made. The arrowpoint scratched his upper arm as it whizzed past. Kothar lifted a foot, drove his heel into sagging wood; the door burst open.

He dove into the room, barely seeing the hanging drapes, rich arrases from Avalonia and massy wooden furniture carved by master craftsmen. There was a hooded chimney wide enough to hold a horse inside it, in which three great logs were burning. Torkal Moh stood before the fire, body braced, a dagger in his left fist, his sword in his right.

"You die, man!" snarled the robber baron.

Kothar rumbled laughter, advancing lightly as a panther on the prowl. The battle-axe swung loosely as he twirled it, while with his left hand he drew the sword from its scabbard.

"Ho, guards!" bellowed Torkal Moh, leaping aside.

The doors at the far end of the chamber burst inward and eight brawny men-at-arms came racing in. Kothar swung his sword, hitting the blade that Torkal Moh raised in defense; so great was the blow that the robber baron staggered backward, thrown off balance by its savage power. Before he could regain his balance, Kothar was half a room away.

The axe swept the air; the swordpoint stabbed.

Two men were down, and now the clash of steel on steel, the hoarse breathing of men fighting for their lives filled the room. Kothar was never still, he leaped and dodged, he fought these men as he had fought the great white bear of his northern homelands, the mighty Naanaak. Naanaak was as lightning with his massive paws, but Kothar had been faster.

Sword bit deep. Axe drank of blood.

Sword blades swung at his dancing figure, missing, slashing only empty air. As he fought, Kothar growled softly in his throat as Naanaak had been wont to growl at the brawny young boy that dared to hunt it on the ice floes. The sound of that growling put an atavistic terror into the hearts of the men-at-arms who battled to contain this wild animal with a sword and a war-axe in his hands. They would have whirled and fled, but they dared not turn their backs to him.

And then Torkal Moh leaped.

His blade was high, coming downward, when Kothar heard his footfall. Not like the ears of ordinary men were the ears of the barbarian. His hearing was a weapon that he used in hunting and in the savage battles of his barbaric world. He heard that sandal slap the flooring and he threw himself downward, flat upon the ground; in the middle of his fall, he swung the axe behind him.

The edge of the war-axe caught the robber baron just above each knee as it swept through the air. It slashed his legs in half.

Torkal Moh opened his mouth and screamed.

He stood a moment, but he was overbalanced. His body fell forward. Both his legs, cut off where the axe had passed, toppled sideways. A gout of blood ran across the carpeting of the room.

The men-at-arms glared in horror at their dying leader as he writhed and twisted helplessly. They swung about and fled for the door before Kothar could come to his feet.

The barbarian panted, feeling the sweat run down his chest and back. He towered above the fainting outlaw. "My sword, man. Frostfire! And the girl, Stefanya! And that amulet! Where are they?"

Hoarse laughter interrupted him. Blood flowed from the lips of the dying man, but there was a mockery in his voice that bubbled through it.

"The dweller has it, Kothar! It hangs from the gifting tree, as a sacrifice to—to—"

The body on the carpet arched. Torkal Moh cried out. For an instant his body was strutted with every muscle taut; then he went limp. Kothar bent, touched his chest with a palm.

"The dweller in the pool? The gifting tree?" he echoed. "The man was mad."

H searched the room, muttering to himself. There were treasures here: gold and silver, a statue of a woman in polished ebony, a lamp shaped to resemble a Makkadonian war galley, golden chains and loops of pearls. Coffers of rubies, small chests filled with emeralds, loot collected over the years was on display here for the eyes of the robber baron. Kothar passed it by, grunting.

The amulet was nowhere to be found.

He went to the stair landing that looked out over the courtyard and saw the wolf-woman staring up at him, surrounded by her wolves. There was blood spattered on her wolfskin and on her cross-gartered breeks, but it was none of hers.

"The place is ours, Kothar," she called.

"Then command it. I go to find the girl."

He ran back through the chamber where Torkal Moh lay, and through the door beyond. The stone steps of the keep, worn with the long passing of time, knew the touch of his feet as he ran down them. On the next floor he found a woman of the fortress cowering in a corner.

His hand tightened fingers on her arm as he dragged her up to her feet. "The girl Torkal Moh captured yesterday? Where is she?"

"I know not," the woman moaned.

A woman screamed from the courtyard. Kothar grinned and jerked his head. "You hear that? The peasants have won this fight and they're ripe for fun. The men and women they've captured will dance for a few agonized hours under their torture. Do you—"

She fell to her knees. Tears ran down her cheeks. "Not—the torture. I couldn't stand the pain. The girl you seek is in the dungeon. Torkal Moh ordered her chained there—to teach her manners."

The barbarian grunted and shoved her in front of him. "Lead, woman. And play no tricks. My sword can kill again, without regret."

She slipped and stumbled ahead of him, down the sloping stairs that went deep under the keep and past what had been, uncounted centuries before, the cellarways to a forgotten chapel built to honor an evil god. The air was musty, damp, and when the barbarian commented on its foulness, the woman nodded her head.

"Centuries back," she whispered, shivering, "they held certain rites to worship—Pthassiass." Her shoulders moved in a convulsive spasm. "Even today—Torkal Moh honors the foul one. He makes sacrifice to it and heaps the gifting tree with loot from his robberies.

"Where is this gifting tree?"

She turned a wan face. "Beside the pool where the dweller is. But— you aren't going to steal those gifts? Surely not! Pthassiass would prevent it. He will take you as he takes the sacrifices!"

Kothar rasped, "I'd dare a thousand dwellers to get Frostfire back. But where's the girl? What part of these dungeons is she in?"

She ran ahead of him, until she came to a vaulted stone archway that revealed beyond it a stretch of flagging and stone walls in which were set chains and a number of wooden platforms. On the platforms were instruments of torture. The stone walls were wet, and there was a pervasive dampness in this deep cellar that made Kothar growl in revulsion.

His growl grew louder when he saw the body hanging in chains on one wall. All but naked, her long brown hair hanging loose and tangled, Stefanya dangled motionless, eyes closed, extended toes barely touching the flagstones beneath her.

Kothar roared and caught the woman by an arm. He shook her angrily, making her cry out in alarm. "The key! Where is it?"

"On—on the wall yonder," she whimpered.

He was across the room, snatching loose the great key ring. Another leap and he was fitting a key to the manacle locks, turning it. His arm went about the girl, catching her as she dropped.

The chains were off, but still her eyes were closed. Kothar swung her up into his arms. "Go ahead of me, woman. Take me to this gifting tree!"

"I—I dare not," she pleaded.

"Shall I hang you here in her chains?"

The woman gnawed a knuckle, her eyes huge and terrified above her hand. Numbly she nodded, whispering, "No—not that. At night the rats come and—"

She shuddered and turned, running ahead of the barbarian. When she came to a small wooden door she turned and stared back at him. "This is the way, through the—the gardens of the god—to his pool."

"Open it."

Her long, white fingers fumbled at the three thick bolts that held the door shut. They came open, one after the other and her hand pulled back on the massive iron handle. The door creaked inward. Kothar stared at a graveled pathway that wound between strange trees and curious plants and flowers, upward along a hill. The petals of those plants and flowers were pulpy, appearing half rotten, and the stalks on which they nodded were scabrous and covered with bloated white fungi.

The barbarian snorted. "It has the look of a garden of the dead," he muttered, "where the roots are sunk deep into the corpses of men and women."

The sky was different, too. There was no longer the clean blue tints of the welkin beyond the fortress, nor any of the fleecy clouds in it that ran before the winds. This sky was grey, ominous, and instead of clouds there was emptiness, a vague suggestion of—nothingness—beyond the distorted trees and plants and flowers. It was as if the garden had been spawned in the midst of emptiness.

Kothar grumbled, "I like not this place. See how the flowers and the leaves turn toward us—as if they watched where we walked!"

The woman cowered back against him so he could feel the trembling of her body. "Sometimes Torkal Moh put a man or a woman in this garden, as a sacrifice to Pthassiass. Nobody ever saw them again."

His sword was not Frostfire, but the barbarian brought it out into his hand, shifting the inert body of Stefanya to his left shoulder where he clamped a hand on her. When a flower or a plant swayed too close, he used the steel to slash it, leaving a bloated corruption that rotted and decayed even as they walked away from it.

To the Cumberian, it seemed that they strode endlessly along that strangely curving walk. The air about them was thick, oppressive. It grew hard to breathe after a time. An oppression of the spirit lay across this eerie garden, a sickness of the soul. It brought gloom and despair with the nodding of its flower-heads and the swaying of the tree branches where there was no wind.

The woman stumbled many times; only the hand of Kothar at her elbow kept her going. Once she whispered, "This also happens to them, I have been told. The ones Torkal Moh pushed into this garden lose all spirit, all will to live. They just lie down and beg to die—"

"…and the flowers and the plants oblige them?"

She began to sob.

"Silence, woman, you're enough to unnerve a statue!" the barbarian snarled. His own nerves were raw and open, he found. Whether it might be a gaseousness which the bloated flowers and the scabrous plants emitted that so upset his system, he did not know, but he would have given much to be safe out of this miasma and on his way to Alkarion.

They came to the crest of the hill at last, and from its crown Kothar stared down at a lake of silvery waters gleaming dully beneath the leaden sky. All around that lake were trees which were white in color, as were their leaves, drained of everything that was normal to all trees. The gravel path curved downward to a little beach where the mere-waters lapped softly and insistently.

To one side of this shelving was a tall, gaunt tree of many branches, but no leaves. Instead of leaves there hung from the gifting tree a profusion of objects, some great and some small, though all were precious. A white vine had twisted itself about the bole of the white tree and dripped downward toward the ground so that the gifting tree seemed festooned with silver.

"Gods of Thuum!" breathed Kothar, almost letting go his grip on Stefanya.

The gifting tree held the treasures of the ages.

First he saw Frostfire, its red jewel glittering as if with inner flames, and from this his eyes went to a necklace of giant green emeralds, each gem of which was worth a small kingdom. Golden chains were draped about the tree limbs, and on each twig had been placed rings holding red rubies, flawless diamonds, rare sapphires and emeralds. Chests and coffers were filled with overspilling golden chains and ingots, silver bars and nuggets lay in vast profusion about the base. This was the wealth of a world, gathered here on this great tree.

"Torkal Moh and his father and his father before him made a covenant with Pthassiass, who dwells in the silver lake. They agreed to heap this tree high with their most precious possessions and send human sacrifices to the garden on which Pthassiass feeds in some strange manner, if the beast-god would guard that treasure.

"In such a way, Torkal Moh and his robber baron ancestors knew that no matter where they rode, their treasures would be safe from attack."

Kothar stepped forward, walking on spilled coins and fallen ingots until he stood below the branch where Frostfire hung. He stretched out a hand, touched the scabbard, lifted it and the swordbelt free of the branch that held it.

The woman at his back whimpered.

Kothar looked where she pointed. The smooth, glassy surface of the mere was disturbed by some titanic something just below its surface.

"Pthassiass comes," she breathed.

The barbarian growled and let his eyes run over the tree. His hand darted out, found the amulet given by Merdoramon at the oasis he had conjured up in the Dying Desert. He slipped its chain about his neck. Then, with the rash impulse of his barbaric nature, that must taunt and mock a dangerous opponent, he selected the great necklace of emeralds and a dozen rings from the tree-twigs.

He hung the necklace about Stefanya's throat. On her limp fingers he pushed rings until her fingers seemed to be all jewels. His blue eyes glanced at the frightened woman from the fortress.

He undid a golden chain, tossed it to her. "This—to help you build a new life, woman."

She almost collapsed under its weight. Her hands closed around its huge links to which they clung convulsively. Back and forth went her head as she moaned, "It will come to stop us. Pthassiass will come. And Pthassiass will kill us."

Kothar undid the belt at his middle, placing the limp Stefanya on the gravel for better ease of movement. About his middle he placed his swordbelt and shifted Frostfire in front of him. His eyes roved the surface of the silver lake all this time, and he saw that the ripples in the water were growing larger.

"It comes," whimpered the woman.

Upward from the unplumbed depths of the silver lake rose a head almost as big as a house. One glittering eye stared balefully at the man and the two women on the shore. A forked tongue ran from gaping lips where great fangs gleamed, outward into the air. From its huge snout dangled thick tendrils of flesh, tinted purple, and down the long neck fluttered a crest of that same purplish tissue.

Seemingly without movement, the thing moved toward the shore.

Kothar bent and lifted the sword he had carried through the battle in the fortress. He hefted it, gauging its weight and the distance between the beast-thing and himself. He waited, crouching slightly, watching the progress of the water-demon as it moved toward the shore.

The woman moaned and collapsed, falling unconscious on the graveled path. At his feet Stefanya never stirred. Kothar ignored them, putting them from his mind as if they did not exist. He would need all his power to prevent that thing from swallowing them all.

More and more of the lake-demon was emerging from the silver waters. Its bulk was titanic, nearly as huge as the entire fortress! How deep that lake must be to accommodate such a being as this! Perhaps there was a subterranean sea beneath the fortress, and this was where the lake-god roamed.

The vast head was stretching outward across the water toward the shore. It cast a shadow on the gravely path and that shadow was over Kothar, broadening as the thick head lowered.

The barbarian hurled his spare sword upward. The steel made a grey glinting in the grey air, speeding point-first toward the single eye of the sea-beast.

Pthassiass saw that blade, but its nerve controls were so sluggish it took time to move its head out of the way. The point of the sword burned itself in a corner of that single eye and the demon-beast bellowed in agony, threshing its long neck here and there, attempting to rid itself of that steel sliver.

And now Kothar noticed a curious thing.

Where the shadow of the sea-beast fell on the bloated plants and flowers and the scabrous trees, those strange life organisms quivered and shook. They raised petals and pistils, leaves and stalks upward toward the writhing neck and the huge head above them as if they would fasten leechlike pores on that slug-like thing and drink its blood.

Pthassiass knew this; its contortions became less maddened. It withdrew its head and neck back over the silver waters and there it convulsed and twisted itself about in its frantic attempts to dislodge that sword that caused it so much pain. Against the silver water it slapped its head, it brought out a great flipper from the silver lake and attempted to reach the sword with it. It lifted its head, blood oozing from its wounded eye and shook its head to free it from its neck.

Kothar did not wait. He grabbed up Stefanya, threw her over a shoulder. He lifted the woman into the crook of his arm and ran lightly up the gravel path toward the distant wooden door.

Once he turned his head to stare back at the agonized sea-demon. It had dug part of the sword from its flesh. In a moment or two the blade must fall to splash into the lake. Then the sea-slag would be stretching out its neck and its great jaws would be gaping to engulf them all. Kothar ran faster toward the door.

When he was within twenty feet of that wooden barrier, he let the woman and the girl slip from his grasp. They lay inert on the gravel path as if dead. Kothar whirled and yanked out Frostfire.

The sea-beast was coming, moving through the water, pushing its head on its long neck outward over the wide graveled path. Blood dripped from its wounded eye, but it could still see. Venom foamed on its forked tongue and spattered the gravel from its gaping jaw where the sharp fangs gleamed.

Kothar breathed, "Dwallka—aid me!"

He ran forward into the shadow of the vast head and great neck until its dimness was all about him. The lake-demon had come in low with its jaw, its bulk was too vast to permit it to move on the graveled walkway, broad as it was. But its long neck could reach as far as the wooden door, and it knew its victims dared not leave the sanctuary of the path.

A drop of venom fell on his arm and stung, but the barbarian was past the head now and the neck was like a titanic black canopy over his head. His fingers opened and closed on Frostfire's hilt. One glance he risked behind him and what he saw made him cry out sharply.

Pthassiass was bent above the inert women, its jaws wide and about to engulf their soft bodies. "I will be too late," the Cumberian thought, and hurled himself forward. His feet flew so that he barely touched the path across which he ran.

The neck was before him, not scaled but of a tough, leathery substance. His arm went back and his blade drove forward in a slashing cut. Deep into that leathery hide and soft blubbery flesh and oozing purplish blood sank his steel.

A bellow shook the garden.

Pthassiass was writhing upward with its neck, attempting to pull it out of reach of the sword that nibbled at its throat, beside the edge of the silver lake where Kothar swung Frostfire like a man demented. Around and about, as if he wove a figure eight with steel, he slashed and stabbed until his body was almost covered with the purple ichor that passed for demon-blood.

And Pthassiass went mad.

Its prey still lay inert on the pathway gravel, but the man just beneath the base of its long throat was slicing that neck to ribbons of bloody flesh. Upward Pthassiass jerked its huge head and became like a flower waving in a gale, its neck jerking and swaying as the sea-thing sought to get back within the silver lake. In its agony, the creature forgot the flowers and the plants and the trees on either side of the broad gravel walk.

Its head swung low above those bloated vegetations as their leaves and petals rose upward toward that thick black throat. The plants and flowers fastened gripping suckers on the bloody throat and they drew it downward.

The sea-demon screamed like a woman in torment.

It was caught, held fast as more and more of the growths fastened leech-like petals and leaves onto its bulk. For a few seconds, as Kothar watched with Frostfire in a hand and the purple ichor dripping from its blade onto the gravel, a tugging war went on between the beast and the living plants. Slowly, slowly, the grip of the vegetation strengthened, perhaps because of the purple ichor they were drinking. Downward drooped the vast head, until the trees could fasten their leafy limbs about it and drag it down even further.

A wail burst from the sea-demon.

Its titanic bulk shuddered, sending waves up onto the shore of the silver lake. Kothar ran back along the gravel path, seeing Stefanya and the woman sitting up and staring in horror at the struggle of the dying beast.

"What is it?" Stefanya wailed.

And the woman answered her, "A thing placed here long ago by some forgotten cataclysm of nature, and hemmed in by the vegetation about the silver lake by a long-dead wizard, whose garden this once was. To punish those who offended him, the wizard made the gravel walk so that his victims died either by plunging into those plants and flowers to escape Pthassiass—or by being swallowed by the god himself."

The woman shuddered. "To control Pthassiass, so that he did not emerge and attack the wizard himself, those plants and flowers were put about the lake. Fenced in this way, Pthassiass became content to roam his silver lake and feed on those whom Akthan the wizard fed to him.

"When Akthan became old, he allied himself with the great-great-grandfather of Torkal Moh, inviting him into his little castle, which was enlarged into this present-day fortress. Their enemies they fed to Pthassiass and their stolen treasures they set upon the gifting tree, that the sea-demon might guard them.

"Now his guardianship is ended."

The head and throat of that which had been Pthassiass lay gently shuddering as the vegetation fed upon it. The feasting would take a long time, there was much purple blood in the body of the fearsome sea-thing. Kothar rasped a curse and put a hand to Stefanya, yanking her to her bare feet.

"Kothar," she breathed, pressing against him. "You live! I saw you stretched out on the road, pegged down—and I saw the rats gathering in the rocks and I—I wept for you."

He hugged her trembling body to him with an arm. "Where's my little spitfire, girl? Where's the Stefanya who leaped on a hobgob and tried to blind him with her fingernails? Where's the gypsy hoyden who slapped me for giving her a kiss?"

The girl quieted with his arm about her shoulders. Against his chest she murmured, "They tortured me a little when I would not bed down with Torkal Moh and threatened to cut his throat while he slept if he forced me." She threw back her head and smiled weakly up at the barbarian. She smiled when he roared his laughter.

"I am a goose, Kothar. But I was so afraid."

She drew back and saw the woman of the fortress standing close by, as if afraid to move. "What about Torkal Moh?"

Kothar explained how he and Lupalina had freed the peasants of Tomillur and armed them, turning them loose against Torkal Moh and his men. "We can go to Alkarion now, you and I. There is nothing to stop us."

They walked toward the open door and through the dungeons to the worn stone stairs leading to the upper floors. The sounds of fighting were gone. All they could hear now was the occasional scream of a woman being molested by some of the peasants. They climbed the rock treads swiftly; Kothar was anxious to find the wolf-woman and be off to Alkarion.

As they came out of the doorway and onto a stone balcony overlooking the flagstoned courtyard, they saw Lupalina standing among her grey wolves, watching the erection of a dozen wooden crosses. She turned at the sound of their footfalls and her stare went directly to Stefanya.

"Chryasala," she breathed.

Stefanya turned to Kothar, amazement written large on her face. "I've seen that woman before, Kothar. In my dreams! It was always she who took me and rode away with me!"

CHAPTER FIVE

Kothar shrugged his shoulders to that curious look.

"She calls me Chryasala," the girl murmured. "Why?"

The wolf-woman was walking across the courtyard flagstones and mounting the stone stair to the balcony. Her green eyes were thoughtful as they went on studying the girl who was pushing closer to the barbarian.

"There can be no mistake," she muttered, as if to herself. "The likeness is too pronounced, too vivid for error."

Lupalina reached out, caught Stefanya by a wrist and pulled her away from Kothar. "Be at ease, girl. I mean no harm," she murmured.

Her hand tore the ruined tunic from Stefanya, leaving her naked in the sunlight. Stefanya cried out harshly and would have whirled to claw the eyes of this woman in the wolf pelt, but Kothar rumbled reassurance to her, seeing where Lupalina looked.

The wolf-woman nodded her head at the Cumberian. "It is not Chryasala—but Chryasala's baby girl—grown up."

She released her hold on Stefanya who would have clawed at her except that now Kothar held her. "Quiet, girl. I want to hear what Lupalina says."

"Over goblets of wine, Kothar," smiled the wolf-woman. "The fighting was long and hot. I'm thirsty—and I could eat some food, as well."

They found a servant or two cowering in corners, and summoned them to serve table in the great hall, on the dais. They clothes for Stefanya, a plain shift, and steaming lamb and cheese cut in wedges, and freshly baked breads. They poured the rich red wine of Abathor from big silver ewers. The sounds of robbers being crucified in the courtyard was faint and far away.

Lupalina said dreamily, "Long and long ago, I was tire-woman to Chryasala, queen of Phalkar." At Stefanya's gasp, the wolf-woman nodded. "Aye, that is the Chryasala I mean, a little spitfire of a thing out of little-known Sybaros that King Thormond fell in love with and wed. In her land, Chryasala was a princess of royal blood.

"They were very much in love, Chryasala and Thormond, so much so that the king neglected his duties. When a man named Themas Herklar, a general of the army of Phalkar, gradually assumed the controls of government, King Thormond paid no attention. He was content to be alone with his Chryasala and make love to her."

Lupalina sighed and used her knife on a slice of meat. She chewed, then swallowed half a goblet of wine. Stefanya was not eating, her hands were clenched into dusky fists on the table's edge and her intent face was faintly flushed.

"Are you trying to tell me something?" she shrilled.

Lupalina smiled her cat's smile, lowering her black lashes to cover her green eyes. "Listen and see, girl.

"In less than a year, Chryasala gave birth to a baby girl—a babe marked with a curious brown splotch just above her left buttock."

Kothar cursed softly.

Stefanya leaped to her feet, eyes wide, lips quivering. Her wide eyes went from the wolf-woman to the barbarian and back again. She shook her head once, as if to clear it of the thoughts that tumbled about inside it, like dice in a gaming cup. "Do you mean to tell me—that is—" she began.

Lupalina broke a slice of bread. "I do, girl. The throne of Phalkar belongs to you. As of this moment, Themas Herklar reigns, though I have heard whispers that he is not as powerful as he imagined himself to be, years back."

Kothar yanked Stefanya down on the wooden bench beside him. "Eat, girl," he growled. "You were a long time in those dungeons without food. You need it."

Without taking her eyes off the wolf-woman, Stefanya allowed him to drag her back onto the bench. She sliced meat and bread to eat, yet always her stare was locked on the features of the older woman.

At last she said, "How can you know this, who runs with wolves?"

Lupalina laughed softly. "I was not always a wild thing such as this. Once and long ago, I lived in Alkarion and was known as Samandra the wise woman. Aye! My body knew the cling of silks and satins, the fevered embraces of young lovers.

"I was friend to Elviriom the wizard in those days, with a reputation as a sorceress myself. Knew I also the mage Thalkalides, though not as well as I knew Elviriom. On a cold night when the snow blew down out of Thuum to cover the streets in a white blanket and as Thormond lay in bed with Chryasala his beloved, there came a knocking on my door.

"It was Elviriom."

Her eyes were wide, looking upon the past.

* * * *

Elviriom stepped into her warm house, shedding snow from his black cloak. He was a gaunt man with cadaverous cheeks, who always wore a half-starved expression that consorted well with his long, shaggy hair and busy eyebrows. He shook the snow from his cloak, staring about him at the fire where a log burned brightly and at the necromantic furnishings of this, her conjurer's chamber.

"You prepare a spell?" he asked softly.

"I brew a mixture to insure happiness for a pair of newlyweds. But what brings you asking silly questions on such a night?"

There was a pause during which they heard the wind howling about the stone and wood house. Elviriom nodded his head slowly, moving toward the open hearth where he stood rubbing his thin white hands together in front of the flames.

"I come to ask an important question, Samandra. Would you help to overthrow King Thormond?" Samandra considered the gaunt man, her head tilted to one side. She was a handsome woman, there was not a fleck of grey in her glossy black hair, and her green eyes blazed youthfully. She sighed and seated herself on a chair that was close beside the hearthstones.

"The king has never injured me," she murmured at last. "What has he done to you?"

Elviriom cackled laughter. "Why, for one thing, he has never paid me fifty thousand gold dinars. And Themas Herklar makes me such an offer."

"Ahhhh," nodded the sorceress.

"He offers you fifty thousand as well, and another fifty thousand to Thalkalides if by our wizard's wiles we destroy the king and queen."

Samandra thought a moment. "Alone, neither of you is able to do this. Even together you have not the sorcerous strength to break the protective barriers Merdoramon the mage, who is much thought of by King Thormond, has erected about their majesties."

Elviriom inclined his head.

The woman went on, "I am not rich, I barely eke out an existence here in Alkarion. And fifty thousand dinars is a vast fortune."

"Then you will join us in the venture?"

"Of course, I will. But I think you knew this before ever you came out onto the city streets on such a night. When do we work our spell?"

"According to the demon calendar, on the birth-date of Albaran, at the hour of the Imp. We shall make three magicks between us, and by their accumulated effect the barrier placed about Thormond and Chryasala by Merdoramon will shatter and our deadly spells flood in."

Samandra frowned. "I do not enjoy this killing, Elviriom. I do it solely for the money."

"Doesn't Thalkalides? Don't I?"

She was not so sure, Samandra told herself, standing there and watching the mage swing his cloak behind him so that it could drape his gaunt shoulders. His pale hand pulled the hood up over his head.

"I say farewell, Samandra," he murmured.

It was not the last time she was to see Elviriom. He came again on a moonlit night, with a parchment in a hand. Before her wondering eyes he unrolled that parchment and in a troubled voice confided that he had cast the horoscope of the little princess, Stefanya.

"I do not like what I have seen," he muttered gloomily, shaking his graying head. "She was born in the moon of the Heart, when the sun passes through the ebon pillars of dark Space, with Venus as the ruling planet."

Samandra answered, "This is a favorable sign, mage."

"Ah, yes—but Mars and Saturn are adverse and see here, this comet in the fourth house. You know what that portends? Dire disaster!"

The woman chuckled. "And it will be dire disaster for the poor thing when her father and her mother die. What better influence could you seek?"

"I must predict death for her. Death! And I see no signs of death—anywhere. She must not live, Samandra! Can you understand that? Unless she dies, our plan to help Themas Herklar is useless."

"She will die. Give her to me, I will arrange for her dying." She saw the suspicion in the bright eyes of the necromancer. "I will cast her into a vat of acid after strangling her. Is this enough of a death for you, Elviriom?"

The magician nodded slowly.

"Aye, for you are in this with us, Samandra. Our fate is your fate. Should the child live to make a claim for the throne of Phalkar in later years, it is you who shall be crucified along with us if she succeeds."

King Thormond and his queen died two days later in a rockslide on the narrow mountain road leading to their hunting lodge. The dust had scarcely settled over their bodies when Elviriom was knocking at the door of Samandra's little house, carrying a packet in his arms that was the child-queen Stefanya of Phalkar.

"I shall stay to watch the killing," Elviriom told her, handing the babe into her arms. Samandra nodded vaguely as she clasped the child to her bosom. She knew how suspicious the magician was, and she was prepared beforehand to overcome his last few shreds of doubt. In the charnel house along the street of Death where also the Temple to Kamol the death-god stood, she had sought long and diligently for a dead babe whose features matched those of the child-queen. At last, she had found one, had bought the body and brought it to her house.

Now as she busied herself with vials and alembics, she transferred the purple placket in which Elviriom had carried Stefanya to the dead body. She slipped the living child into a compartment while her helper, pretty Thoria of the red tresses, distracted the attention of the necromancer. Around the neck of the dead babe Samandra twisted a killing cord, wringing it tight.

Then as Elviriom looked on, she dropped the dead baby into the vat of dissolving acids. For a little while the magician stared down at the hideous bubbles and frothings as acid ate that flesh.

He nodded at last, accepted his cloak from Thoria, and left the house. It was then, even as the door was closing, that the babe Stefanya began to wail in hunger. Samandra held her breath; the mage never heard, but walked away along the flagstones toward his own domicile.

Later that night, Samandra left the city of Alkarion, riding a swift white mare with Thoria at her side on a bay horse and a dozen armed retainers at her back. She galloped for hours through the night and the early morning, until at high noon she came through the little village of Sfanol and to the great hall where the necromancer Zoqquanor lived.

Into the keeping of the magician Zoqquanor she gave the babe, Stefanya. From a wooden coffer she poured gold and silver dinars for her keeping into his big oak chest. The mage rubbed his thickly veined hands together greedily, seeing that flood of valuable metal adding to his riches.

"I want her safe, Zoqquanor," Samandra commanded. "No harm must come to her. She is a pawn in a game of empire."

"Oh, I'll guard her with my life," the wizard agreed.

Without delay, Samandra rode back to Alkarion.

For several years, the reign of the regent Themas Herklar was good and just. He cared for his people, he commanded that no grain or corn be destroyed, but that it should be stored in silos against famine.

When it made too large a surplus, it was to be fed to the poor. He allowed taxes to be lowered and he gave ear to the complaints of rich and poor alike.

But gradually, a change came over Themas Herklar.

Some men attributed this change to a woman with dusky skin and ebony hair who was brought to him by the wizard Elviriom as a gift. It was rumored that the strange love habits and sterile caresses of this dusky beauty, whose name was Ayilla, sapped the regent not only of his strength, but also of his wisdom.

His first act was to increase taxes. He then sold the accumulated grains and corn in the royal silos to the ruler of Makkadonia, whose people faced a terrible famine. He refused to hear the pleas of the poor people, deeming them of no importance to the well-being of the kingdom.

Then, but slowly, he withdrew himself from the eyes of all his people. He spent his days with Ayilla and with the women she bought in the slave marts of Sybaros for his pleasures. He constructed a great park and a palace within it, with a high stone wall about it, and caused a portion of the army to be encamped outside the walls to prevent anyone from entering without authorization.

The reins of government might have faltered, were it not for Elviriom and Thalkalides, the wizards. They ruled in place of the regent. Their hands drew up the proclamations and the decrees, and one or the other carried them to the pleasure palace of the regent and witnessed his signature at their bottoms.

* * * *

The wolf-woman turned a bread crumb over and over between her fingers. Her green eyes stared down at the bit of bread with which she toyed, glazed and staring. Her face was drawn with fatigue, and there appeared under her eyes twin pouches that proved her exhaustion.

"All this I learned in Alkarion, when I was living there," she murmured. "I did not agree with what was done, for I had reason to know that Themas Herklar was under a spell of Hastarth, the goddess of illicit pleasures between man and woman.

"I tried to reason with him when I visited him. My own spells and conjurations are not impotent. I was able to pass the army encamped outside his walls with ease, since I wafted there on the strength of the south wind as a little white cloud."

She straightened and moved her shoulders as if they ached. Her black head she rested against the chairback, staring straight before her.

"I could do nothing with him. He cared more for Ayilla and the women she bought for him in the slave marts than he did for the people of Phalkar and the throne he had bought with murder.

"He sent me away with curses, and he caused word to be brought to Elviriom and Thalkalides of what I had done. I had to flee away from Alkarion on a moonless night. I realized there was little I could do about hiding out were I to go to places like Commoral City or to Romm, for Elviriom would learn of my residence in cities such as that. So I fled into the wilderness.

"I made friends with the wolves by a few simple spells and with them I have dwelt, ever since. Occasionally, I peer into the future, just to keep in touch with events in Alkarion, and so I know about the message Themas Herklar sent to the mage Merdoramon, on a night when he was afflicted with the hideous guilt of his sins. He asked Merdoramon for a protective amulet."

The green eyes turned to Kothar who sat hunched forward on the baretopped wooden table, occasionally sipping cold ale from a leather jack. Her gaze studied the amber cube in which was imprisoned a tongue of blue flame, dangling about his throat.

"You may be too late to help Themas Herklar, barbarian," she murmured. "I know that Elviriom and Thalkalides, in whom the lust for power burns so brightly, have some very special deviltry in mind for the regent of

Phalkar. I haven't been able to learn what it is. They protect their plan with spells which my own enchantments cannot penetrate. The only way for you to learn what they are, is for you to go there."

Kothar grinned. "That I intend to do, wolf-woman."

"Be warned. Your broad back and strong sword arm may not be enough to stop those wizards. They have powers not even Merdoramon possesses, I believe. They can call on the demons of the thousand pits, and on Belthamquar who is the father of all demons. With their help they ring themselves about with barriers that are impenetrable.

The Cumberian grunted, "I'll risk it."

Lupalina eyed him thoughtfully. "I shall go with you, as shall Stefanya. Perhaps in Alkarion I may find a way to aid you. In any event, I owe Elviriom and Thalkalides a debt of vengeance. It has not been easy, these past years, living among the wolves."

Stefanya whispered, "Is this truth, all you have said? Did you indeed save my life when I was a baby? Am I really the lost princess of Phalkar?"

"Aye, girl," rumbled Kothar. "And once I hand this amulet into the regent's hand, I'll see to it he puts you on the throne where you belong."

"I don't know anything about ruling people!"

"Then let Lupalina teach you." He turned to the wolf-woman. "Or shall I call you Samandra?"

"Lupalina would be safer. Nobody knows me in Alkarion under that name." Her green eyes twinkled as she watched Stefanya yawn. "But I think we ought to find our sleeping cots. We will be the better tomorrow for sleeping out what's left of the night."

* * * *

At the Hour of the Ewe they set out the next day for Alkarion. Kothar was clad once more in mail shirt and bearskin kaunake, Frostfire at his side. His horn bow hung by his saddle in its ornate quiver, that held also his long war arrows. Lupalina wore a brocade gown and rode an ivory saddle with her right leg hooked about the pommel, as great ladies were wont to ride, sitting astride the kak rather than by straddling it. Stefanya rode as a serving maid in a blouse and woolen skirt, upon a mule, trailing after the barbarian and the wolf-woman in the dust raised by their horses' hooves. She was an intelligent girl, she understood that she dared not enter Alkarion as the claimant to its throne. An imp of mischief in her made her thoroughly enjoy this lesser role she played.

They went by way of the forest roads, for the wolf-woman knew this corner of her world, since she had roamed it for the past few years with her wolves. The wolves she had set free on the edge of the wilderness, bidding their gaunt leader return to his normal haunts. Now Lupalina went with bent head, for she was reflecting over the years of her banishment and wondering what might lie ahead.

Kothar was the only one of the three unconcerned about the future. The young giant knew only one thing; there was a good prospect of a fight ahead of him. He carried Frostfire at his side once again, and so he was content.

They came through the Dragon Gate of Alkarion just as the sun was setting, reflecting off the gilded dome of the Temple to Hastarth and the spires of the vast palace where Themas Herklar ruled. The streets of Alkarion were wide streets, their cobblestones worn to an even surface over which farm wains and peddlers wagons clattered in a clop-clopping of horses hooves and iron-tired wheels that told of the bustle and activity of this largest of all Phalkarian cities.

Kothar and the women came in through the gate and at a whispered word from Lupalina, who would now reclaim her name of Samandra, turned right at an intersection and sought a less-traveled corner of the metropolis. They went by way of narrow avenues and little traffic, where there was less likelihood of recognition.

Since Samandra was lightly touched by the brushing of the years, since there were few lines in her face and there were many in this city who might know her on sight, she rode with her hood about her face. As a result, her features were in shadow, though her eyes peered brightly from under her long black lashes, studying Alkarion and its people that she might know their moods.

Stefanya held her face and head free to the small breezes that roamed the city byways, acting out her role of maidservant. There was laughter on her lips and a sense of exultation in her shapely young body. From time to time her eyes would dwell on the wide mailed back and fur-clad shoulders of the barbarian, her protector, and a tender mood would come upon her spirits. She sighed often and her wide red mouth would smile to secret thoughts.

At last Samandra stirred and called out softly.

"To your right, Kothar—the alleyway through the mews!"

They swung off the wider street. They passed under the hanging backs of old houses and between little stone fences until Samandra reined up before a small wooden gate. She swung down from the side-saddle and stepped toward that gate and its huge iron lock with a key in her hand.

"Many changes have come upon Alkarion in the years I've been gone," she breathed to the Cumberian who came to join her. She made a grimace of distaste. "This very neighborhood is different. In my time these were fine city homes. Now they're inhabited by riffraff."

The lock opened to her turning hand, and the wooden gate creaked protestingly on rusted hinges. "Oh, my poor garden—look at it! Weeds everywhere. Are any of my herbs left? And the simples? But never mind—I can see to them later."

She led the way along a path overgrown with nettles and vines until she came to a wooden door recessed beneath a stone overhang. This door also yielded to her key, and she stepped inside a large kitchen with a gigantic fieldstone fireplace taking up all one wall, with cooking cranes and pot hooks set into the stonework from which hung dusty pans and kettles. A table stood in the middle of the room, while along the opposite wall skillets and caldrons were suspended from bronze hooks.

Samandra sighed, wringing her hands. "The dust! The cobwebs! Oh, and I've cooked so many good things in this kitchen."

Kothar grunted. "It needs a cleaning, I'll admit."

Her green eyes were wide. "More important than that—my conjuring chamber must be all over grime and spider webs, too! I've been counting on my almost forgotten spells to guide us, here in Alkarion. Kothar! Stefanya! Come with me."

She ran ahead of them into a room filled with furniture that held the debris of the past sixteen years. Up a narrow wooden stair to a floor containing two bedrooms she scampered, skirts to her knees for faster going. On the top floor of the little house she came to a pause and stared at the big room.

Dust lay everywhere, except in the corners where spider webs showed blood-red in the rays of the dying sun coming through the streaked and grimy windows. Samandra almost wept.

"I'll need my herb jars and the simple cases—and my athanor most of all! Oh, this is dreadful. Everything is so dirty, so upset."

"Oh, hush," snapped Stefanya, brushing past the sorceress. "Get out of here, the two of you. Leave this to me. All it needs is a couple of hours' hard work." When Samandra stared at her, Stefanya laughed, head thrown back. "Have you forgotten? I was imp to Zoqquanor during my growing years! Many's the time I cleaned out his necromantic nuisances with a dustpan and broom. I know an alembic when I see one, and I burnt my fingers once on an athanor. So leave me. Shoo, shoo, the both of you."

"The princess of Phalkar—a cleaning woman?" asked Samandra in something of a daze.

Kothar grinned and caught the sorceress by an elbow. "Aye, by Dwallka—the future queen of Phalkar! Her knowledge will help her control her palace servants when she wears the crown."

Stefanya was reaching for a broom as they went through the door. As they moved down the staircase they could hear the swishing of its straws on the dusty floor, and Stefanya coughing. Kothar grinned, chuckling to himself at the tricks destiny can play at times.

Samandra herself cleared the kitchen, enough at least to prepare a meal of the meat she had brought from Raven Garde, and to lay out cheese and bake two loaves of bread in the hearth where the barbarian set a roaring fire.

When they were done eating, and Stefanya announced that the conjuring chamber was reasonably clean, they went up the narrow wooden staircase to the upper floor. Samandra paused a moment in the doorway, confessing herself well pleased by the neatness and cleanliness of the chamber. Stefanya shrugged off her compliments, admitting that Zoqquanor was a hard taskmaster and had beaten her so often for failing to put his vials and ointment jars in order that cleaning wizards chambers was the one thing she did extremely well.

Samandra arched her eyebrows. "We'll test you as an assistant, that we will. Where's the bat's blood? And the wings of horpats?"

Stefanya fetched them, placing the newly dusted urns before the sorceress. Samandra smiled faintly, then asked for her crystal ball. When the girl placed it before her on a silver base, she nodded and bent forward, spreading her hands and moving her fingers in a certain magical manner.

Kothar leaned forward with Stefanya, staring into that cloudy ball which cleared rapidly to the motions of Samandra's fingers. He saw a picture form, slowly at first, as though it were seen in rippling water that stilled to become the reflective surface of mercury.

Three figures he saw, one seated and one standing on either side of the high throne of Phalkar. The throne itself was a masterpiece of exotic sculpture, carved with the leopards of Phalkar, each containing a great ruby as a baleful eye. The arms were of dark wood cunningly wrought to represent the twin serpents of Askard, and each serpent held a great, glittering diamond in its open jaw. A tiger skin from Ispahan had been thrown over the cushioned seat and on the tiger skin sat...

"Gods of Thuum!" breathed the barbarian.

"Who is that?" asked Samandra softly.

It was a tall youth, very pale of skin, yet handsome in a sepulchral manner, with large red eyes and a blood-red mouth. He sat stiffly, his black hair holding the golden crown of Phalkar, set with magnificent gems, his arms outstretched upon the twin-serpented arms.

To his left stood a tall, gaunt man with dark spade beard and black eyes that brooded upon mysteries from under bushy black brows. He was clad from shoulders to slippers in dull black on which was etched in scarlet threads the dread fangs of Belthamquar, father of demons. He never moved. He stared downward at something out of sight of the watchers in the crystal ball.

On the other side of the throne was the mage Thalkalides, a shorter man than Elviriom, and somewhat more fleshy. His shoulders were wide, his graying hair was curled upon a massive head that went well with the thick, muscular arms he showed in a short-sleeved tunic on which was emblazoned the sigils of fearsome Azthamur. Kothar drew a deep breath, his heart thudding wildly. Well, he finally knew that demon-god!

Samandra whispered, "Look now, both of you!"

The crystal ball never moved but appeared to draw back and away from that trio on the royal dais. Now they could see five men in armor with swords hanging by their sides facing the cadaverous young man upon the throne. They wore the mail of the Royal Guards of the Outlander Corps, the leather-trimmed link-armor of the Mercenary Horse. Each head was helmeted, each figure stood as if frozen in awe—or stark terror.

Before these five was a sixth man, in armor trimmed with gold. The sword that hung at his side was jeweled and the black cloak hanging from his shoulders trimmed by golden threads. He stood erect; there was defiance in the set of his head.

Faintly, they heard the voice of Thalkalides. "Jarken Wat, general of our armies, you have defied our orders to invade Makkadonia."

"We are at peace with Makkadonia, sire. And I had not those orders from Themas Herklar, who is my ruler."

"The regent has been deposed, General. But then—you have not heard word of this, perhaps, being on the borderlands with our army as you have been."

This voice was soft, almost that of a woman. But the cadaverous youth who spoke was not feminine. There was a metallic quality about him, for all his pallid appearance, that suggested supernatural strength and powers. The pale young man who sat on the throne of Phalkar continued.

"It is even possible that you have not heard our name, nor learned that I rule now in Phalkar with my uncles, Elviriom and Thalkalides. Themas Herklar is no more. And so you will take your commands from me alone.

"For I am Unus, King of Phalkar!"

General Jarken Wat bowed slightly. "I had not heard, Highness. But what of Themas Herklar?"

The muscular Thalkalides whispered, "It is not good to ask too many questions of the ruler of your country, Jarken Wat! Know only that the regent has been placed in gaol, and that he will suffer the fate of all traitors."

"How may the king of a country be a traitor?"

Elviriom leaned forward, smiling cruelly. "Heard you not my fellow mage, Jarken Wat? It is not good policy to question those who rule! Perhaps you need a lesson in what to expect should you continue to ask of things that do not concern you."

Elviriom waved a hand.

CHAPTER SIX

Out of view of the crystal ball, men came dragging a naked man in chains, for the staring trio could see in its clear depths the figure of that man who struggled against the arms of the guards who held him. The guards dragged the frightened wretch to the foot of the dais.

Elviriom went on softly, "Observe this criminal, General. He has been doomed to be burned alive for his many crimes. But King Unus is merciful. Himself, he shall grant everlasting peace to such an unfortunate.

"Beware, Jarken Wat—that his fate is not your fate!"

The pallid man turned his head and his red eyes stared down at the shivering creature in the iron manacles. Suddenly, red beams leaped from those scarlet eyes and splashed on the naked man so that his body was encased in a vermillion aura that blazed with angry fire. An instant later, the man was a drifting haze of dust motes.

Empty iron manacles clanked on the floor.

"Dwallka," breathed Kothar, staring. "What in the name of his War-Hammer was that?"

Samandra shivered, "I d-don't know. Elviriom and Thalkalides have grown so powerful in my absence—I would never know them."

The general also shivered as he stared down at the chains at his feet. "Saw you ever such power in a man?" asked Elviriom in a silky voice, and the general shook his head.

"Think you, Jarken Wat, that you will invade the borderlands of Makkadonia and carry the leopard banners eastward to the Outer Sea?"

The general hesitated only briefly. His right hand came up to rest against his armored chest. "I hear my king, Elviriom. I shall obey. My armies march at dawn to the east."

The mage appeared to relax, straightening slowly and smiling. "Excellent. King Unus will have many honors to heap upon you when you bring us the griffons of Makkadonia as evidence of its surrender. Now go!"

The general and his captains saluted and wheeled, marching as one down the long audience hall. King Unus watched them with his red eyes as the two magicians who were his counselors eyed each other above his black head that held the crown of Phalkar.

Stefanya whimpered as the scene faded. "Is that my throne? Samandra, whatever am I to do against someone like—that?"

"He has strange powers," admitted the sorceress.

Kothar scowled blackly. "What of Themas Herklar? I was paid to deliver an amulet to him. I mean to do it and discharge my obligation before I tackle a thing like that!" His eyes stabbed at the older woman. "Who is he? Where did those magicians find him? Is he a demon of some sort?"

Samandra shook her head. "I can't say. I will use spells and necromancies to discover his origin and identity. In the meantime…"

Her hands made those curious gestures above the crystal ball. The cloudiness vanished, and now Kothar found himself staring at a pile of straw. On it lay the huddled, trembling figure of an old man. To one side were jail bars, and from somewhere on the damp stone wall a torchlight flickered dimly.

"Themas Herklar," breathed Samandra, horrified.

"That old man?" asked the barbarian.

He stared at long, white hair and a wrinkled face and a body that once was strong and powerful, yet now was emaciated and quivering with weakness. Though he could smell nothing, he sensed the filth and ordure in which that body was stained, clad in rotted, tattered garments as it was.

The sorceress whispered, "I knew him long ago, when he was younger and far stronger. Gods, what have they done to him?"

Kothar grunted, "He did something of that to himself, inside the pleasure palace he built."

"Aye—and those two magicians helped him."

"Well?" Kothar barked. "I must go to him with that amulet, I've given my word to do so. And when I go to him—what shall I say of King Unus who reigns in his place?"

"Ask him questions, Kothar," the sorceress counseled. "Themas Herklar may know something that will let us understand what threat it is we face in Alkarion. Only he can help us now, I think."

She stared at him over the crystal ball that was resuming its cloudy state. "But he is in gaol, probably in the lowest cell of the dungeons. How can you find him there—without danger to yourself?"

"Pah," snorted the Cumberian. "Leave all that to my wits." He scowled. "But I'd best go now, that man I just saw is dying. I want to reach him before grim Karnol, the death god."

Stefanya whispered, "Tell him I live, Kothar! Let him die with that in his head." When they stared on her, she clenched her fists and cried, "He killed my mother and my father! Do you think I pity him? I curse his name! Just let him know I am alive and that I shall burn incense before the crypts of Karnol so that the death god may torture his soul in his ovens forever!"

"Little miss spitfire," murmured Samandra with a smile. "You'll make a good queen in Phalkar, if we can ever put you on the throne."

Before he left the house, while he was tossing his bearskin cape about his mail-clad shoulders, Stefanya came to Kothar and put her arms about his neck. "Guard yourself, Kothar," she whispered. "You're all I have."

He grinned and would have kissed her cheek. But she turned his head with her hands and pressed her lips against his mouth. Then, flushing slightly, she drew back and murmured, "I'll make you general of the army in place of that Jarken Wat if you make me queen, Kothar. I vow it."

He rumbled laughter and, opening the kitchen door, crept out through the overgrown garden into the alleyway. He walked swiftly through the mews, for there was an anxiety in him to be about his business. He heeded not the tempting voices of women who revealed their bodies in recessed doorways, nor the cries of hawkers who sold fruit and cheese and other things not so palatable.

At last he came to the great stone bulk of the city gaol. Here, he walked more slowly, studying the structure, discovering that on three sides it was well lighted, but that the fourth side overlooked a slightly lesser building. This structure was not as high as the gaol, yet it plunged all that one side of the prison into darkness with its shadow.

Kothar slipped between the buildings when the street about him was empty, so that none should see him. His fingers fumbled across the brick-work, finding many of them recessed and others protruding in a sort of crude decorative pattern. His fingers tightened about those bricks as his toes sought grips below. In moments, he was climbing steadily upward.

No man saw him. He came out upon the flat roof, seeing a small, wooden doorway protected by a shed that led downward into the bowels of the gaol. The door was not locked, so he entered, closing the door gently behind him and moved stealthily down the stone stairs.

The barbarian was like a wild animal in his silence. His war boots were of the finest Vandacian leather. They made no sound upon the stone. Down five stories he went like a shadow, hearing only the moaning of tortured prisoners and the snoring of men and women who slept.

A dozing man was on guard at the door that lead into the dungeons. Kothar took him by the neck, holding him until his kickings ceased and his eyes glazed over. Propping him up in the chair as if he slept, removing the key ring at his belt, the Cumberian stepped past him through the doorway.

A short flight of stone steps brought him to a circular room. There were bars on each of the stone walls here, and a smell of unwashed flesh and human sweat. A lone torch flickered, shedding a pale, yellow light. Kothar snorted at the stink, and padded to the iron socket that held the torch. This he took down in a hand and carried with him as he made the rounds of the cell fronts.

He found Themas Herklar in the fourth cell.

Unlocking the door, he stepped inside. The old man stirred as he held the torchlight closer, moaning and raising his withered hands as if to protect himself from a blow.

"I know nothing more, nothing," the old man groaned.

His eyes opened and he stared in terror at the young giant bulking dark and ominous behind the blazing brand. "No! Don't torture me any more. I can't tell you anything else."

"Easy, old man," muttered the barbarian, dropping to a knee. He leaned closer and whispered, "I come from Merdoramon with an amulet for your protection."

His hand eased out the amulet with the blue flame trapped within it. The old man stared at it, not understanding. He shook his white-haired head and tears ran down his cheeks.

"I know nothing of it. Nothing!"

"It is to protect you against Elviriom and Thalkalides and their wizard-ries. The mage Merdoramon gave it to me at an oasis in the Dying Desert and told me to take it to you."

The rheumy eyes lost their glaze, finally, as the old man gasped and struggled to sit upright on his heap of straw. The thickly muscled arm of the barbarian came to aid him. Kothar was about to drop the amulet and the chain into the hand of Themas Herklar when the old man shook his head.

"It is—too late. Keep the amulet, man—so that it may help you get safely out of Alkarion, the Accursed City."

"I came into Alkarion with Stefanya, the daughter of King Thormond and Queen Chryasala."

"Heh? Thormond? Chryasala? Their daughter? But she is dead. I paid good gold to—no! I must not betray myself!"

"She lives, old man. She is in Alkarion to claim her rightful throne—usurped now by a strange being called King Unus."

The man who had been regent of Phalkar stared at him. "King Unus? Aye, I mind him. A demon-being created by the sorceries of Elviriom and Thalkalides. They warned me they would do this—make a king to take my place, even while they tempted me with strange wines and potent drugs from the southland that made my body like that of a virgin youth, and then they brought lovely women to my chambers in my pleasure park and—"

The old man shuddered. His voice was a low wail as he spoke. "They punished me for my sin against Thormond and Chryasala! They did, with the wine and the drugs and the fleshy women who knew all the caresses of Hastarth! I paid the price. I forgot my years and my country to wallow as a pig in the filthiness of the slops. The pleasure park was my pig-pen. I ruined myself.

"And to get more women and more drugs, I gave in to their suggestions that I make them my deputies. The power of Phalkar I handed into their greedy fingers. I wanted no responsibility. All I wanted was the women and my youthful body. Ah, well they understood my weaknesses!"

Themas Herklar wept bitter tears, hunched over in the dungeon.

With pity in his voice, Kothar growled, "Come away with me. Grow better in a safer place. Help Stefanya assume the throne. Make restitution for what you did in the past."

"Too old. I'm too old!"

"Then tell me how I can do it."

There was a silence. Themas Herklar fixed the young giant in his cell with bright eyes that studied his face framed by golden hair and set upon wide shoulders, the deep chest in the shirt of link mail, and his massive arms. For the space of a candle burning from first lighting to full brightness, he stared at the Cumberian.

The old man nodded slowly, smiling for the first time. "Maybe you can avenge me, whoever you are. You bear the amulet of Merdoramon. Wear it against the deviltries of Elviriom and Thalkalides! And now—listen!"

Somewhere in the cell water dripped and a man snored. The voice of Themas Herklar cut through these sounds with an intensity that told Kothar he spoke the truth.

"They *created* Unus. They made him in vats where they stirred the chemicals and other matter which they shaped into human simulacra with their demoniac arts, with the aid of Belthamquar and Thelonia his mate, who breathed life into it.

"Unus is not a man but—a thing.

"Yet, he has terrible powers. Beware of him, young man. First, you must slay the two wizards. They have not the eerie abilities of the thing they made. They are human flesh and blood—no more. But take them by surprise so they cannot work their spells on you.

"Slay first Elviriom, for he is the more deadly of the two. And then dispatch Thalkalides. After them—slay Unus if you can!"

The old man sank back, shaking his head.

"I do not know whether anything can kill Unus. He is unique in all our world. Created by wizards, given life by demons! Who can predict about such as that?" Themas Herklar jabbed a finger at the Cumberian. "But one thing I can tell you—before I die. Beware his..."

Kothar rasped a curse. The old man was gagging, eyes bulging. His gaunt body shook spasmodically so that the barbarian extended an arm to hold him. And then he heard the dry rattle in the wrinkled, old throat and knew he would hear nothing more.

He eased the dying man back onto the straw and waited until the rattle was ended. His hand moved forward, closed the dead eyelids down over the staring, lifeless eyes. Themas Herklar was gone to Karnol to be judged for his sins and punished or rewarded.

Kothar left the cell as silently as he had come.

Like a spirit-being, he moved from the gaol and walked along the dark and empty streets of Alkarion. It was the Hour of the Rat, and those abroad were few, being mostly soldiers who kept the watch or criers who paced sedately with their poled lanthorns, calling out the time. To avoid discovery, the barbarian kept to the recessed doors and overhangs of the buildings past which he walked. Soon he was back inside the walled garden belonging to Samandra.

In the kitchen he rolled himself up in his cloak and slept.

Toward morning, Samandra crept down into the kitchen to light the cooking fire and shake him awake. He told her what had taken place between Themas Herklar and himself and of the regent's words of caution.

"And now you are free of your task," murmured the sorceress, stirring eggs and chunks of meat together in a skillet. "What do you intend to do?"

The youthful giant shrugged. "Put Stefanya on her throne. My task for Merdoramon has been fulfilled—and I seek employment for my sword."

"Then do as I say," the woman said, filling his platter with food. "You shall carry a three-eyed golden foll to the Audience Hall of King Unus this day, in a silver cage."

"A foll? What kind of thing is that?"

Samandra gurgled laughter. "A bird I invented, Kothar—which shall be myself! Ah, I am anxious to see the faces of those two mages when they hear what this golden foll has to say."

Three hours later, as the crowds gathered before the Temple of Judgment, in which King Unus sat as arbiter for the complaints of his people, a brawny young man with golden hair and wrapped in a bearskin cloak came pushing a path through the throng of housewives and merchants, farmers and peasants assembled to hear the decisions of King Unus. He towered a foot above any other man, and there was a scabbard visible at his side, when the bearskin cloak flapped back, that held a cross-hilted sword.

He shouldered his way to the great oaken doors and walked through them, heedless of the snarls and other protests his actions caused, until he was within the gilded Audience Hall itself. His blue eyes scanned the dais where King Unus sat on the royal throne with his advisers, Elviriom and Thalkalides, beside him. Now he lifted the hooded cage he carried and his bull voice bellowed throughout the chamber.

"A gift!" he roared. "A rare gift for Unus, King of Phalkar!"

His speech drowned out the words of the two merchants disputing before the king. The white face of Unus showed annoyance, and the wizard Elviriom bent to whisper into his ears. But Unus could not hear the mage, the crude fellow in the bearskin was bellowing again.

"Never have eyes seen the like of this! So rare is this gift. I have carried it all the way from the Sysyphean Hills as my present to the great Unus!"

King Unus gestured with his pale hand. "Bring the fellow forward, guard. And if this gift be not different, indeed—why then, we'll have the man flayed alive to amuse our people!"

"No need for any guard," roared Kothar, elbowing a path forward, holding the covered cage high above his head. "I can find my way."

He came between the merchants and stood facing Unus and the necromancers. The king made an impatient gesture with his hand.

"Well? What is this gift?"

"A three-eyed golden foll, highness! It speaks words of truth. Its eyes peer into the past, the present and the future—one eye for each!"

"Bah!" cried Elviriom. "There is no such bird!"

"Yet such a bird should prove priceless to a king, lord wizard," said Kothar slyly. "For it can tell the king whatever he wants to know—past, present—or future."

Unus said softly, "Let us gaze upon this marvel." Kothar whisked away the purple cloth from the silver cage and gasps were heard here and there in the hall, for the bird was golden, indeed, and very beautiful to look upon. It preened on its perch, spreading its yellow wings and stretching.

"Greetings, Unus—King of Phalkar," it chirped.

Unus laughed, a cold, unemotional laugh that went down inside the bones of a man and chilled them. He said, "At least it speaks. But can you actually foresee the future, bird of Sysyphea?"

"I can, great lord. I see Stefanya, daughter of dead King Thormond and dead Queen Chryasala, sitting on that same throne where now you sit yourself!"

Shouts and screams rang in the audience hall. Men and women pushed and fought to get closer to this bird which saw such a future. A slow tide of anger rose upon the faces of Elviriom and Thalkalides, but the pallid features of King Unus showed no emotion at all.

"I can order you slain," commented the king, "for such a ridiculous prediction. Know you not that Stefanya died when she was but a babe?"

"Nay, King. Stefanya lives."

Cries and murmurs of fear and wonder went about the Audience Hall like a sonic tidal wave. Elviriom pushed forward on the dais, bending his cadaverous body to stare at the barbarian and at the golden bird in the silver cage.

"Sorcery," he hissed. "This is a wizard's trick!"

"As much a trick as the landslide you caused, Elviriom—to bury Thormond and Chryasala!"

The sorcerer reeled back, stunned. His normally pale face became as white as the snows on the Great Glacier that lies between Cumberia and Thuum. His hand lifted, pointing at Kothar, quivering. "Destroy that man!"

Kothar shouted and ripped Frostfire free of its scabbard. In a single bound he was before the throne, the point of his blade touching the throat of the king.

"Before I die—Unus the usurper dies!" he bellowed.

"Fool!" snarled Thalkalides. "The king will destroy you for your sacrilege! Unus, great lord—wash this barbarian with the scarlet stare of your glorious eyes, that he may pay the penalty for his crime."

Unus said softly, "Nay! It comes to me that this man has brought me a rare gift, indeed. He has shown me that our throne harbors traitors. If you did, indeed, slay the king and queen before me, what proof have I that you might not some day conspire to slay me as well?"

The red eyes that stared at Elviriom and at Thalkalides in turn were baleful and accusing. Kothar lowered his swordpoint, enthralled by the little drama of hate and mistrust at which he stared.

"Unus—I order you!" Thalkalides screamed.

"You made me—king. You gave me certain—powers. My kingship and those powers you hold inside your hands, Thalkalides and Elviriom. I dare not make a move without your consent. I am no king, I am only your puppet!"

"What are you saying?" gasped Thalkalides.

"He speaks truth," chirped the three-eyed golden poll. "Elviriom and Thalkalides created Unus—from flesh they made with certain chemicals and aristols. With the aid of Belthamquar and Thelonia, the demons, they birthed King Unus. This is no man before you, but a creature of wizardry!"

"Slay that bird!" screeched Elviriom.

A guard moved to obey, lifting his spear. Kothar sprang from the dais to straddle the silver cage, grinning wickedly. The guard saw the battle light in those blue eyes and drew back a step, being a pampered royal guard, not a trained soldier such as served under Jarken Wat.

The Cumberian moved his sword back and forth. The men and women near him fell back several paces, crowding in upon those behind them. "Pick me up now and carry me away," chirped the bird at his feet. "We have served our purpose."

He lifted the cage and would have shouldered his way out of the hall but Elviriom screamed, "Stop that man! Make him your prisoner."

King Unus said softly, "The man goes free, Elviriom. I have him to thank for understanding your motives, you and Thalkalides. His golden foll has opened my eyes to the truth."

The king rose and tossed his gold and purple mantle about his shoulders and stood brooding down over the Audience Hall while the two wizards fumed and cursed on either side of him. Only when Kothar was safely through the throng and moving toward the open street, did Unus move down off the dais with a peremptory wave of his hand, indicating that the audience was at an end.

As they walked through the bazaar where Kothar hoped to hide his tracks amid the crowds of people, the bird at his side chirped, "Are we being followed?"

"Aye, by the two wizard's helpers—tall fellows with murder in their eyes and dagger-hilts in their hands, half hidden under their cloaks."

"They must not find Stefanya!"

The barbarian chuckled. "Leave this part of our plan to me, my three-eyed golden foll. It is skullduggery in an alleyway, and at this no man is my master."

He trotted after a time. He had come to a narrow bypath that led through the stews east of the Hall of Judgment. A backward glance told him the two men in cloaks were trotting also, grinning as Kothar went deeper and deeper into the slums.

He came to a door over which swung a wooden sign in the shape of a crudely painted jug of mead, half obliterated by wind and time. Quickly, Kothar dodged aside. He thrust open the door, found himself in a dimly lighted street tavern where half a dozen men crouched over dirty tabletops, clutching tankards of ale.

He set down the birdcage and summoned the slovenly waitress to him. "A jack of cold ale, woman," he ordered.

He had not long to wait. The woman was on her way to the table with the ale in her greasy hand when the door once more opened. The two tall men in cloaks entered. Their eyes flashed at the sight of the barbarian, and they edged their way forward so that they trailed the woman. As she bent to set the mug before Kothar, one of the men grasped her, whirling her and her cry of surprise out of their way.

The two men lunged with daggers.

And the barbarian reached out, stabbing with his hands and catching their wrists. Like iron bands were his mighty fingers as they turned those wrists to drive the dagger points deep into the wooden tabletop. For an instant the man stared at him with surprised eyes. Then they whirled and would have fled, but the hands of Kothar were on their heads, grasping their hair and yanking them back upon the table.

They lay helpless, staring up at him. "Listen, carrion birds!" the barbarian rasped. "I could slay you as easily as not. You know this. I spare your lives on the condition you return to Elviriom and Thalkalides who sent you. Say this to them: that their days in Alkarion are numbered, and that by the Hour of the Bird, doom shall come upon them."

He let them go, and watched them wrench themselves up off the table-top and gather their cloaks about them. One of the two rasped, "Those wizards will fasten a cage to your head, barbarian—with a starving rat inside it!"

Then they whirled and fled.

Kothar grinned and tossed a silver coin at the serving woman. "For the spilled ale, and for a tankard filled to the top in its place. And hurry. The gods have put a dryness in my throat that needs appeasing."

While he sat at ease sipping his chilled ale, the foll spoke to him in a whisper only he could hear. "Are you mad to threaten the wizards? They will unite with Unus and destroy us! Better to return to the house where I can make spells to keep them from finding us."

"I want them to find us. At least, I want King Unus to come," muttered Kothar. "We planted a bee under his royal crown this morning. I think it will sting him into action."

"My idea was to rouse up the people! As it is, all we've done is alert the king and his counselors to the fact that Stefanya lives!"

"Exactly. But heard you not the king? He is a thinking man, that Unus. He desires to rule by himself, not as any puppet. I think he will come seeking us before long. Now be quiet and let me finish my ale."

The king came an hour past noon, shrouded in a worn cloak and hood to hide his white face and scarlet eyes. He came alone, and he rapped with the iron knocker on the street door until Kothar came and opened it.

"You could not hide from me, you know," the king said to Kothar. "I know many spells to seek you out."

The barbarian inclined his head. "To you I extend a welcome, Lord King. It's those wizards I mistrust. Please to enter."

Samandra moved forward to greet Unus, curtseying, resplendent in a gold brocade gown. She looked years younger, thanks to the green malachite on her eyelids and red salves out of Aegypton on her lips. She had set her graying black hair in a cunning coiffure, so that two lovelocks fell on either side of her temples. She was as lovely as any courtesan King Unus had ever seen.

"I came to view the golden bird," said King Unus. "And to accept it as a gift."

Kothar rumbled, "I think the bird will be slain, highness—by your wizard counselors, should I give it to you."

"They would not dare!"

"Ah, but they would," said Samandra softly. "But there is a way by which you may have the bird in complete safety to it."

"What way is that?"

"Destroy Elviriom and Thalkalides," rasped the barbarian.

The king smiled, "Such a prospect is dear to my heart, but I dare not. They are mighty magicians."

Kothar leaned forward, whispered, "But you are the child of Belthamquar, father of demons—and of his mate, lovely Thelonia."

"What has that to do with it?"

"Would they permit their child to be destroyed?"

Unus rubbed his white jaw with a pallid hand. "It may be so, what you say. I have been given great powers, true. But none of my powers is sufficient to destroy Elviriom and Thalkalides."

"Leave that destruction to your demonic parents," breathed Samandra.

The king eyed her. "Can it be done?"

"Very safely, while you stay and watch."

Samandra gestured and King Unus followed her up the narrow, wooden staircase. Kothar waited until they were out of sight before turning and moving toward the kitchen. Here Stefanya waited for him, breathless and big-eyed, huddled inside a huge, woolen cape.

"Come girl," he growled. "You and I must ride!"

"But where, Kothar?" she asked as he caught her hand and half dragged her from the house.

His grin was mirthless. "To forestall the king. Now follow me."

Any passerby who saw them might have thought them barbarian and kitchen wench, for Kothar walked with his arm about her shoulders and laughed and chatted and petted her from time to time. They went through the mews until they reached a stable where Greyling and her bay mare were stalled. Tossing a few copper coins to the linkboy, the barbarian led out the animals and saddled them.

Then he helped her into her saddle and mounted his own. They rode slowly through the city streets lest they attract attention and when they passed under the Dragon Gate, Kothar amused the officer on guard with a tale that came close to making him flush.

They trotted down the road, side by side.

CHAPTER SEVEN

In her conjuring chamber, Samandra led the way to a scarlet pentagram painted in human blood upon the floor. The great sigil was large enough for several people to stand within it, so King Unus came at her invitation to stand and watch her every action. Set inside the pentagram was a horned altar formed of human bone and ashes from a demonic fire, mixed with the sands from the Isle of Magic which stood within the Pool of Life, where demons were said to meet at every Beltane eve.

Onto the horned altar, into a tiny hollow within its top, Samandra poured blood and a bit of water from the Pool of Life that rumor says can be found some miles east of the Sysyphean Hills. Into this blood and water she sprinkled a reddish powder and then a blue salt together with some grains of earth and iron.

The mixture fumed with purplish smoke.

"Belthamquar, father of demons, I abjure thee! Thelonia, mother of demons, heed my prayer! Come to us, your supplicants, great ones of the Other Worlds. Cross the gulfs of Time and of Space and listen to our plea!"

King Unus was silent, but he let the hood of his cloak hang on his shoulders so that the demons, when they appeared, might recognize him. He listened as Samandra went on with her demoniac litany, and he stirred restlessly beside her when it ended and there was no response to it.

"What delays them?" he asked.

"Hush! Belthamquar and Thelonia have far to come… Across the bottomless pits of Eborrol and great gulfs of intragalactic space. Few know this conjuration—it was taken from a shattered shard which legend attributes to Afgorkon himself. To my knowledge, only Elviriom and Thalkalides possessed it—before I stole it from them."

Her smile was almost flirtatious.

Then her hand caught his and squeezed.

A coldness came into the room, creeping past the iron tripods flaring scarlet with their burning powders, avoiding the coffers that held the necessaries of the magical trade, tiptoeing along the floor that was marked with zodiacal and other mystic sigils. It was a cosmic cold, unearthly and terrifying. Its thin tendrils reached out over the pentagram so that Unus and Samandra shivered in unison.

In a far corner of the room, a darkness grew. From a spot of ebon entity it enlarged, quivering with sentience, with life, and with a malignancy that was stupefying. A blackness pulsed.

A sepulchral voice whispered, "I see my son and with him, a strange woman. It is the woman who has summoned us."

"Yet, it is your son who would speak with you, Belthamquar, father of evil, father of demons. Tell him, Unus."

"Will you not wait for me, Belthamquar?"

A woman stood in the opposite corner of the room, a woman supernaturally beautiful, with long, golden hair hanging before and behind her, veiling the nudity of her pearl-pink flesh. She looked at Unus with long-lashed, purple eyes, and a maternal smile hovered on lips that were curved to tempt all men to wicked dreams.

"For if you are his father, am I not his mother?"

Samandra curtseyed deep. "Most beautiful of women, great Thelonia," she breathed. "Your son seeks aid against the sorcerers who made him—with your help."

"A sweet son," murmured Thelonia.

"A bothersome son," snarled the blackness which was Belthamquar. "What is his danger, that he must summon me up out of my myriad hells?"

"It is as Samandra has said, father. Elviriom and Thalkalides have named me king of Phalkar—but I rule in name only. I am their puppet. They can depose me as easily as I might crush an ant beneath my heel."

"You have powers, Unus," breathed fair Thelonia.

"What are my powers—against theirs? They know conjurations to summon up demons such as Azthamur of the hundred hells."

"A lesser demon, certainly," growled Belthamquar.

"Against you, father—yes! But against me…"

King Unus sighed and looked woebegone. To one side of him, Samandra admired his histrionic abilities. He sighed and shook his head and she thought she saw a lone tear trickle downward from the corner of an eye.

"Can we permit our son to be a puppet?" asked the sweet voice of Thelonia.

"Woman-demon, listen to me! There are restraints upon our appearance on this land of men. We can be summoned up, yes. But an unwarranted intrusion… I don't like it."

"Our names will be a laughing stock," cajoled Thelonia.

"No men shall mock me! Nor will they."

"Only if we teach these sorcerers a dread lesson."

"To do that—well, I'm not averse to the idea. After all, Elviriom and Thalkalides got their will of us—without so much payment as the lost soul of a slave-girl to take back to our abodes to amuse us."

"Take *their* souls, instead," suggested Unus.

"Quiet, boy!... Thelonia, what say you?"

"I think it may be done. I would like to practice certain abominations on that Elviriom, who thinks he is above anything on earth or in the cosmic gulfs. Yes, I have a number of little torments that might make me laugh for centimes, with Elviriom as the subject."

"I'd rather have a woman, myself," muttered Belthamquar, and two golden eyes, blazing in the blackness that was the father of demons, ate at the shapely legs and body of Samandra. "Thalkalides will prove of little entertainment."

"Haven't you tired of women yet?" snapped Thelonia.

"No, my dear, I haven't. I find them charming creatures who understand me far better than you do. And besides..."

"Oh, do be quiet—Samandra, heed me. We do as my son asks, for this one time. There shall be no more calling upon us to assist him in his petty little plots here in Phalkar. Is it understood?"

King Unus breathed, "This one time, mother. And father, too."

Belthamquar snorted, Samandra thought. But he growled, "There is an incantation which must be recited to enable us to do what must be done."

Thelonia said, "Repeat after me, Samandra. And you, Unus—cover your ears. I don't want you hearing such language."

Samandra repeated what Thelonia said, word for word, inflection for inflection, and trembled with fear as her lips and tongue uttered sounds never meant for a human throat. As she spoke, she felt the vibrations beginning in the conjural chamber, knew them to be spreading outward across the city of Alkarion even as far as the palace and beyond, to the pleasure park of Thomas Herklar that Elviriom and Thalkalides had made their own.

It was as if Yarth, which was her world, and those myriad hells of cosmic space in which Belthamquar and Thelonia lived, were merging their very outlines. Dimly, as she peered about her she heard the shrill laughter of gathering fiends and familiars, *bêtes noires* and things which defied description. They cluttered at her and made obscene and sometimes threatening gestures until Thelonia waved her hand.

The pentagram where she stood with King Unus rose upward as if supported by the hands of djinns and floated through the house roof and over the mews. Below it lay the city of Alkarion, but no man or woman moved in all that city for madness might have come upon them had they seen what chattered and gibbered just out of reach. The denizens of a million hells had been unleashed by that awesome conjuration, and they ran and scampered across the city cobbles, pausing to finger the body of a particularly toothsome wench or making gestures of ridicule before a plump merchant garbed in velvet and miniver fur.

High over the palace spires and the gilded dome of the Temple of Judgment sped the pentagram. To one side of it floated the demon-mother, Thelonia, while ahead ranged the black sentience that was Belthamquar. Beyond the walls of Alkarion they passed, and it seemed that the old sun that had shone on Yarth for more than twelve billion years hid its light, for the day became grey and overcast and dark clouds gathered above the city.

The pleasure park of Themas Herklar had been built some miles from Alkarion, with a wide road fringed by poplar trees leading out of the Hastarth Gate. Above this road sped the pentagram, and very faintly it seemed that Samandra could hear the terrified wailing of a man.

The park itself was walled. The army camping outside it was as an army of statues, with the soldiers frozen into those positions they had held when Samandra had mouthed that awesome spell taught her by Thelonia. They ignored the bolted gate; they floated above the walls and downward toward the garden paths and the trimmed yew hedges and the plats of flowers that made this corner of the park a paradise for lovers. Marble benches and erotic statues had been carved and placed in little grottos to tempt all who came in pursuit of fleshy pleasures. The love goddess herself might have planned this park, for there were depictions of the sterile and illicit caresses sacred to Hastarth in bronze and marble, everywhere the eye might look.

The palace was of porphyry and marble, of ebony and ivory. It was a masterpiece of architecture, with its many leaded windows shaped in the manner of a male or a female organ, and the entrance itself was…

Samandra gulped. She heard Thelonia laugh and turned toward her. The demon-woman cried, "Which of the two planned that doorway, Samandra? I think he is a very naughty man!" The wailing she had heard was louder.

Out onto a balcony burst Elviriom, half clad in black tunic and with only one sandal on a foot. Behind him, peering from the window, was a fleshy, redheaded wench, a courtesan out of Vandacia. Elviriom saw the black sentience of Belthamquar, the pearly pink nakedness of Thelonia, with horror etched upon his features.

His eyes bulged. His mouth fell open.

"Mightiest of gods! Father of demons! Why are you here?… Beautiful Thelonia, most lovely of succubi! To what do I owe this honor?"

King Unus screeched, "Enough of your cloying tongue, Elviriom. I'm here to exert my powers over you. Where's that other niddering, Thalkalides?"

"Hiding beneath a bed, my son," shouted Thelonia. "Thalkalides— come to us!"

Through the marble wall floated the second mage, clutching a sheet about his nudity, as a dark-haired wanton from the desert world of Oasia stared with wide eyes from a bedroom window. Thalkalides was shivering as with a fit. The sweat ran down his face and his mouth was open like that of a gaffed fish. With a despairing cry he fell to his knees.

"Great demons of the void—where have I sinned?"

"You've sinned against me, Thalkalides—as has Elviriom," shouted Unus. "Me you name king, yet I am no more than a puppet whose strings you pull when the spirit moves you. I am both of you—in one body. I speak your words, I think your thoughts."

"Mighty king," quavered Thalkalides.

"Wise sovereign," babbled Elviriom.

"I would rule Phalkar, and perhaps Makkadonia and Sybaros to the east, as well as Gwyn Caer and Zorador to the west. I shall be the mightiest emperor on Yarth! But I will do this in my own name, in that of Unus the First, the all-Conqueror, the Immortal and the Invincible! Destroy them, father! Consume them, mother!"

Samandra added her voice to that of the king. "This is my vengeance, Elviriom! My revenge, Thalkalides! For what you did to me years ago—suffer now!"

Thalkalides shrieked in unearthly fear, for well he knew the fate that was in store for him. Elviriom reeled, his face an ashen hue, and he might have fallen had not Thelonia lengthened a strand of her long golden hair to hold him upright.

Toward Thalkalides moved the dark intelligence that was the father of demons. With little questing tentacles he searched over the body of the mage, shredding the sheet that hid him until it disappeared in puffs of smoke. And now Thalkalides screamed and screamed as those little ebon tentacles dipped inside the skin of the wizard and, like tiny knives, began to cut away, here and there, severing the skin of the sorcerer from the body within it. Long it took the demon to flay the hide off the screaming, agonized wizard. An evil delight Belthamquar took in the screams and agonies of this man who had commanded his services. By inches he pulled loose the skin, tugging it off over head and shoulders and revealing the bloody ruin of the skinless body beneath.

And when he was done, when the screams of Thalkalides were no more than a bubbling whimper, Belthamquar gathered the empty skin and the life force it still contained into his darkness where that voice was raised anew in tormented shrieks and outcries.

"Are you pleased with your revenge?" Unus asked softly.

Samandra nodded, unable to speak. Her very soul was frozen inside her body as she understood at last what manner of vengeance a demon may take.

Now it was the turn of Thelonia who lowered herself onto the balcony beside gaunt Elviriom who stood staring at this lovely she-demon in utter horror. Her soft laughter rang out as her hands touched the skin of the gaunt wizard. The few bits of clothing on his scrawny frame burst into flames and fell away, leaving him naked.

Then Thelonia put her hands on his chest and slid them inside his body. Up to her elbow went her hands and now Elviriom screamed even more than Thalkalides had screamed, for the hands of Thelonia were remaking and remolding his body inside his skin, breaking bones and pulling ligaments, working cartilage and gristle as a sculptor works wet clay.

She changed the face and the body of Elviriom and all the while the mage screamed his painful agony at that living vivisection. Only the powers of the she-demon prevented him from losing his mind at what was happening to him.

And when she was done…

A giant toad crouched upon the balcony, and its eyes were the eyes of Elviriom. It croaked piteously, but it was forced to obey the snapping fingers of the demon-mother, and leap where she commanded it, hopping after her as she rose upward until she hung in the air beside the pentagram.

"Farewell, my son," she murmured.

She cried a word and…

Samandra reeled dizzily, reached out her hands and caught hold of King Unus to steady herself. They were back in her conjural chamber, she saw with tired eyes. Belthamquar and Thelonia had come and gone, and with them they had taken the two wizards.

King Unus stepped from the pentagram, nodding his head and smiling coldly. "It is done, what you promised, and I am grateful," he said softly.

She was stepping off the pentagram when he brought his hand out from under his cloak. There was a long dagger in that pallid hand.

To the hilt he plunged it in her belly.

CHAPTER EIGHT

Kothar and Stefanya rode at the gallop along the dusty road to the forest world that borders Phalkar and Makkadonia. They spoke no words to one another, for the grim scowl on the face of Kothar kept the girls lips tightly closed. From time to time she glanced at him and found that her heart thudded excitedly at sight of his muscular bulk and craggy good looks.

"If I am queen in Alkarion," she thought, "I would like Kothar to be my king. I am in love with him." She flushed to her thoughts, which was unlike Stefanya, for she had been brought up from babyhood to young womanhood by old Zoqquanor who was a wizard dabbling in many evil and esoteric matters.

The steady tattoo of their hoofbeats carried them along a dusty road, past a wide meadowland and back into the forest. Here they galloped through shafts of golden sunlight beating between the leafy branches. And now the girl noticed that Kothar moved his shoulders and shifted in his high-peaked saddle, as though imps of deviltry stabbed at him with barbed faery-spears.

His growled words were soft, yet she heard them clearly. "I do not like it. I have the feeling that we are being followed."

At a rise in the road he slowed his pace, reined in and stood in the stirrups, staring back along the read they had come. There were no travelers on that road, as far as Stefanya could see.

"But who would follow us?" She hesitated, then asked, "And—why?"

His eyes bore at her. "Why? Haven't you figured that out yet? Don't you know where were going?"

She shook her head, puzzled.

"Have you forgotten Zoqquanor in a deep coma somewhere in the gorges of Gyrolois? Do you remember when Torkal Moh attacked us, staking me out and robbing me, and carrying you off with him? The comatose body of the old magician was on a spare horse. They pitched it into a gorge, didn't they?"

Understanding came to her. She put her fist to her mouth and gnawed on it in worry. "Yes," she nodded. "They saw no value in it—I told them we carried it to the burial ground Zoqquanor had picked out for himself long ago. They heaved it between a couple of rocks."

Kothar jerked the reins of Greyling and touched him to a run with his war-booted toe. "Then we ride to find him and keep him safe."

"Keep him safe? You mean, keep me safe!" She was hard put to keep up with the tireless grey warhorse that the barbarian rode. Her bay mare was tired and stumbled from time to time. She did not think Kothar had heard her, but he spoke again, slowing Greyling so that she could come even with him.

"Yes, keep you safe. Both as a woman and as future queen of Alkarion. King Unus plots against his wizard counselors to destroy them with the help of Samandra and the demon-gods she summons up.

"Do you think Unus will be satisfied with that?

"You are as much a threat to him. Aye, by Dwallka! For you are the princess of Phalkar, the throne belongs to you. When Samandra and I agreed that we must announce this fact to Elviriom and Thalkalides to draw their action—when Samandra turned herself into the three-eyed golden foll—we knew that we were taking a chance.

"Well, Unus has done one thing we expected. He's turned against the wizards. Now he'll come after you. There's no need for him to seek you out. I'm sure that before he destroyed Elviriom and Thalkalides he made certain that they employed their necromantic arts to learn where you were hidden all those years of your absence. They must have discovered about Zoqquanor—and how he laid a spell upon you so that when he died, you died.

"All Unus has to do is locate Zoqquanor!"

They galloped through the cool forests and along the marshland road, then over a wide, vast prairie. The bay mare fell farther and farther behind, but now Stefanya did not mind, for she knew that only Kothar could protect the body of Zoqquanor if King Unus came seeking it. She herself could do nothing to aid him.

And then the gorges of Gyrolois were before them, grim and grey, jagged and rising upward from deep ravines and forming peaks of brooding granite. It was a wasteland of rock, with only the pebbled road to suggest that man might exist anywhere on such a world. They clattered along the road, and then the barbarian drew rein.

His eyes scanned the roadway, seeing the holes where they had put stakes to hold him down, half-filled now by the winds that roamed the gorges. Somewhere nearby, Torkal Moh would have dumped the body of the magician.

Dismounting, he moved from rock to rock, staring downward into the crevasses and the gullies, letting his stare range across the jutting laccoliths and the soil creeps. He leaped from crag to crag until finally he gave a bellow and pointed.

"There, Stefanya! Wedged into a crack about twenty feet down."

She came running to stand on the edge of a rock formation and watch as the barbarian swung over its lips and went downward, hands and toes seeking and gripping for holds. Perched on a jut of stone he tugged at the body of Zoqquanor until it came free of the rock grip that held it.

To his shoulder he threw the body, but it was so stiff it hampered his climbing. He was forced to tighten a rope Stefanya tossed to him from his saddle, and tie the magician to his broad back.

When he stood upon the roadbed, the girl came to him and loosed the ropes, easing the body to the ground. They stared down at the waxen face and white beard and long hair of the sorcerer. To Kothar, it seemed that he was dead and frozen, as if by long immersion in the ice of a northland glacier. Stefanya stared at him with wide eyes, remembering the curse he had laid upon her living flesh.

Then the Cumberian growled, "Listen!"

She heard nothing at first. Then, very slowly and weakly and from far away, she detected the sound of pounding hoofbeats. The girl turned, put a hand to her forehead as her eyes ranged back along the road which she and the barbarian had galloped.

There was a horseman in the distance.

He rode a white beast that ate at the road with its long legs, with a speed beyond the strength of normal flesh and blood. It was a demonic thing, that white stallion that ran more swiftly than a horse should run. And sitting straight upon its back, wrapped in a purple and gold cloak, sat King Unus.

Stefanya whirled. "What sort of mount does he ride that moves so swiftly? It covers miles within seconds!"

"A horse from hell," Kothar grunted. "A beast the wizards must have conjured up for him."

He drew Frostfire and stepped out upon the road.

King Unus came as does the gale, sweeping along the road without pause, without halt, a blaze of whiteness that was horse and rider. With fantastic strides the animal came on, blurring with motion, but there was a motionless quality about it so that it seemed he glided rather than ran. Yet, his hoofbeats made a thunder that crashed and rocked about the ears of the man and girl who stood staring downward.

Then the horse was coming along the road right at them. They could see the red eyes of the king in his dead-white face as he stared from them to the body of the magician, and back again. White hands reined in that strange animal that took the appearance of a gigantic horse, and then the king swung down to stand beside it.

"You have done my work for me, Kothar. My thanks."

The barbarian drew Frostfire and growled, "Zoqquanor lives, Unus. And he stays alive."

"Fool! The magician and the girl die here, this day. Stand back if you would live. I can destroy you all."

The barbarian leaped, his blue blade flashing in the sunlight. So swift was his lunge, so powerful the stroke of his sword, that the keen edge of Frostfire slashed through the purple and gold cloak, severing its threadings. Part of the cloak fluttered to the ground as Unus leaped back.

"I warned you, barbarian. Now…"

The red eyes grew and burned. Scarlet hellfires came to life within them and a beam of redness sprang from those eyes to the Cumberian, and splashed upon him so that he stood in an aura of redness. Stefanya screamed. She had seen in the crystal ball how King Unus had dissolved a criminal with that scarlet bath from his unearthly eyes.

Yet Kothar was not harmed by the brilliance swathing his huge body. Instead, he hurtled forward and again his great blade slashed.

King Unus had been confident that he had seen the end of the Cumberian. He was turning away when Kothar leaped. Now he dodged, instinctively lifting a hand as if to ward off that flashing steel. Through the arm went the edge of Frostfire, severing it slightly above the elbow.

Unus reeled back, screeching in surprised alarm.

"You should be dead! Kothar—what demon protects you?"

Kothar leaped, but now Unus was warned. He dove sideways and dodged that steel and though no blood dripped from his arm-stump, he felt pain. His pallid face was twisted in terrible rage and his lips mouthed imprecations dreamed in hellfires.

As he fled, Unus waved his lone hand. Upward from the ravines and the gullies of these gorges came chunks of rock flying through the air toward the barbarian. One hit Frostfire, drove it from his hand. A second hit the middle of his broad back and rebounded from his link-mail. A third slashed across his head, leaving a bleeding furrow.

The barbarian went to his knees.

He fought wizardry, he knew.

King Unus had inherited, or learned, a little of the necromantic skills of his creators. And well he used them, summoning up the rocks of the earth and hurling them in an awful bombardment on his enemy. The king stood with widespread legs, his head thrown back, and his eyes blazed brightly as he shouted out words that Kothar could not understand.

Yet the barbarian saw the result of those words.

A vast fissure opened in the road. He was lunging forward, hand reaching out for his sword hilt, when that fissure was spawned before him. Downward into that crevasse went his magical blade.

And then a wind appeared to catch it and the sword flew upward. To the outstretched hand of King Unus flew the blade. The king wrapped white fingers about it and laughed, head thrown back, and the victory was his.

For Kothar felt tiny tendrils wrap about his arms and legs and he knew they were tentacles out of some demoniac world that Unus summoned up. He crouched there on the edge of the crevasse and he saw the king move forward toward the dead body of the wizard Zoqquanor.

Stefanya leaped to stop him, was met by a hand across her face that tumbled her backward, sprawling on the pebbled roadbed.

With a cry of hate, King Unus let his red eyes blaze and a thin needle beam of scarlet drove deep into the chest of the comatose wizard. Deep went that deadly redness, until it pinned the wizard to the ground.

Stefanya screamed and caught at her chest. She writhed like a woman dying from a sword thrust. She flopped about, flailing the air with her arms as her legs and neck held her arched above the ground.

"Dwallka—aid me," growled Kothar.

Through the air the barbarian launched himself, tearing himself free of those tiny tendrils, just as Unus was turning to face him. His mighty arms went about the king, pinning his arms to his side, rendering the sword useless. Kothar tightened his arms.

And King Unus screamed in agony.

Back went the royal head. Wide stared the red eyes, sightlessly at the sky. He hung limp and lifeless, and the barbarian felt the short hairs on the back of his neck stand up. Mighty was his bear-hug, massive were his muscles. But no man, no matter how strong, could have killed Unus this swiftly!

Puzzled, he opened his arms. The inert, dead body of that which had been King Unus flopped upon the ground and lay motionless. The barbarian found his eyes caught and held by a bit of burning garment. Below that, where the cloth had burned away, there was the mark of a blue flame on the white skin of the dead king's chest.

Kothar knelt, parted the scorched clothing. There was no doubt about it. The print of the blue flame was there, stamped indelibly upon the white flesh.

Wonderingly, the Cumberian stared down at himself, saw the amulet that Merdoramon had given him at the oasis in the Dying Desert. By the gods of Thuum! So this was why the red death had not affected him! And why, when he placed his arms about King Unus to crush him, he had died so swiftly.

Merdoramon had placed a counter-spell inside the amulet that dangled on its chain from his neck. The blue flame was the magic that warded off the incantations of Elviriom and Thalkalides—and since King Unus was their creation, formed by their necromancies—it worked against him, as well!

Kothar turned his head, saw the dying Stefanya in the dirt. The wizard was gasping; the barbarian fancied he could hear his death rattle. His eyes scanned the road, seeing no crevasse in the road, no rocks that had been hurled at him. This too, was the wizardry of Unus. He swung on Stefanya, understanding bursting in him.

The amulet was in his hand as he landed on his knees beside the dying girl. Zoqquanor's death had been caused by the magical abilities of King Unus. Perhaps the amulet would protect Stefanya as well!

He draped the chain about her throat, let it dangle downward so that the blue flame pressed against the psychic wound that was killing her. There was no response; Stefanya lay there lifeless. Kothar rumbled anger in his throat, and his great hand closed into a fist with which he beat the air.

"Kothar," Stefanya whispered.

Her eyes were open, resting tenderly on his face. Her sun-darkened hand reached out, caught his own and held it. "What happened to me?"

"I put Merdoramon's amulet about your neck."

He told her how he had killed King Unus and how it had been the amulet that protected him and had slain the king when its blue flame had touched his flesh. Stefanya allowed him to lift her to her feet, and went with him to stare down at the dead wizard, Zoqquanor.

"It was the only way you could have been saved," Kothar growled. "If Zoqquanor had died in any other way except by the magics of Elviriom and Thalkalides through Unus—you would be dead."

There were tears in her eyes when she looked at him. "Come with me to Alkarion, Kothar. Help me rule Phalkar wisely and well." Then, as if she remembered something out of those days and nights they had been together, she added, "I shall hire you to be my prime minister. Will you sell me your sword, barbarian?"

He chuckled and clapped her behind with a big palm. "Get on your horse, Your Majesty. It's a long ride back to Alkarion."

And in Alkarion, they went first to the house of Samandra. A long time Kothar rapped on it with his dagger pommel before the door opened and Samandra looked at them. She smiled, lifting a hand to brush back her hair.

"King Unus stabbed me before he went to slay Zoqquanor. Had I not suspected he might do just that and prepared a spell to counter the effects of his dagger blow, I would be dead. As it is, I still feel weak."

"Ride with us to the palace, Samandra. You shall be my foremost lady-in-waiting. And the only one permitted to practice black magic within the boundaries of Phalkar. Legally, that is."

And so Samandra rode with them to the palace. As she rode, her eyes brooded on Kothar who went with sunken head, deep in thought. Troubled he was in heart and spirit, she knew. When Stefanya was surrounded by the servants and palace guards welcoming her home, the sorceress drew the barbarian aside.

"She is infatuated with you. Has she offered you her throne?"

"Not yet. I'm to be prime minister."

"You'll hate it."

"I know, but I haven't the heart to hurt her."

Samandra smiled and whispered words of wisdom.

At midnight, while the palace slept after the splendid banquet with which Queen Stefanya had welcomed General Jarken Wat and the noblemen and rich merchants of Phalkar to her hall, Kothar the barbarian crept from the silent palace and mounted his warhorse, Greyling. He rode him out of Alkarion, content with his lot.

He sang as he passed through the Dragon Gate and trotted along the road to Makkadonia. Frostfire swung at his side. He was no king, doomed to rot upon a throne, despite the fact that he might have a beautiful woman at his side. There were not enough treasures in the Phalkarian strongrooms to tempt him to give up his sword.

Ever since Afgorkon, the long-dead mage, had given him the sword—with a choice of keeping the sword and riding penniless through life, or foregoing Frostfire and accepting wealth—it had been this way. It satisfied Kothar the barbarian.

His hand touched the red jewel set in the sword hilt and wrapped long fingers about the braided hilt. It was a caress, that gesture, as though he stroked the smooth flesh of a beautiful woman.

KOTHAR AND THE WIZARD SLAYER

CHAPTER ONE

Where the seawaters lapped the rocky shore of Norgundy, a tall man wandered. He was clad in black cloak and nether garments that swayed with the breezes coming off the Outer Sea in a strange, writhing fashion, as though these garments might be alive. His step was firm, his eyes bright, as Luthanimor the Obsessed searched the seastrand for those purplish shells that gave him the power to summon up the demons of the deep.

A great magician was Luthanimor, one versed in the spells and cantraips of his world. But he was fearful, for odd tales had come to his ears of late concerning the deaths of other necromancers, men as great or even greater than he when it came to dooming a man or a maid to the seven hells of Eldrak or summoning up the cacodemons to destroy a warrior or a castle.

"Hastarth, send that I may find them," he whispered.

His head bent low as his eyes scanned the seashore where the ocean waters ran, frothing and bubbling before they sank down into the sand or ran out upon the wide shelf of beach sands. With but a few of the purple shells called myradex, he might summon up Omorphon, who would tell him how to protect himself against assassins.

Luthanimor did not see the thing that followed him crawling between the rocks, nor the long dagger it clutched in a rotting hand. Ever and always the lich watched the tall mage; ever and always it slithered closer, closer, making no sound on the rocks and on the stretches of sand. When the necromancer bent low above the shingle, the dead thing that followed him with the knife came to its height and ran, on decaying feet that made no sound, across the sand.

The dagger went deep between the mage's ribs. It was withdrawn, yanked back, and driven deep a second time. Luthanimor stiffened, his mouth opened as his bulging eyes stared sightlessly on the gray sky.

He slumped and fell, to lie lifeless.

* * * *

In great Romm, in a cobblestoned alleyway of that metropolis, Nebboth the warlock walked in the sidling gait that earned him the name of Crab among his fellows. A thin man with graying hair growing on a huge skull above a wry neck, he was forever shivering from cold except on the hottest days. He wore a black cloak and a hood up about his head, to shut off the cool winds sweeping across this poorer corner of the city.

Nebboth rarely came to the slums, he had servants to perform such menial tasks for him. But this night, he was seeking something special, two small girl children, sworn virgins, whom he would sacrifice to dread Eldrak in return for certain favors. Nebboth did not trust his hirelings; the children might be virginal no longer if he were to send huge Damthos after then. He would go himself, the lusts of the flesh no longer troubled him.

He was used to the sight of ragged men, of beggars and thieves who stalked these narrow byways for what they might beg or steal from honest folk. His sharp eyes darted into dark corners and recessed doorways, but he did not heed the tall, thin corpse in the torn burial robes, whose hand held a thin rope entwined about it.

Only when the mage stepped into a doorway set deep in a stone wall did the carrion thing move forward, snapping its right hand so as to free the thin cord. It whipped the cord in the air as the mage stepped into the doorway, thrust the door open. Before Nebboth could make a move, it wrapped the cord about his neck.

Its bony hands drew the cord tight while Nebboth clawed at the thing that was digging into his neckflesh, stifling him, cutting the air from his windpipe. Blue in his face was Nebboth, and the contortions of his lips and the flaring of his nostrils told of his agony.

For a few more seconds, life remained in the necromancer. Then he gave a great shudder and went limp. The lich released its hold, gathered up the thin cord, and rewound it about its hand.

It opened the street door, peered left and right, then broke into a lurching run along the cobbles.

* * * *

One by one, all over Yarth from the flatlands of Zoardar in the northwest to Zoane in Sybaros on the Outer Sea, from the snowy peaks of the Sysyphean Hills to the pyramids of Pshorm, the magicians of this world were meeting death. A bloody dagger, a worn length of killing cord, a sword or an axe, the weapon varied though the deed did not.

Anthalam in Vandacia, grim old Vardone of Ifrikon, many were the mages who went to join their ancestors in these early days of the Month of the Dragon. Fear was a blight among them, for the deaths that came to them tiptoed on unseen feet, hung poised on seemingly invisible daggers, for no man saw the coming of his death, always it was out of the shadows or the darkness.

In a tomb that housed the dead body of Kalikalides the magician, lay a sleeping woman whose long red hair fell over her white shoulders and down the stone walls of the ancient tomb, where her body rested atop the bier slab. She turned and twisted in her sleep. Uneasy was that necromantic slumber; her eyelids quivered, and the scarlet fans that were her lashes threatened to open at any moment. Her red lips moved, parting, and she uttered wordless little cries of dread and alarm.

In her dreams, Red Lori stood before the great stone throne where sat the dead mage whose tomb she shared. Kalikalides brooded down on her, but he shook his head and his lips quirked in what was meant to be a smile.

"My help cannot undo what has been done, Lori."

"It can prevent—more deaths! Lord Kalikalides, have pity on them all. Your friends, your fellows, Luthanimor, Nebboth, Anthalam! All of them dead—slain by wizardry! A wizardry that comes from whence—no man knows.

"Soon all will be dead, all!"

"Except him who sends the slayers!"

"Ahhh—and who is it?"

In her dream she leaned closer, breathing harshly. The dead mage drummed fingertips on the broad stone arm of his stone throne in these charnel regions, making a faint, rhythmic sound even as he frowned.

"I do not know. He has covered his steps well, whoever he is. He has put a wall of demons about his deeds which even my eyes cannot penetrate."

"Then let me go, release me from the silver barrier Kothar placed upon your tomb door!"

A savage fury shook her as Red Lori spoke. Hate for the barbarian from the far northlands, the blond sellsword who had placed her here and sealed the edges of the tomb with molten silver, ate inside her. Before that, he had brought her captive over his shoulder out of the dark tower where she worked her incantations to aid Lord Markoth against Queen Elfa of Commoral, and had given her over to a silver cage hung high in the audience hall of the queen.

Kothar himself had freed her of the silver cage when she caused a she-demon named Ahrima to bring him to Commoral, but his barbaric wits had succeeded in imprisoning her once again, this time in Kalikalides' dank tomb.

"Free me," she whispered to the lich of the dead magician. "Free me, so I may help those of our wizard brotherhood left alive."

Kalikalides pondered, chin on fist. He sighed and in her dreams began to speak in his sepulchral voice. "Indeed, I like it no better than you, fair Lori. Magicians and warlocks should be sacred folk, freed from fear of the assassin's knife. But what may I do? I am long dead, as well you know."

"You know ancient spells. There must be one that will pass my body through the silver barrier."

"None! There are none."

Red Lori sank weeping in stark rage to the stone floor, her hair like a scarlet mist about her body. Angrily she beat her white fists against the flaggings.

"Cursed be the name of Kothar! May his bones rot in his flesh and may his flesh stink with the suppurations of ulcerated wounds! May Omorphon sink his serpentine fangs in his liver and never let him go. May—"

"Hush, woman! Your eternal babbling disturbs my thought—and I am even now recalling an old spell, an incantation long forgotten by me…"

"Will it pass through silver?"

"Not your body, but a part of you. A spirit body that will appear to men in all respects as if it were real flesh and blood."

Excitement made Red Lori tremble. "It is enough," she breathed. "I know a way to join flesh body to spirit body! All I ask is to go out of this place into the world—where Kothar lives!"

"You must forget vengeance for a while!" warned the magician, leaning forward on the stone throne from which he ruled the world his magic made before he died. "Were Kothar to suspect, he could blast your spirit self merely by touching you with that same silver which keeps you penned in here with me! Avoid angering him, Lori—if you would live and be free."

Between grating teeth she snarled, "I will be like a puling maiden. I will serve him like a doting slave girl. I will even—faugh!—make love to his barbarian body if it will help me."

"Pleasantly, Lori—pleasantly!"

She made herself smile. The smile transformed her lovely features, that had been contorted with rage and shame, into those of a young girl. Young was Red Lori when she smiled, like a shepherdess or a milkmaid in the meadow. Her mouth was a scarlet fruit sweetly curved and ripe for kisses, her red tresses like a shimmering veil hiding the white flesh of her shoulders and upper arms.

"See you do, witchwoman. The barbarian is no fool. If you intend to go to him—"

"Oh, I do—since I have a need for his sword and his muscles. Aye, I shall be the virginal innocent—until he gives me what I need to set myself free in truth."

"So be it. Then listen; this is what you must do."

Her slumber was troubled now, and she frowned, tossing slightly so that the worn velvet wrapping that covered her against the chill of the tomb slid down to reveal her ripely curving body clad in the Mongrol blouse and leather skirt which she had worn when she stepped into this tomb. Words came from her lips in broken phrases, at the sound of which the air grew cold and gelid in the stone sarcophagus. Faster she spoke and faster, committing those dread sounds to memory.

The cold woke her.

Red Lori sat up, clutching the velvet wrapping tighter about her shoulders. On the painted ceiling and walls of the crypt she could see the glittering hoarfrost and the hanging icicles which told her that her dream had been a reality of sorts. Her spirit had left her body, had gone into that charnel world of Kalikalides' own creation, where she had spoken with him.

Under her breath she whispered those words, shivering to the intense cold they summoned up. Now she knew that it had been no true dream but a journeying of her spirit into another realm. Kalikalides had placed a key in her white palms, a key which she would turn with words, to transport a part of her into the outer world.

Lying back, throwing aside the wrapping, she stretched out upon the top of the stone bier which held the rotting remains of the dead sorcerer. She understood now the reason for the cold, it was to hold her flesh in eternal ice while her *ka* went searching for the barbarian. Without its spirit, the flesh might putrefy; the cold would prevent this, would keep her body as it was now, while her spirit was still inside it.

"Great Thissikiss, lord of ice, of snow, of cold that numbs the soul! Hear my plea! Come unto me, come across the abysses and the voids of space and time that separate us! Take into your icy paws my body, shelter it from evil. And so benumb my every sense that my spirit may go forth, free of this fleshy trapping.

"Thissikiss, hear me!

"I call you by Titicomti and by Alchollos, by Belthamquar the demon-father, and his dread mate, Thelonia!

"Come to me, Thissikiss. Come! Come! Come!"

From far away she seemed to hear the rumble of ice floes one upon another, caught the moan of the icy blast of wind that ranges the snowclad hills and dales of fabled Hyperborea. A frozen breeze swept the chamber, and where it touched, the hoarfrost lay in thick white sheets. Her own body was beyond sensation, she realized. She felt neither heat nor cold nor did any odor touch her nostrils.

She was frozen flesh.

Aye, frozen solid by Thissikiss, yet still—alive!

For her spirit self could move, and rose and walk about this chamber, though her body was naked, with only the long red hair to hide her blue-veined flesh. She stood in the mausoleum and threw back her head and let soft laughter rise from her lips toward the icicled ceiling.

Free! At long last—free!

"My thanks, Thissikiss. Keep me safe within your paws."

She mounted the stone steps leading upward from this subterranean vault to the upper level and moved toward the great stone slab that was the tomb door. Around this stone Kothar had placed the molten silver, sealing it, past which she could not go. Yet now she knew the way to travel beyond that barrier, in this shape that had substance and outline of a sort, though her true flesh and blood body lay frozen like unto death on the bier slab.

Red Lori lifted her hands and bent her head, placing her lovely features within her cupped palms, the better to concentrate her thoughts. She must make no error, without flaw must she speak the cantraipal formula that would permit her to slip from this tomb into—that other place where she would go.

She began to chant those words softly, almost to herself.

And the world around her reeled.

CHAPTER TWO

The sun beat down with fury upon the golden sands of the desert which ran from the great rock scarps of the Haunted Regions as far eastward as the vast meadowlands of Sybaros, and which, some men said, once had been an inland sea-bottom. On that vast sand sea, a horse and its rider moved slowly, steadily southward toward a range of low hills marking the southern boundary of this vast wasteland.

The rider was a huge man in mail shirt and with thick, sun-browned thighs showing between a plain leather war kilt and tan leather war boots. The muscles rolled in his arms and his long blond hair was caught in a leather thong knotted to keep the hair from getting in his eyes, for the wind whipped across these sandy wastes in a steady blow.

Beneath him the big gray warhorse moved with steady gait, walking leisurely in the heat, with a faint jingle of ringbits and harness brasses. A sword with a red gem in its hilt, long in the blade and with a gently curving crosshilt, gathered sunbeams to it and reflected them.

There were reflections of that same strong sunlight off metallic surfaces in the distance, where the rocks made a jagged carpet around a thin ribbon of road. Kothar the barbarian had seen those dancing motes of sunlight hours before; he had frowned suspiciously and watched them with hard blue eyes. His warrior instincts told him those bits of unusual brightness must be made by spear points and helmets where a body of men lay hidden among the crags.

Did any but himself know why he rode this way, southeastward through the desert sands and toward the rocky pass leading into Tharia? He had kept the secret to himself, trusting no man.

And yet—those bright sparkles amid the rocks spoke to him of an ambush in which he was to play the part of victim. He growled low in his throat, loosed the blade in its ornate scabbard, and shifted so that he might bring the quiver of arrows hanging behind him within easier hand-reach. The great horn bow, which had been a gift of the merchant Pahk Mah when he had rescued his daughter Mahla from the ensorcelments of Red Lori, was unstrung but close to his left thigh.

He rode on, alert and waiting.

Where the sand made an upward slope before merging with the rock-land of the Tharian Pass, he drew rein and reached for a water skin hung from the saddle pommel. He yanked the cork, tilted the bag to his lips.

"Half a mile ahead, Greyling, that's where they wait."

His mouth twisted into a wry grin. An itch was in his palm to hold his sword Frostfire against his enemies, he had been peaceful too long in Zoane and Atlakka, those cities of Sybaros where he had first learned of the ancient grave of Kandakore. Apparently others had heard of the grave and of his search for it.

Kothar lifted the horn bow into his hand, strung it with muscles bulging in his long arms—for the horn was tough and bent not easily—so that he might set the catgut string in place. Bow in his big left hand, he toed Greyling to a canter.

The hidden men planned to surprise him, but the barbarian swordsman would furnish the surprise. At least, this was his plan. But as he rode forward, he soon heard the ring of weapons clashing ahead of him and the shouts of warring men.

"By Dwallka, they've marked another for the slaying!"

His laughter boomed out and now the war-horse went at the gallop along the abandoned roadbed, for few travelers moved along this highway that had been built when Kandakore had ruled in long-forgotten Phyrmyra. From the hide quiver he drew out a long war arrow and fitted it to the bowstring.

The clash of ringing swords was close, now. As Kothar rounded the bend in the old highway, he saw one man fighting off a dozen, a slender youth in mail and helmet, with a broken sword in his hand. He was dismounted and moving backward toward a high stone boulder where he could make a stand.

Kothar bent his bow, let loose the arrow.

Straight it flew, to bury itself in the chest of a burly man with a black beard. Again he fired, and now a lean man dropped. The grass grew thinner about the lone youth who fought so bravely with the broken sword. Some of his attackers turned toward the giant in the mail shirt galloping down on them.

The barbarian fired two more arrows, saw two more men drop. Then he was casting the bow aside, drawing Frostfire. The long blade lifted as he reined the gray horse to the side of the road and sent him thundering past three of the men who leaped for him.

A shearing swing of the steel and one man fell headless. Past a second bandit he drove the stallion, and this time the point stabbed into a throat just under a mail apron hanging from a helmet.

The galloping horse was past the melee now, turning to the hand on the worn leather reins. Kothar saw that the young man had thrown aside his broken sword, had snatched up another blade from the fingers of a dead man and was leaping forward on the attack.

The bandits did not wait to stand before these swordsmen. They scattered, running in among the rocks, slipping and sliding a path across them until they disappeared in the distance. Kothar reined up Greyling, let the horse snort and dance until its battle fever cooled. The youth before him stared up at the rider in the mail shirt and grinned.

"My thanks, warrior. It was touch and go for a while there, after I broke my blade on a helmet."

Kothar stared down at a slim young man whose face was split with a reckless smile, whose long brown hair hung to his shoulders. He wore a mail shirt, a sword belt about his middle. His red leather boots were dusty and split, here and there, by long usage. On the far side of the road was a sack he had dropped when the bandits came charging from the rocks.

"The name is Flarion," the youth informed him, bending to cleanse his bloody steel on the cloak of a fallen cutpurse.

"You don't look rich to me," the barbarian rumbled, dismounting to wipe his own blade dry. "So why should those bandits have attacked you? Unless you have stolen jewels in your sack or hidden on your person."

"Not I! I lost all I owned in a game of dice in a Grandthral tavern. Now I'm just a wanderer. Like yourself." His grin showed fine teeth in a nutbrown face.

Kothar scowled. "They must have been after something."

"Oh, they were, they were. My life. I—er—angered a fat merchant by making love to his pretty wife before I knew that the merchant was not on caravan but merely in his counting house, and soon due home."

His laughter rang out, carefree and careless.

"By Salara of the bare breasts! She was a woman, that one. Ignored by her fat husband. Too bad he interrupted us. I was about to make her disclose the hiding place of her jewels. I could have used the coins they'd fetch in a shop I know."

The brown head tilted sideways. "And you? No man rides this old road any more, unless he's running from an angry husband of King Midor's soldiery."

Kothar chuckled. "Or bound into Tharia to the haunted ruins of Phyrmyra, where Kandakore is said to have ordered his burial ten thousand years ago."

Flarion gaped, jaw dropping.

"The lost tomb of Kandakore! Is that your goal?"

"I'm tired of an empty belly, of a purse that's so lean all it holds is air. It's been a month since my throat tasted ale, or anything but a slab or two of dry bread and drier cheese. Gods, for a bit of meat and mayhap even a beaker of wine! The sellsword business is poor, these days."

Flarion muttered, "They say his tomb is haunted."

"Aye, by ghouls and goblins, or worse."

Brown eyes glinted through narrowed lids. "The old tales don't bother you? You'd risk being drained of blood or eaten in some dusty mausoleum?"

"If I could get a handful of gems or golden coins, it would be worth the risk."

He did not add that Afgorkon the Ancient had given him the choice of owning the sword Frostfire and little else; and that since he bore the sword, he had never been able to own more than a few silver deniers to rub together in his purse. Afgorkon had lived, a most potent sorcerer and wizard, more than fifty thousand years ago. His spirit still existed in a world of his own magical creation, across the abysses of astral space.

His curse was as strong today as the big barbarian over whom it hung, however. So Kothar carried Frostfire while poverty was an ache in his empty belly. He paused now, letting go the edge of the dusty cloak that had served to clean his blade.

"And you? Where are you bound?"

Flarion shrugged. "Anywhere. I have no goal, except to find a wench to kiss and a pallet to bed her on after washing the dust from my throat with a panniker of Tharian ale. If you want company, I'm your man. If you'll dare ghouls and hobgobs, so will I."

"If the old stories are true, the tomb of Kandakore holds much treasure, more than enough to make two men rich beyond their dreams."

"Kandakore hid his tomb well, the tales say."

"Where treasure is hidden, there are maps to show its hiding place."

Flarion snorted. "Aye, I know maps like that."

"But not—like this."

The barbarian reached into his leather belt-wallet, drew out a folded bit of parchment, tossed it across to the waiting youth. Flarion caught it deftly, opened it, his fingertips running over the smooth surface.

His eyebrows arched. "Sheepskin?"

"Human skin, or I miss my guess."

"Gods, maybe there is something to the old tales, after all. I suppose you've heard them, that Kandakore empowered Ebboxor, who was his mage, to build his tomb well and hide it, then mark its location on the skin of his favorite slave girl."

"I've heard rumors and legends."

Flarion knelt in the dust and spread the map on the road. "I wonder… if this be the skin of that girl, then perhaps…" His fingertip scratched at a thin black line that showed where a road had been, long ago. "Dried blood, treated in some manner…by Ebboxor? It might be. And if this really is human skin, and I think as you do that it is, then…"

His grin was broad. "Then by Salara's creamy bosom, I think you've got hold of something. How'd you come by it?"

"In Makkadonia where I was serving as sergeant of guards, following a little adventure of mine with Queen Stefanya of Phalkar, whereby I set her on her throne. It seems that King Horthon of Makkadonia has a few hated enemies. Among them was a certain Jokathides, one of the richer merchant princes.

"Well, King Horthon sent a few of his chosen guardsmen to loot the cellars beneath Jokathides' vast town house, which is so big it's practically a palace. At one time, his basements were part of the palace of the Sassanidon line, which ruled Makkadonia long ago.

"We looted it, all right, and helped ourselves into the bargain to a few treasures we felt Horthon wouldn't miss. But Horthon is no fool, he knows what poor wages he pays his warriors, so he had other warriors intercept us before we could leave the cellars with our loot. The men were searched, all their little trinkets were taken away from them."

Flarion laughed softly. "But—not you!"

Kothar rumbled laughter. "Well, I admit I heard what was happening, so I started off into another corner of the tunnels so I could hide the few things I'd managed to take. I went into another part of that basement where we hadn't been, and from the dust on the place nobody else had been there since the Sassanids were dust, I'd wager. A part of the wall was cracked, broken."

He had peered into the darkness beyond the crack, smelling the dankness of old age, the mustiness. His hand slipped, and he saw that the brick against which he leaned his weight was loose. A few moments later he had made a hole wide enough to squeeze through, and when he was inside the hidden chamber, he struck sparks from flint and steel, lighted his tinder, and held up his small lamps.

There were tumbled chests and dusty coffers here and there, with bars of gold and silver making small mountains. Dust lay thick over everything, so that he choked and coughed and had to spit to clear his throat. He moved about the chamber, examining everything. On the metal clasp of a small coffer, he had found carved the name: Ebboxor.

A blow from his dagger pommel snapped the rusted lock. Opening the coffer, Kothar found the parchment inside it. One touch of his fingers and he had known that this was human skin. Spreading out the vellum, he saw there was a map scrolled on that smooth surface.

Kothar chuckled. "I hid the thing flat against my chest under my mail shirt. It was so thin, nobody among the royal guards suspected I carried anything there.

"Soon after, I found an excuse to give up my employment and set out for these rocky wastes, beyond which the tomb of Kandakore is hidden."

"If you were in the royal guard, why is your purse so empty?"

"I spend the coins I earn as fast as my fists can close about them. I can't gather treasure and keep it—Afgorkon the Ancient sees to that!—and so I enjoy life when life is good. When it isn't, I cut new holes in my belt."

Flarion nodded, folding over the map and handing it back. "I know the feeling. But if you've a mind to share your luck in exchange for a sword to stand beside your own, Flarion's your man."

Kothar watched while the youthful mercenary picked up his traveling sack, tossed it over a shoulder. Kothar put a foot into his stirrup, swung up on his horse. From here, the ride to the fabled tomb of Kandakore was but a league, not too far for a man who had walked across the western desert of Sybaros, all the way from Grandthal.

Their way led through the rock country and down a long slope toward the ruins of ancient Phyrmyra. The grave he sought was in Phyrmyra, if his map were true. As they came to a crown in the road, by standing in his iron stirrups the barbarian could make out the few columns and the tumbled building stones that were all that was left of once-great Phyrmyra, faint in the distant haze of twilight.

"We'll camp and eat, first," he said to Flarion trudging beside him in the dust. "There's a fountain in the city that still gives water, travelers have told me."

"There's also a curse on Phyrmyra," grinned the youth, shifting his sack to the other shoulder. "Something about a leech that sucks the blood from a man and leaves him to die in raving madness."

The barbarian snorted. "I never heard anything about a leech. The traders I've spoken with said only that there was an evil in the old city which made them happy to shake its dust from their boots. They didn't linger long."

"We'll have to linger if we want to find that grave."

The barbarian merely grunted.

The came along the road into the twilight of the day, when the setting sun was a red ball low in the west beyond the Misty Swamps and the lands of the baron lords. The jagged rocks were behind them, while before them was a great plain where stood lonely orthon trees and berry-bushes, which gave ripe fruit now as they had when Phyrmyra had swarmed with people.

It was a quiet, dreaming kind of day, and Kothar found himself beset by memories of past encounters with demons such as Azthamur, Abathon and Belthamquar. Those dread beings from beyond the spatial gulfs had good reason to hate Kothar the barbarian; he wondered if one or all of them might come to him in Phyrmyra.

He moved his shoulders angrily, as if to rid himself of phantoms. His hand touched his sword hilt lightly, then fell away. The gibbering imps of his imagination would not let him go: Something waited for him in the ruined city, of this he was sure.

The city stood a mile eastward of the road which at one time, according to old legend, had run through its foreign market square. Now the columns and fallen pediments of the ruins showed only where a palace or a temple had been, with smaller buildings around it. Kothar turned Greyling toward the dead city.

Beside him, Flarion stumbled.

"Hells of Eldrak," he rasped. "What's this?"

His toe kicked sand, showing part of a bone gleaming whitely in the dusk of evening. Flarion spat. "A dead man, his skeleton."

There were other skeletons, the barbarian saw, shifting his glance downward and along the sands where his companion walked. Whitened bones, bits of ribcases, a hip bone, ulnars and tibias here and there made a trail out of Phyrmyra toward the road.

"They can't hurt us," he snarled.

Flarion laughed softly. "What made them bones—can! Still, for a treasure, a man must take risks."

They came among the standing columns and the fallen stone lintels in the first night darkness, with the stars glittering overhead and a wind moaning off the plain. "A dismal place," thought the barbarian, glancing around him as he came down out of the kak, "and if it were not for the map and the tomb it shows, I'd bed down on the clean dirt beside the highway."

He tossed a food bag to Flarion, with a wineskin. He unsaddled Greyling, rubbed him down, fed him oats in a leather pouch. The tinkle of water caught his ears, he turned from the horse and moved along what had been a wide road once but was no more than blocks of stone, tilted and awry, between which the sands had settled.

The water was coming from a rock wall out of which a worn stone conduit jutted. The water was probably forced upward from pressures below the ground, he told himself. He was about to sip when a voice breathed words into his ears.

"No, barbarian!"

Kothar jerked erect, hand on his dagger pommel.

"Who spoke?" he growled. Soft laughter mocked him, and the barbarian showed his teeth in a cold grin. "Red Lori! I'd know that laugh in the deeps of hell where it belongs."

"The water—slays, Kothar!"

He scowled at the conduit, at the crystal stream flowing from its length. He turned and glanced at Greyling and at Flarion, crouched before the fire which he had begun with dried twigs collected from below some orthon trees.

"You have water in your skins. Use that. Drink not this, on peril of your life."

He rubbed his blond head with his hand, scowling. He knew Red Lori well enough to understand that she considered him to be her own special property, to be executed and tortured in her own good time, to pay him back for the things he had done to her.

He knew also that she was still imprisoned in Kalikalides' tomb in Xythoron. Well, she had come to him at other times in his wanderings over the face of Yarth. Inside ale tankards, in the leaping red flames of his campfires, in dreams, he had seen her beautiful face and heard her words inside his head.

"You have seen the skeletons. Those belonged to men who came here parched with thirst and drank the waters of Phyrmyra. Be warned."

Kothar scowled, shrugged. He turned away, went back to the campfire, where Flarion was turning slabs of meat above the flames on a crude spit. "Ware the water. It's poisoned," he muttered, reaching for his waterskin.

"Now how would you know that?"

"I have a personal demon all my own. She helps me stay alive, from time to time. It is a whim of hers, because she hates me very much."

The mercenary considered this, squinting up at the giant on the other side of the fire. He nodded slowly. "If you say so."

They ate sitting on the ground, slowly and with relish, and drained more than half the contents of the wineskin. Cold was in the air here, for with the passing of the sun the ground lost much of its heat, and the wind was off the sea to the west, tainted with salt and chill.

With a muttered word, Kothar reached for the fur wrap that served him as cloak and saddle blanket. He drew it about his huge body, lay down with his feet toward the fire. A moment more Flarion waited, then drew a worn military cloak from his own sack and lay back, eyes closed.

The fire crackled, popped.

Kothar slept as does an animal, with only half his mind, his ears alive to the night sounds about him. Once during the night he rose from his fur wrapping and placed more twigs and branches on the fire. He stood a moment, staring about him at the distant rocks, the vast plain on which ancient Phyrmyra had rested. Then he slipped back into the fur wrapping.

He did not see the men who waited among the rocks and watched. They were crouched low with the rocks between them and the distant ruins. They could not be seen, but they watched the wink of red that was the campfire.

The morning sun was minutes old when the barbarian stirred and threw aside the big bearskin covering. He lay a moment, staring at the blue sky shot with red streamers. Then he was up and moving about the little camp, building up the fire, lifting the spade and pick he had brought with him from Zoane.

The smell of roasting meat roused Flarion, who came to stretch and yawn beside the flames, then bent to mix flour from a sack and water from his skin container, placing the biscuits on flat rocks to bake. He took the map Kothar handed him and spread it out on the ground so they might examine it while they ate.

"Here," said Kothar as he munched, tapping the human skin with a forefinger, "is The Temple of Salara. You'll note that it's right beside the water fountain. Now eastward from the temple, five hundred paces, is the statue built to honor Kandakore."

"And below the statue, his grave."

"We'll dig when we're done eating."

Kothar swallowed a final sip of wine before tossing the skin to his companion and rising to his feet. In his big hands the spade and pick seemed almost tiny as he walked across the tumbled flagstones of this old city square toward the wind-eroded remnant of what had been a carving of the love goddess.

His eyes measured the distance between the statue and the flowing water of the stone pipe. Five hundred paces; he marked them off slowly, thoughtfully.

With his spade, he dug out dirt and sand until the base of what had been a statue of Kandakore was revealed. He labored for close to an hour until the sweat dripped from his face. Then Flarion came to spell him.

When the flagstones all around the statue were cleared, the mercenary leaned on the spade. "There's no opening in the flagstones," he pointed out, tapping them with the edge of the spade.

"I can see that for myself. It comes to my mind that the statue itself may hold a clue as to its opening."

"You mean, it could be lifted, to disclose a hole?"

"Something of the sort, yes."

They strove until their muscles creaked, but the granite base could not be budged. Kothar snarled and moved back, walking all around that stone weight. The sun was higher in the morning sky, it cast dark shadows beyond the base. Kothar studied those shadows a moment, frowning, running his eyes along the edges of the giant block.

There appeared to be a space between the statue and the flagstones, just the merest fraction of an inch. The barbarian knelt, let his eyes run there. He nodded, rose to his feet.

"The base doesn't set flat," he said. "It's raised above the flagstones. Now I wonder why."

"Could we put a metal bar under it? Wedge and lift?"

"No, no. Perhaps the statue swings."

They set hands to the warm stone base and thrust hard. Nothing happened. "The joinings may be rusted," Kothar growled, and heaved again.

They were rewarded by the faint rasp of old metal. At the same time, the block gave, slipped sideways. Flarion yelled encouragement. They dug their toes into the sand tranches between the flagstones of this square, and their muscles swelled.

Slowly, as rusted metal grated, the thing moved, ponderously, with a muffled clank of hidden machinery. And Kothar felt the pavement under his war boots sink.

"Get back," he cried, pausing to stare downward.

A section of the pavingstones was tilted at an angle, forming a trapdoor. Dirt and sand ran down into the small opening before the stone base. Flarion moved to the other side of the block, put palms to its roughened surface.

"We can get better purchase here," he called.

Kothar nodded, stepped around to join him. Once begun, the further moving of the rock slab on its metal fulcrum was much easier. In moments it was swung completely sideways. The section of pavingstone had fallen downward, hung on stone hinges. As he came around to stare down into that dark abyss, he saw stone steps inset into a rock wall.

He swung down onto that ladder, began to descend into darkness. Flarion was on hands and knees, following his progress. "Do you have a lamp of some sort? A torch in your bags?"

"I was hoping to find a torch or two down here. There's a small oil lamp in my gear. Will you fetch it?"

Flarion ran, snatched up a tiny brass lamp, touched flame to its wick. With the lamp in hand he went down the ladder until he stood on a stone floor beside the Cumberian.

"Gods of Thuum," breathed Flarion, staring.

They stood inside a small chamber the walls of which were painted to represent scenes and incidents out of the life of the long-dead Kandakore. Here he stood with a foot upon the neck of an enemy bowed before him, there he sat his throne, receiving gifts from groups of travelers from foreign countries. A long marble table held jars and pots in which food had been sealed.

Beyond this dusty antechamber stood a door studded with brass fittings, proclaiming the fact that beyond the door was the burial tomb of Kandakore the Unconquered. For uncounted ages, this room had known not the footsteps of men, it had stood lost to the world, remote, part of the almost forgotten, fabulous realm of Phyrmyra.

Kothar shook his shoulders against his awe. He moved toward the door with Flarion at his heels, clasping the lamp. A touch of the hand pushed open that brass-hung doorway on its copper hinges.

Flarion lifted the lamp, held it high.

"By Dwallka!" bellowed Kothar.

A woman sat on the bier slab, knees together, hands folded in her lap. She wore the garments of a Mongrolian maiden, leather jerkin thonged to contain the fullness of her breasts, a short leather skirt, neat leather sandals. Long red hair tumbled down over her shoulders. Her face, in the golden lamplight, was very lovely.

CHAPTER THREE

The barbarian stood paralyzed with shock.

"Red Lori!" he bellowed at last, in utter amazement.

"You know her?" Flarion wondered.

"Kothar," breathed Red Lori, "my darling!"

She came off the stone bier slab, ran to the Cumberian and flung her bare arms about his neck. Against his lips she pressed her mouth, then seemed to shrink from him.

"Forgive me!" she whispered. "I could not help it. I've been here so long—put here by a wizard's curse—alone in the dark…"

"Poor girl," breathed Flarion.

"Damned witchwoman," growled Kothar.

Kothar fought the emotions inside his giant frame. That touch of soft lips to his, the momentary brush of female flesh and the clasp of bare arms about his neck angered him, because he liked that kiss, that embrace. And he knew Red Lori too well not to know that it must be part of an act. She wanted something of him.

Flarion reproved him. "How can you say such a thing, Kothar? She's been here because of a curse. And—she loves you."

"Oh, I do. I do!" Lori nodded, glancing from the younger man to Kothar. "I've always loved him, even when he was carrying me out of my dark tower in Commoral City to have me placed inside a silver cage."

There were tears in her eyes as her white hands wrung together. Her warm green eyes pleaded with the Cumberian. She took two steps toward him, let him feel the softness of her body, putting both arms about his middle and hugging him. Her perfumed red hair lay pillowed on his mailed chest.

"Now you have found me, Kothar. Take me with you, out of this place. I beg it of you. Do you want to see me on my knees?"

The grip of her arms loosed and she sank downward to kneel before him, face upturned, eyes wet, tears moving down her cheeks. Kothar stared down at her, knowing dully that he was lost. He could deny this woman nothing. There was an affinity between them. The Fates had made them enemies but the Fates could not control the wild thudding of his heart at her kiss, nor still the male flames in his flesh that leaped at contact with her body.

"Here, now. Get up, Lori."

His huge hands lifted her until she rested against him on tiptoes, her palms spread on his shoulders, her wet eyes smiling, echoed by the sweet curving of her lips. Slowly her hands crept upward as her bare arms lifted to clasp him about the neck.

"Darling Kothar," she breathed.

The barbarian was of half a mind to turn her and whack her backside with a big palm, but it had been a long time since a woman had pressed herself against him. He admitted grudgingly that he found it a pleasant thing. Her moist red mouth was close, slightly parted, as if begging for his kiss.

Kothar growled his helplessness against her allure. His arms tightened around her slim waist, his mouth closed on hers. He held her, swaying slightly, while Flarion stared at the ceiling of the tomb, at its painted walls, at the stone sarcophagus that held all that was left of King Kandakore.

Lori pushed away, flushing, lifting her hands to set to rights her long hair, smiling tenderly up at him, eyes shy and half hidden under her long lashes. She seemed like a maiden newly fallen in love. There was nothing of the arrogant witchwoman in her manner.

"What brought you here, Kothar?" she whispered.

"Treasure," answered Flarion. "But there's nothing here."

Red Lori pulled her green eyes away from Kothar's stare, turning to glance about the burial chamber. "This tomb is sacred to the death god. The royal treasures are kept in another place."

"Where?" asked Flarion.

"Why do you know so much about the burial habits of the Phyrmyran kings?" wondered Kothar.

"The demon who put me here told me of them," said Red Lori hurriedly. "He—ah—taunted me with the fact that in the next room was enough gold and jewels to buy half a world, while I must remain here, shut in and starving."

"You can't have been here too long," rumbled Kothar, running his eyes up and down her curving body, so blatantly exposed in the scanty Mongrol garb.

Lori laughed at him, lifting her arms about her head and turning to let him see what he would of her shapeliness. "Not long, no. I have an appetite for food, but I'm not starving."

Suspicion awoke in Kothar, who still did not trust this redheaded woman. She had vowed vengeance on him, she had hated him with a furious savagery; he did not believe she could have forgiven him so easily for locking her away with dead Kalikalides.

And yet—Her bare legs shone in the lamplight under the short leather skirt, admirably rounded and enticing. Her hips swung with a wanton little wiggle, her body was all sweet curves and smooth white skin as she ran past the stone bier toward a farther wall. Her hands and fingers fumbled there until Flarion went with the brass lamp to show her the raised stone-work she sought.

She turned a stone flower and part of the wall opened with a creak of unused hinges. Flarion cried out, pushing the lamp into the opening she had revealed.

"Kothar—look!" he cried.

Lori turned, held out her arm to the big barbarian, clasping his fingers with her own warm hand, leading him through the opening.

They stood in a room as large as the burial chamber. Golden statues of men and women and beasts stood in orderly rows beside a painted boat in which the mummified body of a sailor sat with the helm in a dusty hand. Metal and wooden coffers lay upon long tables set flush to the walls.

The floor was unmarked, covered by a thin layer of dust. Flarion pointed at it, shouted, "No one's been in here since they closed the place. No grave robber has ever found this place. It all belongs to us. To us!"

He ran to a table, put down the lamp so he could lift the lid of the nearest coffer resting there. He gave a cry when the lid went back. The lamplight showed hundreds of round golden coins—dildaks, they were, the forgotten coinage of ancient Phyrmyra. Each one was worth a fortune because no other coins like them existed in the present world. And also tiny bars of that same precious metal placed side by side. Flarion dug his fingers into that treasure hoard, letting coins and bars sift between them.

Red Lori drew Kothar to another coffer, extending her hand and raising the carved lid to show him red jewels and blue gems, precious diamonds and green emeralds. The ransom of ten emperors stood on this tabletop. Kothar growled his delight in what he saw, he lifted out a great ruby, held it to the lamplight. It glowed and sparkled as if with inner flames.

"It's too bad you cannot keep it," she whispered.

His eyes sparked. "Ah! You know about my curse?"

"You can keep no wealth but Frostfire, your sword. Oh, yes. I know all about Afgorkon and how he gave you the blade under a *geis.*"

The barbarian lifted her hand and dropped the giant ruby into her palm. "Then you keep this, Lori. It matches your hair."

Her red-nailed fingers tightened on the jewel. Her glance at him was curious, enigmatical. "You would do that? Give me this ruby?"

"Why not? Help yourself." His hand waved around the room. He chuckled, "One of us might as well share these riches. You and Flarion take what you will. I'll content myself with a few coins here and there, enough to keep Greyling and myself in food and shelter."

Lori narrowed her eyes, tilting her head to one side as if to study him more closely. "There is a way, you know…by which the spell of Afgorkon may be removed."

He shook his head, snorting. "No man dares do that. Ulnar Themaquol told me as much, that time I solved the riddle of Pthoomol's labyrinth. Other mages have hinted the same thing, Kylwyrren of Urgal among the rest. There is no way for me to own anything but Frostfire."

"And I say there is, barbarian!"

A little of her old pride glared out at him as she straightened. She was a sorceress of no mean repute, he told himself. She had been the helpmate of Lord Markoth in that king's desperate fight against Elfa of Commoral. She had almost bested Kazazael, who served the queen in that struggle.

"How may it be done?"

"Take you what you will, and then do what I shall say," she bade him, turning away to cross the chamber until she stood before the painted solar boat in which the embalmed sailor sat. She stood there, searching the boat, it seemed, for something which should be there.

Kothar shrugged, turned to the table. He said to Flarion, "Take only what you need. Gold and jewels weigh heavily on a walking man."

"I'd bring it all with me if I could. Gods! Saw you ever wealth like this? Kandakore must have been a happy man."

"Legend says he died loveless and hated by his people. No, Flarion, I don't think wealth alone makes a man happy."

The youthful mercenary grinned. "Then let me be unhappy, but loaded down with so much wealth one man could not spend it all in a long lifetime."

Kothar filled his leather belt-purse with gold coins and bars, and with a few of the larger jewels. Its sides bulged when he was done. He turned to look at Red Lori.

The girl was holding a golden scepter in which was set a magnificent diamond. Her fingertips caressed the carven length of the scepter, lingered over the huge gem. Her eyes lifted to stare at Kothar when she felt his look.

"With the help of his court wizard, Kandakore is said to have stolen this scepter from the demon Bathophet," she said softly. "It possesses strange powers. I choose it as my share." Her cheeks dimpled in a smile. "It may come in handy when I recite the spell to Bathophet which will free you from Afgorkon's curse."

The barbarian grunted. Deep in his heart he did not believe there was any such spell. Surely those master magicians, Ulnar Themaquol and Kylwyrren, would have known of it. But because he wanted to believe, because of the gold and jewels making such a satisfying weight at his belt, he nodded.

"Then keep it, and whatever else you see."

She shook her head. "I choose you, Kothar, to be my share. And with you, your purse. That is one reason why I am so anxious to cast my spells to Bathophet. Whatever is yours becomes mine, as it were."

She laughed softly, eyes glowing. The Cumberian felt like a slave selected for the buying. He had no way to sway the Fates, he must go where bidden by this red witch, do as she would have him do.

He felt a momentary anger at this loss of his male independence. But Red Lori came close and ran her soft fingertips across his lips, and the big barbarian shivered and stared deep into her green eyes, losing himself in their promise of delights to come.

Flarion said, "I can carry no more."

They went up the stone ladder, Flarion leading the way and following him, the girl. Kothar mounted easily after them. They came out into the sunlight of high noon, with the air about them sweet with the fragrance of growing things. The sky seemed bluer, the day more lovely, because of the treasure each one carried.

Flarion came to join Kothar in his task of pushing the statue base back into place so the trapdoor would lift and lock. Now no wandering beggar would find the golden hoard which they considered their own.

Kothar said, "We stay the day, and hunt for food. We will sleep the night here, then travel in the morning. It is a long ride to Thoxon in Makkadonia."

"Why go to Thoxon?" Flarion said.

"Better to cross Tharia and head toward Zoane," Lori nodded.

Kothar glanced at her. "Why Zoane?"

"Zoane is the largest city in Sybaros. There I can find what I'll need to prepare those spells to Bathophet for you. Zoane borders the sea, and it is in the sea that the lost tablets of Afgorkon are to be found."

Flarion laughed. "And Sybaros is a rich country. King Midor always seeks for soldiers to enlarge his army against attack by Makkadonia and Tharia. I have my sword to sell, so have you, Kothar."

The Cumberian shrugged. "It matters not to Kothar where Greyling walks. I'll get my bow, there must be a few hares in this wilderness to furnish our supper."

He went on foot out onto the plain bordering the ruins of Phyrmyra. The vast flatland harbored no shelter for the great stags and doe that abounded in the northern forests. Here were merely hares and other small game such as the toydeer and the addabear. Kothar was a master hunter, he walked more softly than the wind, he could freeze and wait for his prey like a statue.

Between some low bushes he sighted two big leaper hares. They nibbled the succulent fruit and the stalks of a nearby berry bush. They did not see him, and he was downwind of them. Carefully he placed an arrow to its string, sighted. He released the catgut string, saw the arrow soar and drop.

One of the hares toppled over, impaled on that long wararrow. The second animal froze in surprise and terror for the instant that the barbarian needed to nock and release another shaft.

He came back into their little camp oddly proud, listening to Lori exclaim over his prowess with the horn bow. Flarion had found a little stream some distance away, had filled their skins with cool liquid. Enough flour was left in Kothar's saddle bags so that the girl could make small bread loaves.

They feasted together as the sun was setting.

When darkness came, Kothar lifted his fur wrap and extended a hand toward Lori. She smiled faintly, let him help her to her feet, and walked with him into the darker shadows away from the fire where Flarion was curled up and ready for sleep.

"You share my fur," he growled, spreading it on the ground.

Her eyebrows rose. "As free woman?"

He turned to stare up at her. "Of course. You're no slave."

"You saved me from Kandakore's tomb. It is the law of Yarth that when a man has saved a woman's life, she belongs to him unless she purchases her freedom with a gift." Her green eyes mocked him.

"Have you a gift for me?"

She shook her head, smiling. "I shall not give you the scepter which you said I could have. And that is all I own."

"Make a gift of your body," he told her softly.

She smiled at him, head tilted to one side even as her white fingers began untying the thongs of her Mongrol jerkin. He could not read the emotion in her slanted green eyes but he had the uneasy feeling that she mocked him, though she said pleasantly enough, "Now that is a good idea, Kothar of Grondel fjord. I shall offer you my body."

The leather thongs were undone and her breasts pushed into the opening of the jerkin. He was faintly surprised to find them so full. Then she shoved down the garment and her leather kilt and her nakedness was a gleaming ivory loveliness in the darkness. Kothar sighed, not caring whether this woman taunted him or not; he had to have her flesh in his embrace.

She laughed and stepped to him, throwing her arms about his neck and letting him feel the moist warmth of her lips. They swayed a moment, clinging tightly, before the barbarian dragged her down onto his bearskin cloak.

The fire winked and glowed in the night.

* * * *

The tip of a sword at his throat awoke the barbarian. He opened his eyes, but lay still. His slightest movement might drive that steel into his throat. Flarion? Was it Flarion who stood over him with a sword in his hand? Had the possession of the gold and jewels driven the youth to madness?

"Get up, you," said a harsh voice.

The sword point went away. Beside him, a naked Lori would have clothed herself in the Mongrol garments, but a foot kicked them away and a man laughed. Kothar rose to his feet slowly, growling.

Flarion was standing beside the fire, scowling darkly. Five men—Kothar recognized them as the bandits whom he and Flarion had driven off in the Tharian Pass—stood grinning at them. Behind him, Red Lori was tugging at a corner of the bearskin cloak to hide her body.

"You've found treasure," muttered the man with a sword in his hand, grinning. He bounced the leather belt purse in his hand. As the Cumberian watched, he opened the bag, poured out a stream of gold coins and jewels onto the ground. "Where's the rest of it?"

Kothar shook his head.

A scarred man snarled to one side and lifted out a dagger. "I know ways to make him talk."

"No, Fithrod, no violence—not yet, at least." One of the bandits approached the leader, the tall man with the pointed steel helmet and chain mail which he had taken from one of the southland caravans. He offered him the sack in which Flarion had put his own coins and jewels.

"A pretty haul," nodded the leader, watching his fellow bandit pour that treasure close to the small pile which had come from Kothar's belt purse. "Enough here to keep a dozen men in wealth the rest of their lives."

"Then take it and let us go," Flarion snarled.

"Why should we do that when it appears you know the secret of old King Kandakore? Show us the treasure and I'll kill you swiftly, without pain."

Against his arm, the Cumberian could feel Red Lori shuddering. Before she had lost her witchlike powers, she would have made short work of these bandits. A few words, a gesture in the air, and a demon such as Asumu or Omorphon or even Belthamquar, who was the father of demons, might have come at her summons to swallow the thieves. He himself was unarmed—Frostfire was thrust into the belt of the man in the pointed helmet. So was Flarion.

"Stake them out," the bandit chieftain snapped.

Two men threw Flarion to the ground, extended his arms and legs. A third man ran for wooden pegs, hammered them in with a rock. Leather thongs were attached to his spread-eagled arms and legs.

Kothar was quiet. Unarmed, he would be no match for the bandits. Yet he had no intention of lying down obediently while they tied him down for the sun to bake or to allow their knives to slice him into bloody gobbets. And so he waited, tensed, not betraying his mood.

"The girl now," said their leader.

And Kothar leaped.

His left fist drove into the face of the bandit chieftain as his right hand closed about the jeweled hilt of Frostfire. With a savage yank he tore it free of the leather belt as blood spurted from the crushed nose his fist had struck. The blued steel came into the sunlight.

Kothar was moving before his sword was completely free of the belt, he was grasping Red Lori, swinging her off the ground and onto his hip as his sword's edge slashed downward across a bandit's shoulder. Instantly Frostfire was turning, parrying a blow from a scimitar, then thrusting deep into the belly of a third outlaw.

The clang of steel on steel was music in the ears of the giant barbarian. His martial spirit reveled in these sounds of combat, the harsh breathing of fighting men, the stamp of feet along the ground, the rasp of swordblades where they met in mid-stroke. He parried effortlessly, seeming to handle two swords at once as his massive muscles rolled beneath his tanned hide. His keen eyes, trained to swift observation along the ice fields and forested hills of the northern lands from which he came, saw openings through which Frostfire darted like the tongue of an angry snake.

Back and forth between the ruins he surged with the redhead hanging onto him, gasping at times when the steel came close to her fair skin, eyes wide under long red lashes as her naked body felt the powerful play of his own. Her arms were clasped about his throat, yet not too tightly, as she sought to make herself less of a burden for him.

As he fought, the Cumberian drove the bandits away from the youth stretched on the ground between the pegs, fearing they might slay him in an attempt to make Kothar surrender. His blade wove back and forth like the bobbin of a loom, stabbing, slashing, thrusting. Where he had been, lay the bodies of dead men, mute testimonials to the fury of his sword.

Against a marble pillar he cornered the bandit leader and the last of his men, and there he slew them with two savage swipes of his steel. A headless body leaned its shoulders against that column as a head went bounding off across the ground, gouting blood; Kothar drove Frostfire through the chest of the chieftain until its point grated against the marble behind it.

His left arm loosed its grip, Lori sank down onto her bare feet. "You fight with the fury of a desert storm, Kothar," she whispered, awed.

He grunted, "Go put some clothes on, girl, before the sun burns your backside for you." His palm clouted a soft buttock, making her stumble.

Her laughter rang out as she whirled to face him, lifting her long red hair in her hands. "You and I—we could rule the world, if we wanted! You with your fighting ability, I with my necromantic wisdoms."

He eyed her dubiously, "If you still possess those powers, why didn't you use them?"

She shook her head. "I save them—for a greater need."

"What need?"

"I may not tell you—just yet."

She scampered toward the sleeping fur and her leather jerkin and skirt. As she drew them on, she watched the barbarian kneel and slash the bindings that held Flarion.

They found food in the leather bags the bandits carried, and water in the skins attached to their belts. Kothar crammed one of the sacks full and tied it to Greyling's saddle. Into the kak he hoisted Red Lori when they were done eating, and turned his face eastward toward the sea.

Flarion trudged beside him. "Where do we go?"

"To Zoane in Sybaros."

Zoane was the largest and richest of all the wealthy cities of rich Sybaros. It was a port city on the Outer Sea, its galleys and sailing ships plied those salt waters as far south as the Oasian jungles, as far north as Thuum, and to distant Isphahan in the east. Its taverns were floored with semiprecious stone tiles, its streets with slabs of marble. Its palace and its smaller castles were breathtaking in their loveliness. No man who ever saw Zoane walked away without a touch of awe deep inside him.

Flarion shrugged. "Zoane or another, what does it matter? I'm a rich man, and I can spend my gold there as well as elsewhere. Still, prices are always high in Zoane."

From her perch in the saddle, Lori laughed. "Come with us, young Flarion—and be richer than you dream!"

He turned and grinned up at her. "What schemes are you plotting in that pretty red head of yours?"

"I ride to find death—and slay it!"

Flarion gaped at her, thinking she jested.

Kothar merely scowled.

CHAPTER FOUR

The tavern was alive with sound in the smoking light of a thousand candles as the men at the wooden tables pounded the tabletops with wood and leather ale-mugs. The slap of bare feet on wet wood, the tinkle of zither strings, the hoarse shouts and the shrill laughter of drunken women, wafted out into the marble streets of the city by the Outer Sea. Three travelers, each wrapped in long woolen cloaks against the mists off the water, paused at the door of the tavern, listening to the sounds, sniffing at the odors of roasting beef and cooking lamb.

Overhead swung a wooden sign carved to resemble a dolphin, painted black. The smallest of the three travelers waved a pale hand. "It is here, the Tavern of the Black Dolphin, that we are to meet him."

Kothar rumbled, "All this secrecy for a ship? I could steal you one with less trouble."

"It isn't any ordinary ship I need, Kothar."

The barbarian hunched his massive shoulders impatiently, went to stand at the partly opened door, looking into the seaside alehouse. His eyes saw the naked woman who danced on the table-top, but he paid her no head; his eyes were turned inward as if to search his own mind.

For more than a week they had been on the road to Zoane, joined together in good fellowship, with something more than fellowship between himself and the red-haired witchwoman. Yet now that they were in Zoane, Red Lori had fallen secretive, mysterious. She made plans without consulting him, without so much as a by-your-leave. He felt anger growing and was surprised to find that a faint jealousy lay inside him, as well. Oddly, he wanted the girl all to himself, he did not want to share her even with the plan she had in mind.

A soft hand touched his. He looked down, seeing her green eyes staring oddly at him. "I have my reasons, barbarian," she whispered. "Bear with me for a little while."

He shrugged and stood aside so that she might walk ahead of him into the tavern. Flarion came after them, treading lightly, staring with bright eyes at the belly dancer who flaunted her flesh in the candlelight, stamping and pivoting on the tabletop.

Red Lori chose a table close to the wall, where her gaze could scan the faces of the roisterers. Kothar sat to her right, Flarion slipped onto the bench to her left. A serving maid ran to greet them, tray and wiping cloth in her hands.

"Ale," rasped the Cumberian, "and wine for the woman. And don't forget the food platters."

Flarion said, "Fetch the ale in large tankards. We've thirst enough to empty an ocean, girl. And who's that dancing so excitingly?"

"Cybala," smiled the girl and turned to go.

Red Lori chuckled as she saw the eager interest of the youth. "Go talk to her, Flarion. Offer her gold as you will—but bring her to the table."

In surprise, the mercenary glanced at the redhead. "Bring her here? But why?"

"We have a need for her."

Flarion scowled. "I can understand why I might have need for her, having been traveling companion to you two lovers all the way from Phyr-myra, but why you have a wish for her company is beyond me."

"It will be clear, in time. Just fetch her."

The girl on the tabletop paused, arms upflung and head thrown back, her ripely curved body quivering. She was olive-skinned and with long black hair, and though she was younger even than Flarion, there was an eternal wisdom in her black eyes and in the languishing smile on her red mouth. She posed, letting the shouts and the applause roll around her. Then she bent, lifted the thin wrap that she had tossed aside when mounting the table and threw it about her nudity.

Hands reached for her, voices called. She ignored them to step down onto a chair and to the rush-strewn floor. She moved through the voices and the hands, and marched toward a narrow, curtain-hung doorway on the far side of the big common room.

Suddenly, a slim mercenary in worn leather and a mail shirt was before her, eyes worshipful. She paused, frowned, went to turn aside.

"She would speak to you," said Flarion, pointing.

"She?" In surprise Cybala halted, eyebrows lifting. With female curios-ity, she turned, stared where the youth gestured.

Across the room, black eyes touched green and—were held. As the snake holds the hen, she went rigid, feeling her senses slip away from her. "Come to me," the eyes said. "You have no will, Cybala the tavern dancer. So—come to me." And with a sigh that was half a sob, Cybala let the mercenary clasp her hand and draw her along with him through the throng.

"We would make you rich, Cybala," said Lori softly, when the girl was beside her on the bench.

"And in return for such wealth?"

"We have a need for you."

The green eyes still held her in thrall, the dancer found. There was a strange languor in her flesh born not of the physical world but of the mind. Almost against her will, she asked, "But what may I do for—such as you?"

"You will learn—in time. What will it cost to buy your bondage from the tavern owner?"

"He took me in when I was starving, and fed me. I could always dance, I was taught by slave owners from Oasia when I was a little girl. Always, I have earned my bread by dancing—ever since my first master was slain in a street brawl and I was turned loose to earn my keep."

Red Lori held her palm out to Kothar. The barbarian took two small gold bars from his belt purse, dropped them into her hand.

"Will these buy your freedom and pay your debts?"

Cybala nodded, eyes wide. "That will be more than enough. One such bar will do it."

"Then keep the other, Cybala. Flarion, go with her in case of trouble." Red Lori turned to the Cumberian. "She will please him whom I shall summon up."

"You intend to sacrifice her?" Kothar asked, dismayed.

As if she had not heard him, the witchwoman murmured, "She is a pretty little thing, still young and probably—innocent. Yes, yes, he will like her."

"You can't do it," Kothar rasped, hitting the table.

"Then let us say, we bring her along for young Flarion." Her red lips quirked to a smile in her lovely face as she studied the grim face of the barbarian. "You are a thief, Kothar, a man who has raped his share of women and slain more than his share of men. Why then, this sudden delicacy?"

He shook his blond head. "I don't hold with human sacrifice."

"Then we'll buy a lamb when the time comes."

He glowered at her, feeling a stab of the old distrust moving in his veins. He had let himself be distracted by her lovely face and ripely curved body. He should have realized that Red Lori was still a witchwoman, a sorceress, no matter how sweetly she acted toward him. Come to think of it, how had she come to be within that tomb, alive and well, as if—waiting for him?

"A demon laid a curse on me," she reminded him, patting his hand with hers when he questioned her. "I told you so before, and now I see you didn't believe me." The fingers tightened, claw-like. "Our sea captain comes, barbarian!"

A brawny man with a scar down his right cheek, his black hair close-cropped about a bullet skull, came swaggering across the floor, striped jersey tight on a massive chest, his ragged leather sea-breeks tucked into high boots. Around his middle he wore a brass-studded belt from which hung a long dagger and a cutlass. He paused at sight of Red Lori and her beckoning hand, then nodded and moved toward her on catlike feet. He lifted off the mist-wet cloak he wore, dropped it as he crowded his bulk in beside the Cumberian.

"I got your message, I'm Grovdon Dokk of the ship *Waveskimmer.* The cost will be ten gold pieces."

"Abrupt, and to the point," smiled Lori. "It's a bargain."

"It's robbery," growled Kothar.

The captain looked at him, eyebrows arched. "Is it yourself or the lady who's hiring me?"

"Pay him, Kothar," smiled the woman.

The barbarian growled under his breath but he did what the witchwoman ordered. "I still say it's robbery, man. Ten gold pieces could buy me such a scow as you probably command. Do you know the seas hereabouts?"

"Better than I know my face," Grovdon Dokk nodded, clinking the golden pieces between his hands and smiling at them. "And I'll have you know I run a tight ship, with accommodations for four guests."

"Diving gear?" asked Red Lori.

"And men to dive, if you need them, at no extra cost. I'm a fair man, you'll see. When do we sail?"

"We'll come aboard about midnight."

The captain knuckled his brow to the witchwoman and stood up. "I'll go along then, to make things ready. If you could tell me where it is we sail, I could plot a course."

"I'll tell you when we're under way."

Kothar watched the sea captain move off with his rolling gait. He growled, "You're cursed mysterious. Why must we keep it such a secret? Is the treasure greater than that of Kandakore?"

"Infinitely greater, barbarian, as you'll learn when you see it." Her smile dimpled her cheeks as her green eyes glowed. "Perhaps it is the greatest treasure in the world."

Flarion was moving toward them, drawing the belly dancer in his wake with a hand on her wrist. He carried a leather bag, thrown over a shoulder, that bulged with the things Cybala had so hastily thrust into it, which was all she owned in the world. He pushed her onto the bench beside Red Lori just as the serving maid came up with their tankards and a goblet of red Thosian wine.

With them she brought a wooden platter of steaming meat, with wedges of bread and cheese placed around them. Kothar pushed a gold coin at her as he reached for the food.

Cybala whispered, "What am I to do?"

"Amuse Flarion," snapped the redhead.

The girl glanced sideways at the youth, eyebrows arching. Her shoulder lifted and she sniffed, dismissing him. Flarion flushed and stared down at his food.

When the clepsydra showed the hour to be close to midnight, Lori pushed an empty platter away and reached behind her for her heavy woolen paenula. "It is time to go, to board the ship."

Kothar tossed his fur cloak about his massive shoulders, moving ahead of the others so that his giant frame could clear passage for them between the diners and the revelers. Here and there a hand reached out protestingly when the patrons of the tavern recognized Cybala in a traveling cloak with her dusky face half hidden in its hood.

But Kothar was there to push away a hand, and Flarion was close beside the belly dancer to discourage an overly resentful man with a fist in the ribs or an easily drawn dagger. Cybala walked with heavy steps, half dreading that which she went toward so easily. This going was not of her own will but by force of the green eyes that had looked deep inside her and caught hold of her soul. Only Red Lori went with an easy stride. This was her doing, this night and its events, and those which would follow. Only on *her* lips was there a smile, and only *her* feet trod lightly, with satisfaction in the way of their going.

The mists had come in off the Outer Sea, the cobbles and the marble paving slabs were wet with water. The two moons of Yarth were hidden behind dark clouds. The slap of a rising tide against the pilings and the bulkheads echoed the faint pad-pad of their boots as they hastened through the gray fog and the dampness, which the sea wind made swirl about their persons.

Red Lori reached out, caught Kothar by his sword belt. "Not so fast, Cumberian. We others have not your long legs. It would be easy to get lost in such a fog."

Kothar slowed his pace, letting his thoughts run faster than his feet. He knew the witchwoman was moving on a course that might not be pleasing to him. Yet she had promised to rid him of that curse of Afgorkon by which he could own no treasure but his sword Frostfire. He was a little tired of an empty belly for days on end, when his belt-purse was as flat as his middle. He would relish golden coins clinking in that almoner, and the prospects of hot meals and cold ale every night.

And so he plodded onward through the grayish mists, deeply sunk in reverie, headed nothing but his own troubled spirit, until—

"Haiii!"

Two men up ahead in the mists, one leaping at another with the gleam of bared steel in a hand. The second man, tall and lean, shrank back, crying out in dismay.

"Die, damned sorcerer! Into the depths of Eldrak's seven hells with you!"

To see was to act with the barbarian. He lunged forward, glad of this bit of action with which to dispel his gloom. His hand darted out, closed fingers on the wrist of the hand that held the dagger. His muscles bunched, swung the man sideways off his feet and into a building wall.

A face contorted by rage and fear stared at him in horror as the man sought to free his wrist. Haggard eyes half sunken in a skull-like face peered up at the towering barbarian. A thin mouth writhed blasphemies.

"Let me go, fool! I but rid the world of a thing better dead—a misshapen excrudescence of utter evil! Let be, I say!"

"What is it?" gasped Red Lori.

Cybala shrank backward, found an arm about her lissome waist. Her eyes turned sideways, studied the profile of the youthful warrior beside her. His sword was in his hand, there was a faint smile on his lips. Cybala was breathing harshly, leaning her weight deeper into his embracing arm.

He glanced at her; their stares locked.

The dagger fell clattering to the cobbles of the narrow alleyway. With a hoarse cry of fear, the man who had held that dagger turned and ran off into the fog. They heard his footsteps pounding, then fading before the surging rush of the surf not far away. The wind moaned as it swept around the corners of these buildings.

The tall, lean man in the black mantle still leaned against the damp bricks of the house wall, breathing harshly. The barbarian bent, picked up the fallen dagger.

"Why did you let him go, northlander? He was death—that one! Saw you not his face, his eyes?"

Kothar scowled. "Now why should he have tried to kill you? What wrong have you done him?"

"No wrong, not I. For I am Antor Nemillus, mage and necromancer to Midor, King of Sybaros!" He came away from the wall, drawing himself to his full height, his flashing eyes stabbing the mists toward Red Lori and Cybala, and drifting over Flarion for an instant.

His thin lips quirked into a smile as he swung back to the Cumberian. "I owe you a great debt, barbarian. Name your price for your service, and be not humble in your demands—or I'll take it as an insult. The life of Antor Nemillus is worth a kingdom to that man who saves it."

Kothar shrugged, then became aware that a hand tugged at his cloak. He turned, saw Lori oddly shy, almost cowering back into the warmth afforded by the bodies of Cybala and Flarion.

"Safe conduct, Kothar—safe passage for us anywhere in Sybaros and its adjacent waters," she whispered.

Antor Nemillus heard her words and laughed harshly. "Are these my rescuers? More cut-purses with their doxies? Ah, but—no matter. Even a thief can earn a reward for a great service. Here—"

A hand fumbled in a belt pouch, brought out a copper disc inlaid with enamels of varying colors. "My sigil, known the length and breadth of Sybaros, on land and on the sea. It will save you even from—the king's guardsmen. But use it wisely or—it may bring your doom."

The lean man folded the fur mantle about his narrow shoulders and went striding off into the fog. A few moments the barbarian watched him, then those rolling mists hid him from sight. He glanced down at the copper piece he held, studied the intertwined enamels on its surfaces that so much resembled a serpent folded back upon itself.

"The amulet of dread Omorphon," breathed the woman.

"Oh? And will this see us safe against soldiers and lesser wizards?"

"It will. Give it here."

The Cumberian slid the disc into his purse and grinned. "Nay, now. Let me keep it, my red beauty. I'd feel safer with its weight on my person."

She laughed up at him, caught his hand and squeezed it. "Trusting Kothar! Always you see specters where there are none. But come, it moves toward midnight."

They went swiftly through the mists, light-treading, and with their cloaks flapping about them as the wind blew more strongly at the pier where *Waveskimmer* was docked. A sailor in a striped jersey and ragged culottes was waiting for them beside a crude plank. He steadied the plank as Red Lori and Cybala ran across. When Flarion and Kothar were on deck, he moved across the plank himself, and lifting it, secured it to two pins inset into the forerail.

"I'll show you to your cabins," he muttered.

Waveskimmer was a brigantine. The two masts towered high over their heads as they made their way aft behind the sailor, the sea wind rustling between the yards and snapping the shrouds in their chocks. The salt smell of the sea was everywhere. The ship appeared to sway slightly underfoot as the waves heaved and swelled beneath the keel.

"A rough night," whispered Cybala.

The seaman heard her, laughed. "We're still tied to the dock, mistress. Wait until we get out beyond the reefs. There'll be rough water there or I miss my guess."

Cybala moaned, and Flarion took advantage of her momentary weakness to slip an arm about her middle. His own belly was none too steady, he was a landsman, not a deck-swabber. He followed where the others led, enjoying this moment of intimacy with the black-haired dancing girl, the touch of her middle, the awareness of swaying hips that brushed his own, her sweet scent and the soft breathing that seemed like music to his ears.

A white door opened, revealing a small cabin lit with a single candle. "Your room, master," he said to Kothar and nodded also at the woman. "With bunks for you and your lady."

Red Lori swept into the chamber, letting her cloak slip onto a table. She took the lone candle in a pale hand, touched its flame to other wicks set here and there. The light flooded the compartment, showed it neat and trim, with two bunks set into opposite walls and a table between, riveted to the wooden bulkhead.

She turned, ripely curved in the leather jerkin and short skirt, and gestured at the sailor before he could close the door. "I'll want to see your captain, Grovdon Dokk. I must tell him how to set his course."

The barbarian followed her out into the companionway, up a flight of wooden steps and into a cabin set under the quarterdeck. Oil lamps burned brightly as Grovdon Dokk wrote with a scratchy quill pen in his open log.

He glanced up frowning as they entered, but nodded when Red Lori made their mission known. Stepping to a table fitted with boxed compartments, he selected a scroll and bore it to a table, unrolling it, spreading it out.

"Where away, lady?"

A red fingernail scratched the parchment. "Set your course here, captain." His surprised look made her smile. "Yes, it is empty sea. But it is there I would go and—cast anchor."

Grovdon Dokk rubbed his stubbled jaw reflectively. "You pay the fee, I'll not quarrel with you. But it seems senseless, lady. To travel to the islands now, or even south into Ispahan, would make more sense."

"To you, perhaps. Not to me. It is there I would go, and where you shall take me." The fingernail tapped the chart imperiously, and Grovdon Dokk shrugged.

Kothar waited until they were in their cabin before he muttered, "I'm of a mind with the captain on this, red one. What do you expect to find on the open sea?"

"Not on, dunderhead. *Under!*"

His face brightened. "Ah! Sunken treasure. Of course. A ship, eh? A galleass that went down beam-end first in a storm? A treasure ship of King Midor, that was making its way homeward from the spice islands?"

Her laughter rang out as her fingers went to the lacings of her placket. In a moment they were undone, and he caught the sheen of candlelight on creamy skin as the blouse slipped from a rounded shoulder. She preened a little before him, proud of her beauty, her desirability as a woman.

"None of those, Kothar," she said softly. "What we seek has not been seen by men for many thousands of years."

He sat up straighter on the bench where he was easing off his war boots. "No ship? What, then?"

"The lost city of Hatharon, Kothar. Aye, that city where Afgorkon was born, where he made his spells, where he enchanted the world about him. The greatest magician of them all. Even today, fifty thousand years after Afgorkon lived, his fellow mages revere his name."

She was lifting her short skirt, stepping out of petticoats, thrusting down the velvet placket with the loose lacings. Her body was firmly ripe, so lovely as to make the barbarian feel the tide of his manhood sweep through his veins. Long red hair hung to her hips, her skin was pale satin and gently rounded here and there.

"Girl, I don't understand you," he rasped.

She turned her face, staring at him inquiringly.

"You should hate me, by all rights. Since we met in Commoral in your magic tower, I've turned your wickedness away from those you'd injure. It was my fault you were hung in a silver cage, and later I put you into that tomb with dead Kalikalides.

"And—yours isn't a forgiving nature."

Her laughter rang out. "You are mine, barbarian. I've told you that—even while imprisoned in that silver cage. You'll recall how you saw my face in the bottoms of your tankards and peeping out from your campfires? How I talked to you even then?"

"Aye, you said I was yours to do with as you would."

"And you still are." She took the sting from her words by stepping closer, bending to catch his cheeks between her soft palms and setting her red mouth to his. "I think you have always belonged to me, Kothar—even while you were fighting me in my tower, battling the demons and goblins with which I sought to kill you."

"You fire the blood in a man," he rumbled.

Her nimble fingers eased the lacing of his mail shirt, held it so he could slip out of it. She aided him to remove the leather *hacqueton* he wore beneath the mail, and playfully tweaked the blond hairs on his deep chest. She was like a dutiful wife, he thought, tenderly loving and heedful of his every wish.

He could not still the uneasiness inside him, however, even though he feasted his eyes on her nakedness and his lips tingled to her kiss. This was not like Red Lori; it was as if—she played a part. He would almost rather see the anger-flames in her bold green eyes and hear her soft voice grow shrill with curses on his head. Yet a part of him relished this attention she gave him, even as his body hungered to draw her down between the sheets on one of the bunkbeds.

Then he was naked as she and she was clasping his hand, drawing him toward the bunk, bending to blow out the candles one by one until only the moonlight came into the cabin to silver their bodies. Kothar caught her to him, held her close as his mouth feasted on her lips.

They toppled sideways onto the covers.

* * * *

Some time during the night the barbarian woke to find the ship creaking, dipping to the swells of the Outer Sea as its great sails filled with the blowing winds. The rocking was pleasant to him, snug in this bunk with Red Lori within the crook of an arm. He grinned and drew her even closer. Let the gale moan and the ship lift and fall to the surge of the sea waves, he was content.

Morning was a golden radiance in the cabin as the barbarian threw back the covers and leaped to the middle of the room. Behind him Red Lori squirmed and muttered protestingly as she sought the fallen blankets and drew them closer.

Kothar said as he drew on his kilt, "It's long past dawn, girl. Come share a platter of fish with me."

"Go eat, you big ox. I'd rather sleep," she murmured.

He studied her flushed face, the thick red hair spread on the pillows. By Salara of the bare breasts, she was a woman, this one! Her embraces were all any man might want, her kisses things of fire. Never yet had the barbarian sought to ally himself overlong to any one woman. Those he had known in his wanderings—Miramel, and that tavern girl in Murrd, Mellicent, and Laella, who was a dancing girl out of Oasia, and Queen Candara of Kor, and the brunette woman, Philisia, who had been a king's mistress in Urgal—had been but passing fancies, linked with the dust of the lands of their birth, so far as he was concerned.

But with Red Lori, it was different.

He shook his head against what he considered a streak of softness in himself. A sellsword and wanderer had no time to spare for such sentimental things as love and marriage, nor a family, either. He was a mercenary, with his steel blade he earned his livelihood.

And with the curse of Afgorkon forbidding wealth to him, what sort of woman would even consider him for a husband? Nah, nah. A woman might take him for a lover, but nothing more.

In this frame of mind he went up deckside, to pause and study the gray sea heaving on all sides. The ship rode easily, its prow cleaving the frothing waves, the white sails bellied outward with the wind. To his surprise he saw Flarion leaning against the starboard rail, staring dead abeam.

He put his hand to the youth's shoulder. "Come join me in a platter of fish, comrade."

"I have no appetite."

"The ship rides smoothly enough."

"It isn't the ship."

"Ah, then it must be the belly dancer. She wasn't kind to you last night. Did she consign you to your own bunk? And stay in hers until morning?"

"Something like that, yes."

"It's just as well," the barbarian growled.

Flarion swung around. "Now what makes you say that?"

Kothar shook his head. He could scarcely tell the youth that Red Lori had marked the girl for sacrifice to one of her demon-gods. Better to let him suffer now, for a little while, then later when her death would put Cybala forever beyond his reach. He himself did not intend to let the red witch carry out that plan, but he knew her well enough to realize that if her mind were set on Cybala's death, then Cybala would die.

He moved off down the deck, his nose telling him where the galley was, the smell of cooking fish stew and broiling fish steak making his mouth water. The oceans teemed with succulent game fish, ripe for eating over hot coals or an oil flame, and few ships that plied the Outer Sea carried more than salt pork and flour and condiments in its food bins. The sea was all around them, and any sailor could dangle a line with a baited hook.

He found half a dozen men at the galley benches, and selected a wooden mug, filled it with the stew, caught up half a loaf of bread and perched his big bulk before a wooden table. He ate voraciously, for his great body needed much food to sustain it, and twice more he filled the wooden bowl before he was content.

He went out on deck and stood watching the sea toss and surge beneath the keel. He felt no sickness, he was like iron in his middle. After a time, Red Lori came to join him, wrapped in her woolen cloak.

The wind blew her red hair free, so that it tickled his face when he bent to hear her words that the same wind threatened to bear away with.

"I say that once there was a continent below our keel, Kothar. Or part of a continent. This sea here covers what was once part of Sybaros and Tharia, a massive plateau that stretched outward for many miles. At its tip, jutting into the ocean, was the port city of Hatharon."

"Where Afgorkon was born."

"And where he practiced his wizardries. In what remains of his ancient lodging, in that tower where he kept his chests and scrolls, I hope to find his famous coffer of magic formulas and special incantations."

"And once you've done that?"

She looked up at him, laughing. "Then I can free you from his curse, barbarian. And—do what I must do."

"What goal have you set yourself, Lori the Red?"

"To save the magicians of Yarth! Or haven't you heard that someone is slaying them all, very coldly, very systematically? Aye, last night in Zoane, when you rescued Antor Nemillus, was an instance of the wickedness now flourishing in the land."

Kothar scowled. "Why seek you Afgorkon's belongings?"

"He was a wizard. He must help his kind. I would summon him, Kothar, speak with him. If anyone knows how to stop this slayer of sorcerers—he will!"

The barbarian remembered the lich in the hidden tomb within the forests of Commoral, who had given him the sword Frostfire. An unease sat in his middle as he let his memory run on that rotted thing that had been a living man five hundred centuries ago.

"He will not like it," he muttered.

"But he will come. Oh, yes. He shall come to my call."

"Only at a price!"

"The girl, Cybala. She will appease him."

"Flarion won't like it," he rumbled. "The boy's half in love with her. He moons over her constantly."

Her green eyes flared. "You think he'd—kill me—to save her?"

The massive shoulders lifted and fell. "You do what you think is right, to save the lives of your fellow sorcerers and wizards. Perhaps Flarion may do what he thinks is right, too."

She bit her lip, frowning thoughtfully.

The ship *Waveskimmer* ploughed on through the salt waters of the Outer Sea, sails fat with wind, yards and masts straining to those gusts that hurled its prow through the heaving waves. These same salt winds stirred the long blond hair that hung below the barbarian's shoulder, which he tied behind him during battle, and made him draw his thick cloak tighter to his shoulders. He rode the heaving deck on solidly planted war boots, a scowl on his face.

There were human undercurrents all about him that he did not like. He did not trust Red Lori, for all that he was half in love with her. There was an attitude the witchwoman seemed to have—of waiting, sniffing at the air, like a wolf on the hunt—that made him itch between his shoulder blades. And Florian, half mad himself with love for the belly dancer, with hate in his eyes when he thought of Red Lori. Ah, and Cybala? He could not read the dancing girl. What emotion gripped her as she lay in her cabin bunk at night?

"We near our goal, Kothar. Look there!"

A slim forefinger pointed at the waves. Kothar repressed a cry of surprise. These waters were blue, clear as the crystalware of Zoardar. And not so far down in those limpid depths—surely those were gardens he was seeing? He leaned his weight upon the rail, peering downward.

"Aye, barbarian. The pleasure gardens of Afgorkon—or so the legends say! Built upon the side of an ancient mountain that did not sink as completely as did all the rest of this land. Here are his artifacts, his impedimenta, the equipment which enabled him to become the most famous wizard of all."

His eyes saw marble statues, rows of dead trees, petrified now, with sea coral and swaying anemones where flowing hibiscus and lovely roshamores were wont to grow upon a time. He made out something that had been a labyrinth of tall hedges, a stone walkway wending in and out of these once-lovely places, part of a colonnaded temple, shattered and long in ruins.

"It is not so deep here," the witchwoman murmured at his side. "A good diver can fetch to that place and back and bring me what it is I want. Grovdon Dokk! To me!"

And when the captain was at her side, knuckling his brow, "Anchor here! Then send to me your divers," she ordered.

She paced up and down until two dark Tharians, lean men with their nakedness hidden in breechclouts and belts that held long knives, stood before her. They had deep chests, powerful muscles. Men such as these earned their living off the coral banks beyond the Tharian sea-strand, diving for sponges and occasionally a wreck or two submerged among the bottom stones.

"I seek a chest of many colors," Red Lori murmured, "a coffer in which—hermetically sealed—are certain parchments I would have for my own. It has runes worked onto its top, in bright enamels and rustless metals. You shall know it by its brilliance. It shall draw you as might a lantern lighted below the waves. Fail me not, and two gold bars each shall be your prize."

The Tharians grinned and went to the opening in the railing where a plank was affixed so they could dive deep. Kothar watched them, his eyes moving from them to the waters that appeared oddly cloudy, murky, where the anchor had been dropped. This cloudiness extended outward, hiding the gardens, the statuary and even the columns of the temple to some forgotten god.

The men dove.

Down they went, until they disappeared in that cloudy stirring of the sea bottom, which swallowed them up as if they had never existed. Red

Lori went striding up and down the deck, hammering a fist into her palm in her excitement, but the barbarian never moved, never took his eyes from that strange murkiness that seemed so—menacing.

The water clock dripped away the minutes.

Overhead, the sun moved across the sky. It hid behind a cloud and a chill darkness came upon the shipdeck. Kothar stirred. Was the wind moaning? Rising in its intensity? He shivered and looked at Red Lori, bent above the railing, staring into those deeps with worried eyes.

The captain padded across the deck, his face echoing the anxiety in the witchwoman. "They have not come back, mistress. They are good men, strong divers. They have fought undersea things before. I do not like this."

"They have been gone too long," she nodded.

"Shall we up anchor and sail away?"

"No!"

The word came out of her in an explosion of breath. Kothar stared hard at Red Lori, seeing tears trickling down her smooth cheeks. There was fright in the green eyes that turned to him, and a desperate appeal for help.

"Kothar! Everything depends on my getting that coffer. Everything! Including your hope to be free of Afgorkon's curse!"

The big barbarian shook himself. All along, he had known he would be called upon to go down into those eerie deeps, as if a corner of his mind had told him so. He and Frostfire, daring the wrath of Afgorkon: This was what it meant when the chips were on the counting table.

He dropped his cloak, worked loose the leather bindings of his mail shirt. Lori came close, red-nailed fingers striving to loosen clasps. Those fingers trembled and shook so that he was forced to push her hands aside, chuckling.

"Those waters will be cold. Have hot rum waiting for me, well buttered," he grinned, kicking free of his war boots.

Then he drew Frostfire from its scabbard and vaulted over the rail. He went into the cloudy water, his great chest filled with precious air. The sword dragged him downward until his open eyes caught a blurry glimpse of a ruined marble statue and part of a wall and a stone archway, still standing. Then his bare feet touched bottom.

He must look for brightness, Red Lori had said. The coffer that contained the parchments glowed, she claimed—or so the tale had it. But there was no brilliance here, no hint of any light but that which seeped from the surface. Yet he moved forward, under the arch, eyes darting here and there.

Once, out of the very corner of an eye, he caught a flash of light, but it was blotted out. Yet he swung that way, swam forward toward the tumbled stone blocks of what had been a wall, blue and dim in this sea-bottom world.

And then—A thing of blackness, ebon and threatening, rose up from those walls, a great jet outline—something bulbous, without shape, unknown and mysterious—and a length of something equally black tugged at his ankle. He fought against it, he lifted Frostfire—slashed.

Frostfire bounced on that rubbery blackness.

Another tentacle and another came to wrap around his arms, his torso. Strong were those ebon things twisting about him, like constrictor snakes out of the Oasian jungles. He fought them with his own titanic thews, his muscles bulging, rolling and heaving, trying to slash with his swordedge, seeking to thrust its sharp point into that rubbery black hide.

Kraken! The vast beast of the sea deeps that dwelt in sea caverns and the long-forgotten ruins that dot the floor of the Outer Sea. A creature large enough to attack a ship, a being of a hundred thick tentacles each able to shatter the mast of a large ship.

He hung helpless in those things as they drew him between a stone archway, past two tumbled statues, toward a black hole in the side of a crumbled stone wall. There was a light ahead of him by which he could see the titanic bulk of the sea beast.

Its maw gaped wide to swallow him.

CHAPTER FIVE

Two big eyes stared unwinkingly at him as the ivory beak of the octopus opened wide. Its squat, vast bulk rested against a stone structure that had been an altar, long, long ago. And on the altar was the coffer. Even with his lungs about to burst from lack of air, with his head reeling, Kothar knew the intertwined enamels, the reddish glow of that rustless metal.

The tentacles brought him upward toward that open maw.

Kothar struggled; he freed an arm, twisted Frostfire, stabbed. The point did no more than prick one of the bulging eyeballs, but the pain must have been sharp, because the tentacles flailed him sideways, away from the terrible beak.

The Cumberian felt stone at his back, crunching into it. He did not see what it was. Some statue or other, he guessed. His right arm went high, holding Frostfire.

Through the water, he heard the faint clang of steel on stone. Instantly, his arm felt the shock of that blow, a quivering began in his fingers that went into his wrist and forearm, then upwards to his shoulder. From his shoulder, that queer tingling ran throughout his body.

And—his flesh began to glow!

Blue he was, all radiant blue—and that body brightness added to the strange light of the enameled coffer. A strength such as he had never known came into his flesh. He writhed in the grip of the tentacles, and strangely felt no more the need for air.

He brought Frostfire down in a sweeping arc.

Against the bulbous head of the great kraken he drove his steel. The edge went into that blubbery substance, slashing deep. Deep! An inky fluid ran out of the cut. Blood? Purple because of his bluely glowing body and the red blood of the kraken? Kothar did not know, he wrenched his sword free.

He struck again, again!

Far into that mass he lunged his glowing steel. Whatever had happened—thanks to Dwallka! For now he could fight, he could slay. His barbarian muscles rolled as he struck and cut with the edge of Frostfire until at last its point reached deep inside the kraken's brain.

The tentacles about him loosed to thrash about, striking the stone walls of what had been Afgorkon's necromantic chamber, long centuries ago.

The octopus rose upward, seeking to flee this chamber that was its death room. It reached the archway, quivered, fell atop the lintel stone.

"By Dwallka's war hammer!" thought the Cumberian, sagging against the stone altar. "It was a near thing, that."

His eyes touched the altar, the coffer. From that great strongbox his stare went to the statue behind the altar. It was crudely fashioned, of whitish-blue stone and carven to resemble a man. Perhaps five feet in height, it was little more than a thick stone column with arms and legs cut into its roundness, and a head which was a stone ball set atop the indentations that represented shoulders. It had been that eidolon against which his sword had clanged, filling his body with its eerie power.

The head was faceless. Yet there was a brooding power in the thing, a sense of stone inhabited by something—a god? a demon? a nameless power?—that made the barbarian tense.

This thing had helped him, he told himself. It could not be evil. Yet his barbarian senses shivered as if to the touch of staring eyes. Something, someone, was in that stone and—staring at him.

The water around him was very cold, his blue coloring was fading. He reached for the coffer, gripping it by one of the metal rings set into each end. Coffer in hand, he kicked upward.

He had to swim hard, for the coffer was heavy, and his sword was not so light. He might have made it to the surface quite easily with either the strongbox or the sword, but not with both. Yet enough of that alien strength was in him so that he popped upward into sunlight.

Red Lori leaned across the rail, fifty yards away. At her cry, the longboat was lowered and sailors began to row toward him.

Their hands lifted the coffer onto a thwart. Kothar gripped the moldboard, let himself be towed through the waves toward the ship. The witchwoman herself came to the rail where the plank was fastened, reached down and caught his hand. Flarion was there also, fingers grasping.

He stood on the deck, dripping water. Red Lori handed him a tankard with steaming rum, heavily buttered. He drank deep, draining the mug.

"I almost never came back," he growled as Flarion placed his cloak about his dripping shoulders. "If it hadn't been for a statue down there, an eidolon without a face—"

"Oh!" gasped Red Lori, clutching his arm. "Was it the gift of Belthamquar, the father of all demons? Legend says Afgorkon and Belthamquar were partners in wizardry, fifty thousand years ago! That the demon-father made a faceless idol out of stone, giving it to Afgorkon so that the spirit of the great mage could inhabit it and peer between worlds…"

"I know nothing of that. But when Frostfire hit it as I lifted it for a stroke—I was fighting a great kraken, it must have been the thing that killed the divers—my body turned blue."

Red Lori made a sign in the air, crying out.

"I am a strong man, but never have I been that strong! I glowed like an oil lamp, and my sword did the same. Now I could cut into the kraken, and I went at it until I slew it."

"It is the eidolon of the demon-father! I know it! You must fetch again, Cumberian. Bring it up to the deck."

"Not I. I've had my fill of watery deeps."

"Please, Kothar! I beg you!"

Her green eyes ate at his stare. They seemed to swell, to grow larger and larger. They swallowed him up until he stood in a green haze, helpless and without a will of his own. Strangely, his flesh was no longer cold but warm as if the desert sun baked him.

He nodded, unable to prevent his saying, "I shall go for the statue."

"Now, Kothar! Now!"

He turned, without Frostfire and still in that strange daze, to the rail. His cloak fell from him as he stood on the moldboard and leaped. Once again the waters swallowed him up.

Behind him, Lori made a gesture at two of the sailors. "Throw over a rope so he may make a loop from it. Quickly, quickly!"

Kothar sank swiftly, like a stone. He came down past the limp body of the dead kraken where it sprawled across the lintel stone, and his bare feet touched the tiles of the dead wizard's chamber. The statue was where he had left it, brooding across the altar as it had for the past fifty thousand years. He walked toward it, lifting his hands to clasp its sides.

It weighed heavily, so that he was forced to mount to the altar to lift it even an inch, "I can never rise to the surface with this," he thought. "I'm on a fool's errand."

Then he saw the rope dropping toward him and took it. Making a loop he affixed it to the statue. He tightened the coil about the eidolon, jerked twice on the rope.

He rose upward, the statue following more slowly.

When he came to the deck, he found half the crew engaged in tugging at the free end of the rope. Kothar grinned, showing his strong white teeth.

"Fifteen men to raise that thing," he said to Red Lori, "and you'd have had me do it by myself. Give me more of the buttered rum."

Cybala went to fetch the tankard with the steaming liquid. The barbarian drank slowly, eyeing the witchwoman. She seemed changed, prouder and more arrogant; her chin was high, her green eyes blazed triumphantly. He felt vaguely disturbed and uneasy.

Then the eidolon was bumping the hull and she ran to direct its lifting, her own hands reaching out to clutch it, keeping it from hitting the ship. Her wise eyes scanned its bluish-white stone when it was placed upright on the deck, her fingertips quivering as they almost caressed it.

"Take it to my cabin," she ordered.

It took ten men with a leather sling to move the statue, to bump it down the companionway and into the cabin Red Lori shared with Kothar. The sailors set up the statue between two bulkhead supports, where a hanging lamp creaked on its chains.

Red Lori sat before the eidolon, chin on fist, studying it. At her feet was the enameled coffer. The barbarian was in a far corner of the cabin, slipping back into his clothes.

"I didn't think it existed," she sighed at last.

He came to stand beside her chair, buckling on his sword belt. "And what are you going to do with it, once you're done with your mooning?"

"It can make me the most powerful woman on all Yarth, barbarian. This eidolon can look across the gulfs of time and space, search out secrets for me that are lost to our mightiest wizards. For the eyes of this thing, and its face, are in the spaces between worlds, in demon lands and magical countries. It can see things no man knows, and report them to me."

He glowered down at her red hair. "And what will you do with such secrets? I believed you were done with wizardry."

She turned her lovely face up to him, and she smiled. "What would you have me be, barbarian—a milkmaid on a farm or a shepherdess on a grassy hillside? No, no. Long ago, ever since I was a child, I have been delving into the books of the necromancers, I have cast spells. I almost gained what I wanted from Markoth, but you prevented that, and Queen Elfa hung me in her silver cage."

She shook her head. "My first problem is to...but never mind that. Go you and eat. Leave me to my dreams."

With a growl, he went to the galley and ate, and there the captain found him. Grovdon Dokk was a worried, anxious man. He held his seaman's cap in his hands as he flung himself onto the bench opposite the barbarian.

"You look like a good man in a fight, Cumberian," he growled.

Kothar grinned at him, hoisting Frostfire between his legs. "I've done my share and more, true. What enemy do you expect to meet out here? Pirates from the isles?"

"My crew, man. They're talking mutiny."

Kothar paused with the last bit of bread and sausage halfway to his lips. His blond brows rose. "Mutiny? Now why should your men rebel against you, captain?"

His thumb jerked over his shoulder. "It's your woman in the cabin, barbarian. That coffer she brought abroad, with the faceless statue, is upsetting the crew, that's what."

"I'll go talk to them."

"Best have that long sword of yours handy when you do. The men are afraid, and frightened men don't reckon odds. Can the lady cast spells?"

"She could, but whether she can now, I wouldn't know."

"Too bad. She might have charmed them with a cantraip or two. As it is—"

A sullen roar broke the stillness of the seas. A woman screamed. Kothar vaulted the table and raced for the door, yanking his steel free as he ran. Up the companionway steps and onto the deck he raced, only to slide to a halt.

Red Lori was being held high above the heads of half a dozen brawny seamen, half naked, the clothes torn from her writhing, struggling body.

"Kothar," she screamed. "Aid me!"

He rasped curses as he leaped forward.

"Stay back, mate," yelled a scarred forecastle man.

They dropped Red Lori to the deck, and the scarred man fell to a knee beside her, dagger out, point touching her soft throat. The Cumberian scraped his war boot soles on the deck-planks as he came to a stop.

He was helpless, he knew that. For himself, he would have dared a dozen daggers, but he could not risk the witchwoman's life. His fingers tightened on Frostfire's shaft so that the skin showed white above the knuckles as he stared hard at the seaman crouched above Red Lori.

"Let her go, man," he cried hoarsely. "There'll be no magic, no wizardry performed on board this ship if you do. You have my word for it."

The other seamen jeered at him, shaking fists and brandishing daggers of their own. Ugliness glared at him out of their eyes and hard faces.

"The witch dies!"

"We want no part of her spells!"

"We be honest sailors, we don't hold with deviltry."

Red Lori was very still. Only her eyes were moving, turning toward Kothar where he stood in agonized helplessness on the deck. Those eyes pleaded with him, begged him for rescue. He felt them touch him, appeal for his help.

Think, man! There must be a way to save her.

At another time, he might have turned away from those green eyes that stared at him so fearfully. But that was when Red Lori had hated him. Now—she felt differently toward Kothar the barbarian. She had lain in his arms, very loving, very affectionate. He could not shake the taste of her kisses, the ardor of her body, from his mind.

"Hand over your sword, mate," yelled a sailor.

"Aye, the sword. Toss it here!"

They clamored, their voices hoarse and savage.

Kothar shrugged. "All right, then—take it!"

He drew back his arms to toss it. But instead of the easy throw they expected, his arm flashed downward. And as his moving arm came down—he hurled Frostfire straight at the scarred man. Like an arrow it sped through the air.

Kothar followed it, leaping off his feet.

The blade went deep into the chest of the kneeling man. At the same instant, the barbarian slammed into three of the seamen, toppling them backwards. As they went over on their backs, Kothar dodged sideways, barreling into the legs of two men who were bending to sink their daggers into his flesh. His big hands reached out, caught at two legs, yanked their owner sideways and into the bodies of two other seamen.

He was on his feet, big hands balled like clubs and striking as hard. Red Lori was up and running, he saw from the corners of his eyes. A dagger slashed his arm, another opened the flesh of his thigh. In another few seconds he would be buried under men and a dozen daggers would be drinking his blood.

Then the captain was beside him, lashing out with a capstan bar, and Flarion stood on the other side of him, blade darting, thrusting.

Three sailors were down, motionless. Two others were reeling back, hands clutched to wounds, blood seeping between their fingers. The rest gathered into a group, snarling, their own daggers bloody. The captain nursed a slashed chest. Flarion moved the fingers of his sword hand, all blood red from a cut on his forearm.

"Give them amnesty," called Red Lori from the quarterdeck.

"Never," snarled Kothar.

"A boat, captain," cried the witchwoman, leaning across the deck rail. "Allow them the longboat and food. They can reach the coast of Tharia in a good two days and nights."

"A boat, a boat," the men shouted. "And food! Biscuits and meat, with cheese!"

Grovdon Dokk nodded his head. "Aye, aye. But what of us, lady? Those of us left aboard can't sail this ship!"

"No matter," shouted a big seaman.

The men ran across the deck, bare feet slapping wood, and laid hands on the ropes and davits from which hung the single lifeboat of the brigantine. An instant later, with a creak of pulleys and the hum of cording, it was swaying downward toward the water. Kothar stared at the men, tumbling over one another in their eagerness to get down into that boat.

Three of the more longsighted of the crew ran to the galley, carrying back sacks filled with meat and bread, and a few wineskins. Cook was with them on their last trip, the barbarian noted.

Then oars were being shipped and the longboat was pulling away through the waves, lifting and dropping. A ragged cheer went up from the throats of the men crowded from its prow to the rounded stern. Grovdon Dokk watched them go, and spat to windward.

"Cursed rebels," he snarled and glanced at the dead bodies littering his deck. "I have to give them proper burial," he muttered.

"Flarion and I will help," the barbarian offered.

All that afternoon they sewed canvas sacks to wrap about the bodies of the four dead men. Toward sunset, as the captain read from the Book of the Ten Gods, one by one Kothar and Flarion let the bodies slip into the sea, weighted down by leaden balls. Cybala came to stand in the afterdeck companionway, wrapped in her paenula, eyes dark and brooding, but Red Lori was nowhere to be seen.

The ship was still anchored above the house and gardens that had been Afgorkon's, long ago. It was motionless here, becalmed, as the moon rose and flooded the glasslike surface of the waters with its silver radiance.

Grovdon Dokk muttered to the barbarian, "I don't like this stillness, it isn't natural. I begin to wish I'd gone with the others. And how are we to sail *Waveskimmer*, two landsmen and myself? Will you tell me that?"

"I can't guess," Kothar muttered.

He was tired. It had been a hard day, what with his diving and that fight with the kraken and bringing up the coffer by himself; and later, quelling the mutiny before Red Lori got herself killed, and then stitching up the death bags. He would sleep well enough tonight, by Dwallka! Yawning, he nodded at the captain.

"I'm going to find my bunk," he said. "I'd advise you to do the same."

"Who can sleep? This is my ship, barbarian. I make my living with it. And she's stuck out here, nine miles from Kantar shoals, with never a bit of breeze to flap her sails. I don't like it. Maybe the men were right, maybe that redhead is a witch with a curse on her head."

"She isn't. Wouldn't she have used a spell to free herself from the sailors, if she were a witch?"

Grovdon Dokk rubbed his stubbled jaw. "Mayhap. And mayhap not. I'm an honest man and honest men don't know which way a witch's mind runs."

The Cumberian moved along the deck to the companionway. As he passed their cabin door, he heard Cybala and Flarion arguing. Like husband and wife, he thought. He felt like yelling to the mercenary to throw the girl on a bed and take her and be done with it. It was probably the only sort of argument she really understood.

His big hand turned the knob of his own cabin door. Red Lori crouched before the eidolon, parchments spread across her knees and tossed helter-skelter on the cabin floor. She frowned, staring at the words written on those scrolls, and her lips moved from time to time as she sought to understand their meanings.

"Sleep wouldn't hurt you, either," he growled, getting out of his mail shirt. Seeing she ignored him, he crossed the worn carpeting to peer down over her shoulder.

"You're in my light, Kothar. Go to sleep."

"Can't you read, witchwoman?" he jeered.

She looked up at him. "Not this script, not easily. The language in which these parchments are written is fifty thousand years old. There have been some changes since then."

"I thought you sorceresses knew all those ancient languages."

"We know some, yes. These are very old. But I begin to understand them, a little. It is slow going at first. It will go faster, very soon."

Kothar stretched, yawning. He kicked off his war boots, sitting on the edge of his bunk. Red Lori was lost to him for the night, he could see that. She was bent above those scrolls as if they contained the secret of life and death for her.

Maybe they did, for all he knew. He slid into bed in his underbreeks and quilted *hacqueton* and drew the blankets up to his neck.

In moments, he was asleep.

He dreamed he stood in a blue mist, shivering with cold. The mist was speaking to him, whispering strange and troubling words, the meaning of which he should understand and did not. Red Lori was calling out to him, very faintly, or perhaps she spoke those words; he could not tell. He called her name and began walking slowly through the blue mist.

She ran toward him, covered all over with icicles and hoarfrost tinkling to her every stride. She was weeping bitter tears and as he opened his arms to draw her close, a sharp icicle gouged his flesh.

He woke up.

He was not in the cabin, he was inside a tomb.

The sweat came out on his sun-browned face. There was blue light everywhere, demonlight such as had lit the mausoleum of long-dead Kalikalides. Now what made him think of that tomb in far-off Xythoron? As his eyes became more accustomed to the azure radiance, he saw a stone bier and on it a body clad in purple and gold garments. It was the body of a young man—No, by Dwallka! The body had only the similarity to youth. This was the mage Kalikalides himself, kept eternally young by certain necromantic spells. Its cheeks were flushed, its lips red as if with life. And standing in a corner of this vault—Red Lori!

But wait. If that was Red Lori, who was it who stood naked to one side of his bed a parchment scroll in a hand, chanting words unheard on earth for fifty thousand years? It too, was the witchwoman.

"Gods of Thuum," he breathed.

For Red Lori was singing, and the other Red Lori, the one in the dark corner, clad in the blouse and fringed skirt of the Mongrol plains-woman, was floating toward her double. Her feet did not touch the ground, it was as if she drifted between worlds. There was a nimbus of light about her and her eyes were wide and staring, yet she came nearer to the redheaded woman with the parchment scroll, nearer, nearer!

The barbarian shivered, aware of some vague voice in his mind bidding him leap to prevent the joining of these two woman shapes. There was danger here, dread danger, of a kind he did not know, being no sorcerer. Yet he felt it with his animal senses.

"Red Lori," he croaked. "Give over your wizardries!"

She paid him no heed, but went on chanting.

Now Kothar could see the outlines of objects inside the cabin, the eidolon close to the bulkhead, the lamp hanging from its chain nearby and under it, bathed in its light, the coffer with the enameled sigils on its top. Aye, and the bunk where the witchwoman was wont to sleep when she was not sharing his own, and the shirt of mail and his war boots where he had discarded them.

The tomb was here, as well, the bier plain to see, and the body on it. There was a blending of two spaces, the barbarian realized, the tomb and the cabin. He was here on the Outer Sea, yet he was inside the black crypt of the dead magician.

He did not understand how this could be, except by necromancy. His eyes saw the decorations on the mausoleum, his nose smelled the charnel odors of the grave, his ears heard Red Lori singing.

The other witchwoman floated closer, closer.

Soon they would join, these women who were but one.

The cold sweat stood out on Kothar's forehead. He reached for Frost-fire, but in this double-space his fingers could not grip its shaft. He sat here on the bed but his sword was forbidden him.

And so he watched.

The Red Lori in the Mongrol garb touched the naked Red Lori. Her hand went into and around that other hand, as her shoulders and hips became one with her simulacrum. Legs and breasts and belly, the two women merged together.

The cabin was warm, suddenly. Gone was the grave chill, the noisome smells, the dampness. A fire glowed in an iron brazier and by its light, and the radiance of the lamp above the coffer, Kothar could see Red Lori clad in the tattered Mongrol garments she had worn when he had sealed her inside the crypt in Xythoron.

She turned and, laughing softly, saw him watching her.

"Aye, Kothar! I am—myself! Free of the mausoleum where you imprisoned me. Alive! And—free!"

"You've been free ever since I took you out of Kandakore's tome."

"No, barbarian—no! It was only my image which has traveled with you these past weeks.

My astral self, which I drew from another plane of existence and brought into our own."

He glowered at her. "So that's why you wanted the coffer. It wasn't to free me from any curse of Afgorkon, not at all."

Her white fingers went into her long red hair, lifted it high above her head as she pivoted, dancing a few steps about the cabin. Her laughter rose upward, softly mocking.

"I am myself, I am Red Lori," she sang. "And Kothar is my slave!" She pointed a red-nailed finger at him. "Yes, barbarian. You are mine, you belong to me. We are not finished, you and I have a further need for your big muscles and your magic sword."

"You can't command me. I—"

"Ah, but I can. I can, Kothar! Before I could not, my astral image lacked the power—which explains why I was so sweet to you, so loving. I twisted you about my little finger, I gave you kisses and—more than kisses—to make certain that you were no more than a lovesick fool!"

He sought to rise from the bed; could not. It was as if invisible chains held him motionless. "You see?" she cried gleefully. "I possess many of my old powers, now. There is no need to wheedle and cajole. No longer!"

She came across the floor on light feet. Her hand slapped his cheek, back and forth. His head rocked to her blows. Between her teeth, she snarled, "I am your mistress! You are my slave! My slave, Kothar the mighty! You are less than a lapdog, no stronger than a midge—without me.

"Oh, yes. You shall obey me. Without question, without argument. When I say run, you shall run. If I say kill, you and that sword of yours shall kill in my name. You cannot help yourself."

She stopped hitting him, brought her hand to her mouth and licked its smartings with her tongue, her green eyes impish as they regarded him. She smiled suddenly and held out her stinging palm, reddened from her repeated slap-pings of his cheeks.

"Kiss it," she ordered.

And Kothar touched his lips to her flesh.

His soul writhed in his body, but he was helpless against her green eyes and her powers. There was an aura about her, much like that blue nimbus in which his body had been clothed when Frostfire had struck the eidolon in time to save his life beneath the surface of the Outer Sea. He could not resist it, nor her commands.

She ruffled his blond hair, suddenly. "Oh, I'll treat you well, for the most part. A master is good to a valuable slave. You are valuable to me, Kothar. So I shall be good to you."

Red Lori turned away, moving with swaying hips toward the cabin door. She opened the door, walked out. Kothar felt the thralldom fall away from him. With a snarled oath, he bounded from the bed, snatching up Frostfire. He ran for the doorway and into the narrow passageway. On bare feet he raced up the companionway and out upon the deck.

The witchwoman stood with upraised arms, the sea wind toying with her hair. Her eyes were raised to the clouds scudding across the sky, through which the two moons of Yarth peeped, round and silvery like demon eyes. There was a faint radiance about her body, a bluish glow that snapped and crackled to the ears in the stillness of the night.

"Io k'harthal mollonthal! Pthond ka thondal pha benth!" Her voice rose up in a series of ululating sounds that made the short hairs rise on his neck. There was an eerie quality to her voice. Those sounds seemed made not by human vocal chords but by those of some alien being; they held Kothar paralyzed.

"Great god Poseithon, whose breath comes to our world as wind and gale and storm, heed my prayer! Io k'harthal mollonthal! Send your breath to me, to this corner of Yarth, according to my need. And gently honored be thy name, lord Poseithon!"

There was a distant moan in the night, a faint whisper of sound that stirred the waves in tiny ripples on either side of the brigantine. The barbarian could see Grovdon Dokk crouched on the main deck, staring at the woman encased in the crackling blue glow. The *Waveskimmer* had lain becalmed. The surface of the sea around them had been glassy, still as any woods pond. Yet now the ripples grew larger, larger, and the ship lifted to the waves that formed. It rose gently, fell easily. And the moan grew louder, louder.

A breeze brushed Kothar, stirring his golden hair, ruffling the fur that trimmed his kilt. The wind was warm, heavy with exotic scents from the southlands, almost musky. Above his head the riggings rattled and the sails shook weakly.

The breeze became a wind, filling the sails.

Grovdon Dokk cursed faintly, stirred from his position and ran up the afterdeck companion-way. The helm was swinging idly, turning this way and that as the waves caught it, as the canvas filled and drove the ship forward. His big hands went to the whipstaff, caught and held it. Forward surged the ship on a steady course, its prow cleaving the gathering waves with a faint gurgle of rushing waters.

The blue radiance faded. Red Lori let her arms drop. She stood a moment head bowed, as if exhausted. Then she lifted a hand, brushed fallen locks of red hair from her eyes. She turned, saw Kothar; stood still, smiling faintly.

"We go to Zoane," she said softly. "On the way, I shall prepare the necessary spells that will animate the eidolon. Come you with me, barbarian."

Her green eyes looked at him as she spoke; they were enormous, staring. He had no will to resist them. He nodded and waited until she crossed the deck planks to fall into step just behind her.

The cabin was lighted by the single lamp hung on chains from the beamed ceiling. In its golden glow the faceless eidolon stood silent, ominous. The barbarian felt the mute menace of that grim statue, his flesh crawled at the thought of what it represented.

Red Lori crossed the cabin floor, lifted a parchment from the coffer. Unrolling it, she knelt before the eidolon. Softly she began to read from the ancient writings. The room grew cold, there was a smell of the grave and rotting cerements in the air. Kothar growled and put his hand on Frostfire.

To the Cumberian, the statue seemed to writhe in protest, to move its stubby arms and legs. It was a trick of the light, he told himself, for the ship was rising and falling to the surging waves as it cleaved a path toward Zoane.

A whisper in the air touched his ears.

"Who calls Afgorkon? Who comes to disturb his sleep after five hundred centuries?"

"I call, great mage, lord of the fifty worlds of Kafarr, worlds of your own creation! I seek your help for your brother magicians, victims of assassins in this land of Yarth, which you knew long ago."

There was a silence. The whisper came again.

"I feel pity for my brothers in magic. Yet Afgorkon has withdrawn himself from those lands which once knew his name."

"His name! This is all I ask, great wizard. Peer into the astral planes surrounding our own. Speak his name only—and leave the rest to me. And to my man-slave, Kothar!"

"Ah, Kothar. Is he with you? Yes, I see him—and his sword Frostfire, which was forged in the primal ooze by certain—devils—of my acquaintance. How like you the sword, barbarian?"

"I like it," said Kothar.

Afgorkon chuckled. "Aye, even though with it, you are pauper! I see it in your eyes, your blade is the only thing in life you love." There was a little silence, then the mage breathed out words again in that hoarse voice, faint with far distances. "I shall look as you desire, woman who has waked me. Not for you, but for the sake of those who are my kin in warlockry."

Red Lori still knelt, and now she leaned forward, touching her forehead to the base of the eidolon, crying, "My thanks, great mage!"

The cabin was still. Kothar realized that the face of the eidolon was not here in this world, but in those many-faceted lands that surround Yarth in which the demons dwell, and those of the elder race of gods in which are reflected, like objects in a dark glass, the deeds done in his world. Long the eyes of Afgorkon looked, long was the silence in the cabin.

"I see death," said the voice of Afgorkon. "Death from the rusted daggers and rotting swords of those who have gone before. Up from their graves they have been summoned by dire spells, to slay such mages as are marked for death by him who would destroy them."

"His name, great Afgorkon? His name?"

"I know not his name. Nor do I see his face in these other megacosms through which my eyes wander. He had protected himself by mighty enchantments against such knowledge becoming known."

Red Lori wailed, "Then how may I stop him?"

"Go you to those other warlocks whose lives are threatened. Gather them together, induce them to perform spells. I will aid them—if I can. The assassin has enlisted powerful forces against us. How he protects himself from my eyes, I do not know—but I will attempt to learn."

The voice died out.

Red Lori rose slowly from her knees, and in the lamplight her face seemed haggard, worried, as she turned it toward the barbarian. "I was sure he could tell me, I was so sure of it! Now…" Her shoulders rose and fell in resigned despair.

"If this means so much to you, why not follow his advice? Go to the magicians who are threatened, employ their help."

She stared at him coldly. "If Afgorkon cannot help, how can they who are not one-tenth the magician he was—and is—in those fifty cosmic lands of his?"

"What have you to lose? Besides, Afgorkon may help you."

She considered him with her stare, nodding at last and sighing. "It may be, yes. If the mage will tell us where the wizards have hidden themselves, then I may send you to them as my emissary, to cajole them into meeting with us and using our combined wisdoms."

Her palms clapped together as if to show that her mind was made up. She swung to the coffer, sorted through the parchments there. Nodding, she selected one, unrolling it and glancing over it at the barbarian with a faint smile.

"I lack many of the magical impedimenta of my black tower, Kothar. But one of these spells will do nicely, along with that scepter I removed from the tomb of Kandakore. It has certain—ah—properties, this scepter."

She lifted it from where it lay beside the coffer and made cryptic signs in the air with it, saying softly, "I shall call on Afgorkon to help me send you to find one of those wizards who are hiding from the world, terrified of the assassin's dagger."

Red Lori began to chant in that same thick voice which she had used on deck when she had summoned up the father of winds. At the same time she went on moving the scepter in the air.

The room grew cold. The barbarian found himself staring at the shimmering outlines of the cabin that shifted and grew hazy, as if the cabin and the woman were fading to invisibility.

Kothar felt a wrench in all his muscles.

CHAPTER SIX

He stood on a vast plain beneath a red sun, amid a scene of awful desolation. Instinctively he knew this was a dying world, perhaps he had been cast through uncountable millennia to those days before the end of Yarth. There were low rounded hills in the background, eroded by wind, rain, and age. The ground underfoot was almost sand, so fine it was, and only here and there were any living plants.

Yet it was not this wasteland that filled him with awe. Rather, it was the dozen or more glowing signs—suspended in the air, blazing as if with fire, though there were no flames—that made a low, moaning noise as the wind blew through them. There was a feeling of strange energies in the air, magical energies that made the sweat come out onto his forehead.

The barbarian shook himself. His hand touched Frostfire, wrapped fingers about it. This was where one of the warlocks of Yarth had hidden himself thousands—perhaps even millions—of years in the future. His spells had carried him through space and time, just as Red Lori had sent him, Kothar, to find this man.

He walked forward below the burning signs. They did not halt him nor even slow him down for their magic was not directed against a living human such as he, but only against the assassins from the grave who served the killer-mage's dread will.

He had not far to go before he saw the seated figure. This man was old, with white hair framing a bald head, his face covered with a long white beard. He looked up as the sand grated under Kothar's war boots, and his dark eyes were big with terror. His pale, trembling hands came up as if to push the Cumberian away.

"No," he wheezed. "No, no…"

"I'm no killer," growled Kothar. "I've been sent by Red Lori and Afgorkon to help you."

"Afgorkon?" The bald head went up, the old nostrils flared. "Aye, if any can help, he might." Kothar spoke of the eidolon and of the enameled coffer that contained the lost arcana of the mage Afgorkon. The old man's excitement grew until he was almost dancing in his eagerness and renewed hope.

"It may be, it could be. It's worth a chance, the risk surely! Ah, to mingle my spells with those of fabled Afgorkon. It would be the supreme triumph of my long life."

He added, "Wait! I will take us back to Red Lori with a spell of my own and—"

The air seemed to burn around them. The sigils hanging in the air blazed more brightly, glowing scarlet. And the old man screamed in stark terror.

Kothar swung around. Coming across the plain in great leaps and bounds were three half-rotting corpses. One was so frayed by time and the grave that it seemed little more than a skeleton bound together by brown, withered ligaments. And it carried a rusted battleaxe in a hand.

"The liches that serve the assassin," sobbed old Phordog Fale. "Nothing can stop them. Run now, barbarian—while you can still save your life. They don't want to kill you, unless you make them. They care only about me!"

Kothar rasped, "By Dwallka! Red Lori sent me to fetch you to her— and I mean to do so!"

He leaped, his sword blade sparkling in the red fury of the blazing sigils above his head. They were being consumed too fast, he understood that; in some manner the killer must have found a way to counteract their protective magic by causing them to burn themselves up. He ran to meet the oncoming corpses with a snarl on his lips.

The steel blade swung. A rotted head leaped from its shoulders. Kothar whirled, slashed at a second, driving his steel between bones and putrid flesh. The liches never halted in their running; dead men all, they could not be killed a second time.

The barbarian swore, his flesh creeping. The old man was behind him, patiently waiting for the death he felt he could not avoid.

They were past Kothar now, with eyes only for Phordog Fale. The Cumberian grinned coldly and ran after them. He ran lightly, swiftly, soon overtaking them.

Now he drove Frostfire in a savage arc so that its edge would bite through thighbones and dead flesh. One lich fell to the ground, and then a second. They tried to run on the stumps of what had been legs but made only slow, snail-like progress.

He caught the third corpse as it was swinging its rusted axe high to bring its edge down at the old man. Frostfire sliced through the rotting wooden handle of that axe; the axehead fell to the ground. The lich whirled, dove for Kothar with its boney hands up to claw.

Kothar cut its arms off.

Then he slashed at its legs until it was no more than the torso of a dead man flopping on the ground. He turned to the others that still crawled across the ground. Their arms he hacked off, he cut them into gobbets with his steel.

Panting, he paused to glance at the stunned Phordog Fale. "Old man, chant that spell of yours that will get us out of here before somebody sends more dead men for me to slice apart."

The old man began his incantation.

In seconds, they were in the cabin of the *Waveskimmer.* Red Lori cried out delightedly at sight of the old man. "Phordog Fale! I haven't seen you since I was a little girl at the court of King Zopar, where you were chief magician. Do you remember me?"

The old man smiled as he caught her hands. "Dear Lori with the red hair, I mind you well. Always you were under my elbow, practicing my spells, memorizing the various cantraips. When you were alone you pored over my books on magic, learning them word for word. And now—you have saved my life."

"You must help, Phordog Fale. Alone, it is too much of a task for me." She went on to speak of the finding of the coffer and the statue, and of what Afgorkon had told her.

Kothar watched and listened for a few moments, but there was a need in him for clean, fresh sea air. He did not care for the stinks of magic and dead bodies. He went up onto the deck where he stood with the salt wind blowing lazily and the ship swaying and dipping as it ploughed through the waves.

He turned his head, saw Grovdon Dokk like a statue at the whipstaff, cloak flapping in the winds. He wondered at the thoughts of the sea captain, with his great ship running before a wizard wind. It was probably not the first time in his life that he had come in contact with sorcery. He called up to the man.

"How soon to Zoane, captain?"

"A day and this night, barbarian. Tomorrow at sundown we anchor in its harbor." Grovdon Dokk spat into the wind. "I like it not, this traveling by a wind that shows itself only on the ship. Look you at the sea."

Gone were the ripples that had appeared at this first onrush of breeze. Now the sea was calm as if *Waveskimmer* lay in the tropic doldrums. Kothar shrugged. After what his eyes had seen, this glimpse of working magic was as nothing. He went down the companionway with a wave of the hand at the bemused sailor.

Red Lori waited in the cabin, where old Phordog Fale rested his aged body on a bunk. The witchwoman snapped at him, "Where were you? I have need for you."

Kothar thought of his advice to Flarion. Perhaps he ought to throw this one down on a bunk too, and take her; it might teach her manners. Perhaps she read his intent in his face, for she lifted her chin like an empress, saying, "You would not dare! I would blast you with a dozen curses, leave you naught but a babbling idiot."

"Is this why you summoned me?"

"I have a task for you. Phordog Fale has told me that Nemidomes of Abathor has also taken refuge against the magicks of the killer-mage. You will go to him, bring him back with you."

"Girl, my belly aches with emptiness. I'll—"

She was crying out the words and the wrenching was in his muscles, agonizing. Under his war-boots the cabin floor tilted oddly as she moved the scepter this way and that in the air.

He stood on the cobbled floor of a tunnel. All around him were bluish-purple walls, seemingly carved out of rock and dirt, rounded and abandoned. To his left were clay cylinders tumbled and shattered. Ahead of him he could make out a reddish light, oddly flickering. The barbarian sighed and began his walk. Somewhere up ahead he would discover Nemidomes of Abathor, he was certain.

His war boots were dusty by the time he came to the end of the long tunnelway, and now he could hear the sound of voices murmuring softly and smell the odors of natron and balsam. He came to a stop, eyes striving to pierce the purplish gloom of this rock-walled chamber. He knew what it was, a charnel house where the dead of Abathor were stuffed with quick lime and bitumen for the better preservation of their corpses. Of all the lands of Yarth, only Abathor spent so much care and money on the preservation of their dead.

His eyes roamed, seeking the shape of him who might be Nemidomes. Most of the men at whom he stared were scrawny, aged beings whose skin was purple because of the spices and unguents which they handled day after day. Among them would be one whose skin was pink. He began walking forward.

It was one of the corpses that betrayed Nemidomes. For the Cumberian saw a dead woman sit up—she had been stabbed in a quarrel, he gathered, because there was a dagger still sticking between her ribs—and yank out that dagger and hurl herself without a sound toward the back of a plump man with shaggy gray hair.

Kothar cursed and leaped.

His arms went around the legs of what had been an attractive woman short hours before, but was now cold, dead flesh. His stomach turned over as he felt that dead flesh against his own. But his hand stabbed out, grasped the lifeless wrist, and hammered it against a cobblestone.

The body writhed and twisted in his arms as it fought him savagely. It did not breathe, being dead, yet it was seemingly alive, making it the more ghastly. Teeth bit into his arm, nails scratched. Kothar grunted, reached up a hand to tangle fingers in long hair and battered that lifeless skull upon the stones. Again and again he hammered the head to the stone until bone cracked. Still the thing fought on.

He ripped out Frostfire, struggled to free himself, made it to his feet. The sword flashed, and as the steel sheared through the dead flesh and bone, the thing flopped across the cobbles.

Nemidomes was panting in terror, watching. The charnel workers were gathered in a circle surrounding the dead thing, crying out in horror.

When he was done with Frostfire, the corpse was in many parts, all of them wriggling and twisting. Kothar stared down at what was left of that which had been a woman and wanted to be sick. He fought the sickness, waiting until the necromantic life which had sustained it faded away and nothing remained but truly lifeless flesh.

Then he reached out and caught Nemidomes by a wrist. As the sorcerer shrank from him, the barbarian drew him nearer to his whisper. "I come from Red Lori and from old Phordog Fale! I'm here to save you from the assassins!"

The plump little man was covered with sweat all over his pink face. He shook in his fear and resisted only slightly when the Cumberian dragged him down one of the tunnelways.

"I t-thought I was so s-safe," he babbled, running a hand across his face, trotting where the big barbarian led, "hiding in the ch-charnel house. I d-didn't realize whoever is trying to ki-kill us magicians is using the d-dead to do it!"

"Well, he is," rasped Kothar, turning to look down at the little man. "Have you any idea who it is?"

Pale blue eyes stared back at him hopelessly as the plump man shook his head, making his jowls jiggle. "No. I thought you mi-might, since you got here in time to save my life."

"You'd better make a spell to get us out of here." He told the magician where the *Wave-skimmer* was located.

The smaller man made some passes with his hands, chanted a few words. In a moment the tunnels were gone and the familiar deck of the brigantine was underfoot. The magician sighed and his shoulders sagged.

Then his worry came back and he stared around him with fretful eyes. "We aren't safe even here, you know. The assassin can see us. That's how he knew I was in the charnel house."

And that Phordog Fale was hiding at the end of the world, the barbarian thought to himself. He caught the plump man by an elbow, brought him down the companionway to the cabin where Bed Lori and Phordog Fale were waiting.

Red Lori said to Kothar, "Phordog Fale and I have been busy since you left to find Nemidomes. We have spoken to Kazazael of Commoral, to Ulnar Thomoquol, to Kylwyrren of Urgal. We have decided to band together, to apply all the magicks each of us knows to throw a barrier around ourselves."

Kothar shrugged. The green eyes sharpened. "You will bring Flarion and the dancing girl. We leave at dusk. Horses will be ready at the quay, where Grovdon Dokk has gone to arrange these matters."

The barbarian found Flarion on deck, with Cybala across the ship from him, staring at the waters of Zoane harbor. His thumb jerked back at the quarterdeck cabin.

"They'll need protection," rasped the barbarian. "They're great magicians, all of them, but they're about as helpless as babies when it comes to standing off a dagger or sword attack. This will be our job."

Flarion snarled, "I want no more to do with it. What've we gotten out of this, Kothar? Not so much as a copper soldan! And what've we got to look forward to? Just hard fighting. I say—leave the redheaded woman and her wizards to shift for themselves."

The Cumberian grunted. "You have the girl."

"Pah!" Flarion spat overside. "That one! Cold as a northern sea, by Salara! She almost ran a dagger into me when I sought to kiss her last night."

"And what did you do? Take the dirk away from her and beg her pardon? Boy, you're an idiot where a skirt's concerned."

The youth looked uncomfortable. "Just the same…"

"We stay. Who knows, maybe you'll make the wench like you yet." He chuckled, eyeing his friend. "You want me to speak to her?"

Flarion looked suspicious. "What are you going to say?"

"I'll send her running into your arms. Just let me handle it my way and don't interfere. Agreed?"

Flarion nodded slowly, and watched the big barbarian cross the deck toward the larboard rail, where Cybala leaned her weight. He saw Kothar catch the hood of her long cloak and pull it back, freeing the glossy black hair of the dancer so that it rippled down her back.

Cybala turned on Kothar like a spitting cat. The Cumberian grinned and grabbed her hair, half lifting her off her feet. The pain was excruciating, and she screamed.

"Save your breath, wench," he growled. "Or I'll bang your head on the railing to teach you manners. I just want a look at you."

He yanked open her cloak, revealing her curving body clad in a short purple tunic that displayed her ripe flesh. She gasped, sought to close the woolen paenula.

"Ease off, girl. Red Lori says Afgorkon will want you as a human sacrifice, I say he won't. I just want to see what he's going to get. After all, he's a patron of mine."

"Afgorkon?" she whispered. "A human sacrifice?"

"The fabled necromancer, yes. He's been dead fifty thousand years, but he still lives. Of course, they'll have to kill you to get you to him—he lives in a world of his own making into which no living person can go. You have to be dead to go there."

The girl went white. Her knees shook so that she had to lean against the railing to stand erect. She whimpered, "You're only jesting. Say you're jesting, Kothar!"

He shook his head. "Not I! Nor does Red Lori. Why do you think we brought you along, wench? What need have we of a belly dancer—except as a human sacrifice to Afgorkon?"

"No," she breathed. "No!"

"I say he won't take you, but we'll never know until you're dead. Too bad, I say. Flarion seems to think highly of you. Why, I don't know and can't guess—but he does."

"Flarion," she whispered, turning her head to look across the deck.

"Don't look to him for help," he told her, and left to walk across the deck toward the companionway.

He grinned as he heard the padding of her slippers as she ran across the planks to the starboard rail where the young mercenary leaned. Turning at the companionway, he saw her clinging to his arm, pleading, lovely face upraised.

He was turning away when his eyes caught sight of a bright shaft of sunlight some miles away. Its blinding brilliance hurt the eyes. This was no result of any sun! This was sorcery. He watched it squinting for a few seconds, then rounded on a heel and dove down the companionway.

He came into the cabin like a whirlwind. "On deck, the lot of you," he growled, waving an arm. "There's a beam of light coming this way—straight for the ship."

Nemidomes cried out sharply. Red Lori made a little gesture with a hand, pushing past the barbarian who swung to follow her. As she came up onto the deck planks she shaded her eyes with a hand, staring northward.

"Aye, it's wizardry," she nodded.

"Do you have a spell to counter it?"

Phordog Fale and Nemidomes were on the deck, staring where the witchwoman looked. It was the plump little man who muttered, "A demon light. There are ways to counteract it but without my scrolls and palimpsests, I'm helpless."

"I'm not," snapped Red Lori, and bent to duck past Kothar.

Phordog Fale was twisting his pale hands together, face crumpled by fright. Beside him, the little man was sweating profusely, the fear of something worse than death in his eyes. The Cumberian snarled and moved around them to go to the cabin after the redhead.

She was kneeling before the eidolon, head bent, whispering almost to herself. He stood in there.

"...destroy us before we...your power and strength only can...must aid us, Afgorkon...the assassin will slice the boat in half, burning us all in flames of demonry...save us...to save the lives of..."

As he watched, Kothar caught his breath. For a moment, the faceless stone appeared to shimmer faintly, and he saw eyes in that stone and a face where a face should be. He shivered. These were not the features of the dead lich that had been the Afgorkon who had given Frostfire to Kothar. This was the face of a youthful sorcerer, proud and hard.

"I see the demon light, it comes out of the seven hells of Eldrak. The sorcery aligned against you and the others is very great, Red Lori. And you are right. That light will burn your ship and everything on it to a cinder!"

Kothar shivered. Red Lori wailed, "Save us!"

"I call upon Belthamquar, father of demons. I summon Eldrak, who has permitted this light to be stolen from his seven hells!"

The voice was strong, like a gale off the northern glaciers. The room was very cold, suddenly. And in that cold, even while he drew his cloak closer about his great shoulders, Kothar thought to see a redly flaming figure standing beside the eidolon. Eldrak of the seven hells? And on the far side of the statue, another demon, Belthamquar!

"Who calls Eldrak?"

"And Belthamquar?"

"I call," came a voice from the eidolon. "I, Afgorkon, friend to you both. Is this the will of Eldrak, of the demon father? Are all the wizards of Yarth to be slain by a common murderer? Even now a demon light swirls down upon the ship."

"I see it," breathed Eldrak excitedly. "It does come from my burning worlds! But—by what right? I gave no permission!"

"Then stop it," snapped Belthamquar.

Eldrak lifted his hands, cried out thickly, half a dozen words that seemed to sear the very air around him. The barbarian heard voices shouting on deck. He could not make them out, but he realized they were cries of relief, of delight. Apparently the demon light was being recalled back into the seven hells out of which it had been summoned.

Cold chills ran down Kothar's back as he stared at these demon lords, these gods of space and time, at their shimmering figures flanking the eidolon and the kneeling, trembling witchwoman. Vaguely he understood that

Red Lori had called upon tremendous forces and that she was terrified of their awe-inspiring powers.

Yet Belthamquar did not concern himself with the girl. Rather he stared upon the eidolon with the shimmering face of Afgorkon. The father of demons was clad in a black cloak, his face was not clearly seen, it was as if a blackness were inside the cloak with the glowing golden sigils etched upon its surface.

"I have not seen this eidolon for five hundred centuries, Afgorkon. Since then, I have assumed it was lost."

"As it was. The woman crouched on the floor, and that big barbarian in the doorway brought it up from what was my necromantic chamber."

The empty blackness turned toward Kothar. Two gleaming red eyes, smoldering with ancient wisdom, studied his big frame. Sweat came out on the Cumberian's face. His animal senses told him he was in the presence of mystery and strange powers. Yet he growled softly, and put his hand on his sword hilt.

There was a dry chuckle.

Belthamquar turned back to the statue. "Who stole the demon light from Eldrak?"

"I do not know. I have tried to find out—and cannot. I know, however, that someone or something is slaying the wizards and sorcerers of Yarth. The dead come from their graves bearing weapons, and where they find the warlocks, there they strike."

Eldrak—who was little more than a pillar of red flame, Kothar thought—said wryly, "Why, if they do that, who will call upon us, offering us sacrifices and rare jewels, plus other things which we enjoy?"

"I have thought of that," murmured Belthamquar.

"And I," breathed the eidolon. "Long have I slept in the worlds I have made, enjoying that which I have created. Yet now it seems I am awake, and aware that I cannot hide away from the call of those who still know life. We must join forces, we three. A necromancer in Yarth is calling upon powers unknown to me, which protects him from my astral eyes.

"If I could search out this protective shield, learn what causes it, I might be able to destroy it and learn the name of him who kills wizards."

"And we shall help," whispered Belthamquar softly.

"Aye, aye," nodded Eldrak. "We shall help!" The blackness and the glowing redness faded to invisibility. The blurry face on the statue disappeared. Bed Lori shivered, still bent before the eidolon, awed and frightened by the terrifying forces her spells had summoned up.

"Red Lori," came the voice.

"Yes, master?"

"Go you with my coffer of scrolls and with this eidolon to the ruins of Radimore in Tharia. Long, long ago Radimore was the focal point of strange powers. It is where this world of Yarth and those nether worlds of Belthamquar, Eldrak, and the other demons once touched, by a happenstance in the time and space continuum. There are our powers best able to be focused.

"And go you soon, if you would live."

Kothar watched the woman shivering. He stepped forward, caught her under an armpit, hoisted her to her feet. She swayed, staring up at him. Her eyes were glassy, she seemed under a terrible emotional stress.

"My body…they drew on my body to give the…the strength to stay here in this world…while they talked…I thought they would—kill me with their energies—"

She shuddered, resting her cheek on his chest. Gone was the proud sorceress, she was no more than a fearful woman. And the barbarian found that his feelings toward her were more tender than ever before.

"Where is this Radimore?"

"A few miles south of Phyrmyra, where you found me. It is a desolate place. Legends claim that the gods hate it because of olden blasphemies that happened there, but this I do not believe, after what Belthamquar and Eldrak said. We must go there at once, Kothar."

"After you have eaten," he smiled.

"I have no need for food."

"Just the same, you'll eat."

She sought to resist but she was so weak she was like a child as he drew her by an elbow out to the companionway and up the steps to the deck. They went forward to the galley, where Kothar found meat and bread and filled a tankard with nut-brown ale from Aegypton. He feasted with her, and to them came Phordog Fale and Nemidomes, still frightened by what had happened, to listen to Red Lori's account of what had taken place in the cabin.

It was decided that they would land at Zoane, that Flarion would hire horses, and that Kothar would remain on board with the others in case the assassin sent more killing corpses. Red Lori must sleep, the mages decided. She would need all her strength for what was to come.

Flarion offered no argument when the barbarian went to find him. He was oddly pleased, Kothar thought, so much so that he grew suspicious. He put a hand on the young mercenary, gripping his wrist.

"Think not to flee away with Cybala," he rasped. "Those three back there in the gallery could find and destroy you with their arts merely by muttering a few words."

The youth nodded. "I shall not run away. Trust me, Kothar."

The Cumberian did not trust him, there was a triumphant light deep in his eyes that told Kothar he had some plan in mind. "I keep Cybala here. You go alone to Zoane."

"As the two moons pass overhead," nodded the youth.

* * * *

The ship lay at anchor in the harbor of Zoane. It was just one among many ketches and merchantmen that plied these salt waters carrying oak to Thuum and rich red wine from Makkadonia to Sybaros and the southlands, herbs and spices from Ifrokone and Ispahan, weapons from the forges of Abathor, slaves from the Oasian jungles. Zoane was a crossroads of his world, a seaport to rank with Memphor, on the other side of the continent. Tar and pitch and the salt winds blended with the musk smell of the teak-wood ships from below the equator. It was a rich city, Zoane, and here came all the evils and wickednesses of mankind to be sold over counting tables as if they were no more than shawls from Mantaigne.

Flarion found Greyling and five more horses in a stable fronting a cobbled alleyway. The five mounts were big beasts and strong. He bought them, guessing shrewdly that they had been stolen. He paid more than they were worth, but Red Lori had been generous with the golden coins she poured into his purse. On a venture such as this, she assured him, gold and jewels meant nothing.

He was leading his purchases back through the narrow byways and cobbled footpaths when he became aware that he was being followed. He turned, searching the shadows with keen eyes, but he saw nothing more than a dwarf scuttling along close to a building wall. He hailed the midge but the creature never halted. After a time, Flarion walked on with the horses' hooves clip-clopping behind him.

Grovdon Dokk had swum to a quay and found a longboat for hire. He had rowed back to *Waveskimmer* and taken off with Kothar and the two mages together with the belly dancer. Because of the weight of the eidolon, Red Lori had stayed with it on the ship until the captain could return for it.

She was paying Grovdon Dokk off with gold bars when Flarion came up with the horses. She paused to say, "We'll need a wagon for the statue. Go buy one. Or steal it if you have to."

In minutes he was back with a two-wheeled cart and a harness into which he fitted one of the horses. He helped Cybala into the cart, then gave Kothar a hand swinging the eidolon up onto the floorboards. The cart creaked protestingly, but it took the weight without snapping a wheel.

They headed west toward the meadowlands beyond Zoane. They could go only as fast as the lorry, so it was at a slow walk that they moved through the city streets. Flarion crowded his horse close to that of Kothar, telling him of the dwarf.

"If he was an informer, we may expect trouble," the barbarian nodded. "Perhaps he saw the gold with which you paid for the horses and ran to tell a thieves' guild. If so, they'll come after us."

But they rode all the night and well into the day without any sign of pursuit. They were deep in the Tharian grasslands, with the hills of western Sybaros a purple line beyond the desert to the north. A wind faintly scented by the high grasses ran here and there, blew about the flocks of birds that dipped and darted, uttering harsh cries.

They camped by a small stream and ate of the food Red Lori had brought from the ship. They slept, with Kothar standing guard.

It was the barbarian who saw the dust cloud far to the east but coming nearer, and it was with a sense of unease that he went to wake Flarion.

"I make it out a body of horsemen, roughly; fifty strong," muttered the Cumberian.

Flarion nodded, then glanced at the big barbarian. "How far is Radimore? Burdened down by the statue, we can't make a good time."

"Then into the cart with Cybala and go as fast as you can. I'll bring up the rear with my horn bow and hope to slow them down."

Red Lori awoke at a touch, nodded agreement with what the barbarian had done. She stared at the distant dust cloud, then at the little cart trundling off across the plain.

"We can never make it in time. Whatever follows us is coming faster than we can travel."

"Then go ahead, you and the magicians. Use your wizardries to summon up help of some kind." Kothar was at his saddle, lifting his horn from its case. "I'll ride rearguard, keep them back with a few arrows. That ought to give you time to reach the city."

She frowned at him. "You're only sacrificing yourself needlessly. Ride with us, Kothar. We do what we can together or—"

His laughter rang out. "Girl, you've done so much magic-making lately that you forget what a fighting man can do. Yonder are some rocks, perhaps half a dozen miles away. I'll ride so far with you. And there I stay, to give you others a chance to reach Radimore."

He turned her, pushed her toward the others. "Wake them, get them into their saddles. And if you love life—hurry!"

CHAPTER SEVEN

They were mounted within moments and soon galloping after the creaking lorry. To Kothar, bow in hand and his quiver of arrows beside his right leg, life was beginning to make some sense. Not for him the consultations of demons and gods, the whispers of necromancers! This was what he understood, a headlong gallop across the plains with enemies behind him coming fast.

Often he turned in the kak and stared at the oncoming dust cloud. He frowned when he studied it, puzzled and uneasy. That dust cloud could only be made by a large body of men on horseback. But what large body of men would be pelting after them this way? Thieves, yes. But there should be no more than a handful of the sly cutpurses who frequented the streets of Zoane trailing them from the seaport city.

Fifty of the footpads banded together to rob half a dozen travelers? It was too incredible to consider. But if their pursuers were not street thugs, what were they? Kothar shook his head as he gripped his horn bow tighter. Well, he would know soon enough.

When they were galloping along the road leading between the rocks, the barbarian drew rein. "Go you on," he shouted to Red Lori, waving a hand. "I stay to hold them up a little while."

She urged her bay mare closer to him, putting out a hand to clasp him. "Be careful, Kothar. Fight your best but—avoid death! Remember," her lips curved into a faint smile, "you belong to me. I don't want anything to happen to you."

Then she was gone after the others, bent above her horse's mane, crouched low in the saddle. Kothar watched her, then swung down from Greyling and began unfastening holding straps. When he was done, he walked in among the rocks carrying the horn bow and a full quiver.

A leather sack with a little food in it was tossed over a shoulder, balanced by a fat waterskin. He sniffed at the air, finding it blowing to the eastward, which would give his arrows more speed. His eyes searched among the rocks as he walked.

When he came to a level spot protected by several large boulders that looked almost like shields to his war-wise eyes, he dropped the waterskin and the leather food sack.

Crouching down, he ate slowly, relishing each mouthful. He had an hour at least to wait for that dust cloud to resolve itself into men and horses. Until then he would fill his belly. Dwallka knew when he would get to take another mouthful! He hid Greyling in a little dip.

Then he settled down to wait, his gaze moving out across the grasslands, finding the dust cloud no longer visible because the horses were pounding along on thick grasses now. Faintly he could make out a large number of dots that turned into men on horseback the nearer they came.

He nocked an arrow to his string.

His sharp eyes saw metal helmets and nose-pieces and mail shirts under surcoats that bore the boar design of King Midor. Astonishment held him paralyzed a moment.

Why was King Midor interested in them?

It was a question he could not answer. And so, when he found himself faced by an enemy to shoot at, he let go the arrow. It flew fast and straight, burying itself in the chest of a horseman. The rider threw up his arms and pitched sideways from the saddle. Three times Kothar shot. Three men were on the ground bleeding out their lives before the war captain threw up his right arm, realizing they were faced by a sharpshooting foe, and yelled for his men to scatter.

The war captain dropped into the high grasses, holding his small shield chest-high so he could see over its rim. He was a tall man, with a lean middle and a deep chest, with very long arms. His face under the nose-piece and cheek-plates of his helmet was swarthy, there was a jagged scar along one side of his jaw. Kothar knew he was a veteran fighting man, known as Captain Oddo of Otrantor.

His men obeyed him implicitly, they were out of their kaks and into the grass within seconds. They made unseen targets now, but Kothar was too impatient to wait until one or another showed himself. He grimaced, not liking what he was about to do, but Red Lori and the others were in bad straits, between the pits of Koforal and the poisonous swamps of Illipat.

He began shooting the horses.

Six mounts were down before the war captain bellowed, "They'll leave us afoot if we don't stop them." Evidently he thought that more than one man was doing the bow work. "There can't be many, I only saw two warriors. At them!"

He sprang to his feet, shield up and covering his head and chest as he ran. His men followed him, imitating his posture. Yet Kothar downed three of them despite their quick shield-play. There were too many to stand them all off, and they ran swiftly as men who feared for their lives.

Kothar turned and sped away.

They saw him fleeing, but they were convinced that more than one man had been shooting those arrows and so they did not rush after him pell-mell and without regard for their own skins. They kept their shields up and their swords ready to stab or slash as they went warily among the rocks.

Kothar ran for the gray horse. Scorning the stirrups he vaulted over its croup and into the saddle. He lacked Greyling into a gallop.

He rode seemingly recklessly, yet there was no finer horseman anywhere in Yarth than Kothar the barbarian. His strong hand on the reins, his shiftings in the high-peaked saddle, eased the way of the stallion between the rocks and along those stretches of flat dirt between them.

He made good time, yet always as he rode his eyes searched the tumbled boulders for another spot from which to make a stand. And when he had come to it, he leaped from the saddle, scrambled behind a big boulder, and waited.

The stallion he let wander. Its reins were trailing along the ground, it would not go far. And now Kothar wet a finger, held it up, testing the wind. He grinned coldly. It was still blowing eastward, it would give his shafts a little added distance and power.

He set arrow to bowstring, waiting. The soldiers would discover soon enough that there were no men hidden among the rocks, they would be after him shouting for his blood. Against only one man, they would grow careless for a little while…

The horn bow bent. An arrow sailed high into the sky. It came down fast, so swiftly that no eye saw it until it buried its feathers in the throat of a young warrior. The man tried to scream, could not, and pitched forward on his face.

The small shields came up, but Kothar was so far away and the arrows moved so swiftly that no man saw them until it was too late. Three more men were down, kicking out their lives, before anyone thought to go back for the horses and ride to meet this archer who shot with such unerring marksmanship.

Then they came between the rocks at a gallop, moving so swiftly that not even Kothar could aim with any hope of success. He flashed one shaft in a man's arm, but wasted four in among the boulders.

He snarled and leaped for his saddle.

Greyling ran as he had rarely run before. Out of the rocks he flashed like a silver arrow along the flat savannah. An hour of such racing and Kothar could see, low on the horizon, what had been the city of fabled Radimore, which was perhaps the oldest city on Yarth. Tales were told of Radimore, that it had been the home of those people who first worshipped the dark god, Pulthoom. It was the birthing place of all magicians, for it had been here in the subterranean cellarways of this city that magic first came into being.

He saw Flarion waiting at the emptiness which had been the city gate eons ago. The youth raked the seemingly empty savannah with his stare, nodding.

"You came like the wind, faster than the soldiers. Greyling is a horse to be proud of."

"The others?"

"Safe enough, for the nonce. Follow me."

They went along the dusty streets until they came to a building set before a city square, its facade covered with grotesque carvings, eroded by wind and rain. Red Lori was there, coming from the building door, with Phordog Fale and Nemidomes at her elbows. In the background shadows he could make out Cybala, hiding.

"I killed a few, the others follow me," he snapped, dismounting.

Phordog Fale shook his bald head framed in white hair. "I fear it's useless. This is a strange city, very strange. There is an evil about it—"

He broke off, wringing his hands.

Nemidomes wiped his plump, sweating face. "What he means to say is—we're doomed. We perish here, the lot of us."

Kothar looked at the witchwoman. She spread her hands. "He speaks truth. There is a curse of some sort upon it, like a miasma from a poisoned swamp." She shivered, looking about her. "It's in the very air, this evil. It—frightens me."

Kothar tried to cheer her with, "But you three are experts in sorcery! Surely the demons will come to you...protect us..."

"We face more than wizardry," muttered the plump little man. "We deal not with demons but with—things of some other world, another place in the universe. They come and gibber at us, when night falls. As if they were—waiting."

The shadows seemed to lengthen as the barbarian watched. He had fought long, he had ridden across the afternoon to come to Radimore. Now it was dusk, and night was gathering darkness in the sky and in the more shadowy places of the ancient city.

"Let's build a fire," he snarled with the barbarian's directness. "The spirits can't harm us in the light."

Flarion laughed harshly. "Can they not? I think they can. Nevertheless, come with us, Kothar."

He led the way through the deserted, moldy hall of the big building to its back entrance, which gave upon a large courtyard. Here a bonfire blazed, its flames red and leaping. It crackled cheerily, yet Kothar could hear a faint whispering, a breathing, above the snap of fire-devoured twigs.

"They come," moaned Cybala, shrinking close to Flarion.

He saw them first as swirling mists, dancing bits of fog that came from windows and doorways and leaped and twisted in their coming.

They whispered, softly and lightly, laughing shrilly, chuckling in obscene ways. All about them were these gray wisps, sentient and wicked. They edged toward the six travelers in hoppings and skippings that made them the more terrifying by their very lightheartedness.

Kothar yanked out Frostfire and strode to meet them.

Lori screamed, but the barbarian ignored her warning to slash sideways at a twisted bit of mist that slid to envelop him. Through the mist went Frostfire as though it slashed at air. Yet the gray thing touched the barbarian and where it fastened unseen claws, wet and slimy, burned with the fury of a thousand poisoned needles.

The barbarian bellowed, trying to shake free.

They were attacking the others. He saw Red Lori down on the ground, writhing and screaming, trying to battle the thing with her hands. And Phordog Fale was backed against a building wall, pushing, thrusting against a nothingness that ate at him.

Flarion used sword and dagger, but uselessly. In moments he was falling, yet still battling. And Cybala was a step beyond him, hands to her pretty face, screaming. Plump Nemidomes was crouched over a fallen bench, seeking to fend off those stinging mists.

It may have been the magic in the sword Frostfire that hurt the gray mists attacking Kothar. For suddenly as he slashed, their obscene chucklings and merry giggles turned to angry cries and shrill snarls. He could see the gray become scarlet, shot with anger. It seemed also that he could make out a serpentine form within the mists, and something so hideously shaped its very existence was a blasphemy against all that was normal and natural.

He also saw claws—sharply pointed, scarlet.

Instead of ripping just flesh, they tore into his mail and through the leather of his jerkin. He fought, though he was covered with a hundred wounds. Frostfire moved almost of its own will, in a figure-eight pattern that cut to left and right through those eerie beings.

They slashed the leather of his belt pouch, and out upon the courtyard paving tumbled the jewels and golden coins and bars that he had taken from the tomb of Kandakore. Along the flaggings they bounced while Kothar fought for his very life.

"Afgorkon! Aid me! Give me—strength!" he panted.

A serpentine red fog screamed horribly.

The claws went away, the beings drew back. Kothar panted, blood running from arms and chest and thighs. His sword was a very heavy weight in his hand, now; he wondered if he could lift it again to defend himself when the things—came back.

Yet they did not attack him again. He could hear their hissing speech faintly, as though from far away, as they retreated slowly from him and—from the others. Red Lori was sitting up, a hand to her fallen red hair, looking about her dazedly. Phordog Fale was slumped against the building wall while Cybala knelt weeping over an unconscious Flarion.

Nemidomes picked himself up, stared around him wildly. "They're—going! Leaving us. But—why?"

Kothar shook his head. Lori came to him, touched his bleeding arm and chest. "They cut right through your mail, the leather of your jerkin. Strange. To me their claws were like tiny teeth sunk into my blood, drinking my life. But you—"

The Cumberian shook his sword. "The magic in this thing hurt them, made them angry. They wanted to make me suffer before they took my life!"

"Why did they stop, Kothar?"

"I called on Afgorkon."

She shook her head. "No, it was more than that." She drew back, staring at the fallen gems and gold that had come out of his belt-purse. She bent down, ran her fingers across an emerald and a big ruby.

Kothar grinned, "My curse runs true, you see. For possessing Frostfire, I was about to lose more than my life. They took away my treasure first."

The witchwoman shook her head impatiently. "No, no. It was for some other reason, I'm sure. Phordog Fale! Nemidomes! Come help me."

They came running, but it was Lori who cried out, hand darting. Her fingers closed about a disc and lifted it toward the firelight from the campfire. It had grown dark, the city was shrouded by night. Yet, with the leaping flames reflecting on the disc, Kothar could see the intertwinings carved on its surface that had reminded him of a great snake, when he had first seen it, in a Zoane alleyway.

"The disc of Antor Nemillus," breathed the woman.

"I recognize it," the barbarian muttered.

Her green eyes glowed up at him. Her breasts moved to her excitement as she said, "Don't you understand? It was this that kept us safe—this!" Her fingers closed around the disc, and triumph flared in her stare. "He gave us—safekeeping with this thing. But those demon beings would only obey—their master!"

Phordog Fale scowled, "But that means—"

"Yes! Antor Nemillus wishes us dead. He sent those—those eerie things to devour us, not knowing who we were, only that we six travelers were dangerous to him. But the servants of Omorphon saw only the disc—Omorphon's self on it. They drew back away from it, thinking us protected by their lord."

She stood up. "We know now! Antor Nemillus is the one who has been slaying the magicians of Yarth! He sent soldiers to slay us before we could reach here with the eidolon! When that failed, he summoned up Omorphon's servants and set them upon us. Aye, he knows three of us are magicians, and that we pose a threat to him."

Kothar said, "But he was attacked in Zoane!"

"Someone learned he was the wizard-killer—sought to do what we've been trying to do—and failed when you stopped him, Kothar!"

"Find that man, then. Learn what he knows."

Red Lori shook her head. "No time for that. Antor Nemillus will know now that we are protected in some manner. He may or may not suspect the cause. We must act fast!"

"But how?" quavered fat Nemidomes.

The woman bit her lip, frowning.

"Magic won't work," grinned the barbarian. "You've tried that. Even Afgorkon with Belthamquar and Eldrak could not help us. Antor Nemillus is too well protected. Instead—send me."

"You?"

"Make a fake eidolon! Let me carry it to Zoane, offer it to the mage with the assurance that I am a turncoat, that I want no more of you. Let him think I would rather be on his side. Then—I'll take off his head with Frostfire."

She smiled faintly. "The barbarian treatment for any danger—slay it! No, no, we must be clever, Kothar. Clever!"

Yet when they had eaten, speaking all the time of plans and plots, they could not come up with any better idea. Lori did not like the plan, she said as much. Yet she could offer no other solution.

"He will kill you horribly, you know," she told him, "if he suspects the truth."

The Cumberian shrugged, reached for his fur cloak and rolled himself up in it to sleep. The witchwoman brooded at him, sighed, then turned her eyes to the fire to sit there, dreaming.

The soldiers of the king came early to Radimore, but they found the barbarian in the gateway with Flarion at his side. Kothar held aloft the safe conduct sigil that Antor Nemillus had given him.

"Why didn't you show that yesterday?" asked Captain Oddo.

"This is the seal of Antor Nemillus. You wear Midor's livery."

The war captain spat. "Same thing, these days. Midor does what his magician says, not having any will of his own. I'm not sure I ought to obey that device you hold—but I don't dare disobey. We'll ride back to Zoane and get further orders. Then—we may meet again."

He raised his hand, shouted to his horsemen. They rode back across the savannah in lines of two, like trained veterans. Kothar watched them go, finding a touch of kinship with these cavalrymen inside him. He was a soldier, a mercenary. At another time and in another place he might have been that war captain.

"Damn all magicians," he breathed.

Red Lori waited in the courtyard for him. "I have prepared a second eidolon," she muttered, tapping a stone statue that Kothar could not have told from the original. "I have summoned up Afgorkon, asked him to keep his eyes and ears on this simulacra. In such fashion shall we be able to keep in touch with you."

She hesitated, biting her lips. "Don't do something stupid in Zoane. Antor Nemillus is a clever mage, which is why I can't use cantraipal spells to send you to him, you have to go in the cart carrying the eidolon. It would never do for you to arrive in Zoane ahead of those soldiers."

An hour later he was moving through the gate, cartwheels creaking as the horse pulled at its harness straps. Kothar sat on the little seat, Greyling trotted at the end of a tether. His bow and saddle, arrow-quiver and sword lay in the back of the cart beside the statue. It would take several days to reach Zoane at this slow pace; before then, Antor Nemillus might well decide to slay Red Lori and the others.

* * * *

Three days later he creaked into the seaport city.

The gate guards passed him through. No man or woman sought to stop or even question him as the cart rattled across the cobbles toward the big town mansion which was the property of Antor Nemillus. Only when he came to stand at the oaken door of that house and knock, was there anyone to bar his way.

Then it was merely a servant girl, with long brown hair and an over-tight woolen tunic which showed off her ripe figure, who opened the door to him and stood aside with a flirtatious glance from her dark eyes.

"The master has been expecting you," she murmured.

As he followed her swaying haunches across a flagstoned lower hall, the barbarian wondered whether the magician knew also of his scheme to slay him. It was in something of a suspicious mood that he came to a stop in a great dining hall where Antor Nemillus sat to breakfast.

The necromancer was in high good humor, waving an expansive hand. "Come join me, man of the northlands. Sausages, chilled ale, freshly baked bread—ask of me what you will. I remember your face, you see, and the night you saved my life in an alleyway."

Kothar pulled back a chair, perched his rump onto it. Two pretty girls ran to place a wooden platter before him and serving trays heaped with steaming meat within easy reach. The magician watched him with sunken eyes in which the barbarian thought to read a sly mockery.

He ate warily, fearing poison, until the sorcerer taunted him for his fears. "I would never resort to anything so mundane as ground glass or hemlock. No, no. Mine is a better way. If I wanted to be rid of you—I could blast you into the vast abysses where Omorphon dwells. It would not be clean death. No!"

The Cumberian believed him, and so he ate more heartily. When he was done, he spoke of the eidolon, explaining how he fetched it from the sea and how Red Lori spoke to it. Of how he fought the soldiers and the mist-beings of the serpent-god he told freely and openly, while the mage popped dates into his mouth and munched, nodding his head from time to time.

"It is so my magical waters have showed me, barbarian. All these things you have done, yes. What troubles me is, why should you desert your friends?"

"Friends! What friends have I, a sellsword? Red Lori I put in a silver cage for Queen Elfa of Commoral. Later, I trapped her in the tomb of Kalikalides and sealed it with silver. Lori hates me, she considers me her property."

"And you would be free of her?"

"I like not magic," growled the barbarian, honestly enough, "but I've gotten into something I like no better than I do spells and incantations. I thought that by coming here and giving you this eidolon I stole, I might buy your friendship."

"And you have, Kothar. But I must make test of this statue, you understand that. It may be a cheat, a mere copy. Eh?"

Kothar did not betray himself. "It may. It—isn't."

"No, no. But we shall test it, you and I."

He rose, his gesture telling the barbarian there was work to be done in his necromantic chambers. Kothar weighed the chances of dragging out his sword and leaping at the magician.

He decided against it; this apparent friendliness of the wizard smacked too much of a trap. He wasn't even sure this was the real Antor Nemillus before him. Lori had warned him against doing anything stupid. He would wait, biding his time.

He followed the mage upward along a narrow stone staircase to an upper floor. There was a great apartment here, walled with stone and with a high, vaulted ceiling from which hung many cages at the end of chains. In the cages were bats and toads, black cats and newts, together with other small animals from which Antor Nemillus was wont to draw the things he needed for his incantations. Long counters were laden with crucibles and alembics, while the walls contained various magical instruments.

In the center of the flagstones which formed the floor, a red pentagram was shaped of crimson stone, before which was placed a prie-dieu on which rested a massive volume bound in leather, thrown open at a certain conjuration. The false eidolon had been set up behind this lectern.

Antor Nemillus invited Kothar to step into the pentagram with him, with a wave of the hand and a friendly smile. "Let me demonstrate my magicks, barbarian—so that you will know you have made the right choice in coming to me."

The Cumberian shifted his sword closer to his hand. The false eidolon would not work. How could it? Antor Nemillus would know he had been betrayed. Therefore, so that the magician-killer might not destroy him with some magical spell, he would run cold steel into his flesh as soon as he made the discovery.

He stepped inside the pentagram, followed by the mage.

Antor Nemillus put his hands on the open book, began reciting from its pages in a deep voice. As those words washed across the vast chamber, Kothar reached for his dagger hilt. His iron fingers locked around its braided haft.

He held the dagger ready, but could not use it.

For this incantation which the magician-killer was using turned the blood in a man's veins to ice. He stood there motionless, unable to do more than see and hear. Though he strained, his muscles were locked in a paralytic spasm.

And the necromancer went on reciting.

The far wall of the chamber turned to fog, drifted away, opening a cantraipal door into those nether spaces where swung the worlds of Belthamquar and Eldrak, Gargantos and Dakkag.

And—the world of—Omorphon!

Swiftly went the chamber across those abysses. Sweat stood out on the barbarian's forehead as his body swayed to the tricks of his eyes. The pentagram was the only floor beneath his war boots. It swept at terrifying speed above those black gulfs of emptiness, racing always onward toward—A glowing, up ahead! A whiteness that seemed to crawl as might a maggot across the dark deeps of space! And in that whiteness—something that twisted and turned, writhed and wriggled. Even Kothar did not need to ask what it was. Or who—was turning its flattened head toward the moving pentagram.

Wicked eyes in a serpent head, wise with the knowledge of the ages' evil, stared at the on-comers. Larger grew Omorphon. Larger, larger, until it filled the universe about them and the pentagram with its two human riders was no more than a midge before those beady eyes.

"I see you, mage. My servants complain that you gave their victims the disc with my symbol on it, as a protection against their—hungers."

"I did, dread Omorphon. Before I knew they were to be victims. These six whom I intended to feed to your servitors are nothing to me. They shall be fed to your fiends yet. I have sent soldiers to fetch them from Radimore."

"It is well. But why come to me now?"

"There is an eidolon in my chambers. I suspect it is not the true eidolon of the mage Afgorkon who lived fifty thousand years ago—"

"And still lives, Antor Nemillus, in his own worlds."

"Ah, does he so? Then perhaps the eidolon is not so false as I imagined."

"There is a way to test it. Long ago Afgorkon and I were—good friends. The spell of stone tongues will make it speak, if it be that true eidolon."

"My gratitude, great Omorphon. And to show my good will, send your servitors to my chambers, where they shall find their feast awaiting them."

The serpent god inclined its head.

Instantly the pentagram was moving back across those vast infinities of space. There was no wind, no sensation of flying other than the fact that the stars moved slowly to left and right of them. Those tiny blue points of light came and receded, and Kothar felt that they were traversing unfathomable stretches of megacosmic emptiness.

The pentagram firmed.

The stood in the chamber of Antor Nemillus once more. And across the great room—grouped together and unmoving as himself—the Cumberian saw Red Lori, with plump Nemidomes and old Phordog Fale flanking her. Flarion and Cybala stood to one side, the belly dancer half fainting in her terror.

There was fear on all their faces, even on the lovely features of the witchwoman. Possibly her green eyes showed more horror than the others, for she knew what was to be their fate, she understood that Omorphon the serpent deity had aligned itself with the mage of Zoane in his quest for supremacy on Yarth.

To die by Omorphon's servitors was not a nice death.

"Kothar!" she whimpered. "Aid us!"

Antor Nemillus turned, smiled at the barbarian. "Tell them, Kothar. Tell them how you stole the eidolon of Afgorkon and brought it here to me."

"I did as he says," muttered the Cumberian.

"And now to test that statue," nodded the mage.

With long, pallid fingers he turned the pages of the book until he came at last to the spell of stone tongues. And he recited what was written there, faintly smiling when he heard Red Lori moan in her anguish, and saw Nemidomes wipe at the sweat running down his face.

The eidolon was silent.

"What?" cried Antor Nemillus in pretended dismay. "Does not this spell work? Omorphon himself said I should attempt it, and that if the eidolon spoke with me, it would prove to be that fabled simulacra of dread Afgorkon.

"So speak, statue—speak!"

The magician waited, shaking his head dolefully. "It seems it is no more than ordinary stone, perhaps it was even conjured into being by Red Lori who has appointed herself my nemesis. Is it so, redhead?"

Red Lori was silent.

"Too bad, too bad. In such case, I must blast it, then summon the servants of the serpent god to—feast."

Cybala shrieked, head thrown back and quivering.

Antor Nemillus laughed, lips twisted in a cruel smile. "The dancer is blameless, I feel, yet Omorphon would not like it if I withheld her from their eating."

The belly dancer moaned and sagged against Flarion, who held her in his arms. The youth was white with the abysmal terror that held him in its grip; like Kothar, he could fight anything animal or human, but he knew a primal fear where demons of the nether spaces were concerned.

And yet, he drew his sword.

Kothar felt a faint throbbing coming to his war boots from the pentagram. He was puzzled by it. It sounded like the beating of a giant heart, but where in Zoane would such a heart exist? Throb, throb, throb! It made a steady cadence throughout the town house.

An tor Nemillus did not hear it, apparently. Or if he did, he was so familiar with it that he paid it no attention. Instead he turned and smiled coldly at the Cumberian.

"Did you know this eidolon was false, barbarian? Are you part of the plot against me, whereby Red Lori would pull me down to death and make empty vaporings of all my dreams? I could use a man like you, but not if you are one of these conspirators. So I abjure thee. Speak!"

Kothar fought the magic that flooded his great body, fought and groaned against the telling, but the magic of Antor Nemillus was stronger than his muscles. His lips writhed back and his tongue curled to life.

"The eidolon is—false! It was made by the witchwoman and given to me to bring to you, that you might betray yourself so we would know you for the magician-killer. It succeeded of its purpose but—"

"But the knowledge will do you no good! For I have condemned you all to Omorphon, who will feast on your energies through his servitors. See!… They come!"

The mage swept his black-robed arm in an arc.

The walls faded. Leaping across the void, sweeping with dizzying speed toward their world, were the eerie beings whom Kothar had battled in Radimore. He saw their curving gray shapes, their fog-like fiendishness, and knew they were all doomed.

He groaned. Underfoot the throbbing was becoming louder, more menacing, and he wondered if these were the sounds made by those oncoming mist beings. He strove against the spell that held him in thrall, fighting vainly to free Frostfire so that he might go down fighting, at least.

Nemidomes was a whimpering mass of wet flesh pressed against a stone wall. Phordog Fale was rigid, eyes wide as if he already looked on that land which is said to exist after death. Red Lori was biting her knuckles, and Flarion stood over the crumpled form of the unconscious Cybala.

They were like hogs to the slaughter.

Antor Nemillus threw back his head and laughed. His laughter only echoed the swirlings of the serpentine things through the vanished chamber wall and onto the flagstones. Cybala awoke, screamed.

And at that moment, thunder shook the house.

CHAPTER EIGHT

So terrific was that awesome burst of sound that Antor Nemillus looked upward; even the gray life-drinkers paused. A brick fell from the vaulted ceilings, missing the barbarian by a foot. The thunderclap shattered their eardrums a second time, and now the building swayed. Antor Nemillus cursed in his pentagram and sprang toward his open *grimoire*.

The stone wall quivered, stones fell.

A great hand—a thing of stone and rock, hideously carved and with strange spells and incantations limned on its rock surface—reached in the opening it had made, and stabbed forward. Blunt fingers closed around the squirming, screaming necromancer.

"Dread Omorphon! Awful being of the nether hells—aid me!"

Antor Nemillus tried to fight it, but his hands could do nothing against the solid rock out of which that other hand was formed. The fingers tightened, and now the magician began to swell curiously at chest and legs, as if other parts of his body were being forced into them by that frightful grip. His face became purple with congested blood. His eyes bulged hideously, a trickle of blood ran from his open mouth.

The magician tried to cry out, could not.

Another hand came into the chamber, making its own opening by crashing through another part of the wall. It slapped at the whirling gray fog-things, smashing two of them flat, and as it did, tiny scarlet bubbles burst and splattered a malodorous ichor across the flagstones. The other serpentine beings squealed, shrieked, turned to flee.

The stone hand was lightning, darting as might a human hand after flies, catching up those things and squeezing them until they plopped and died, gushing that noisome fluid. Only two got away, darting back into the spaces vaguely glimpsed behind the stone wall. The others lay in tiny puddles of their own slime, lifeless.

Antor Nemillus finally burst. His chest and legs—or what had been these portions of his body—were so filled with that which had been in his middle that the skin of his torso and his thighs exploded. Bits of blood and flesh flew here and there.

The stone hand holding his body opened its fingers. The dead magician dropped to the flaggings, lay inert. And the spell on Kothar went away.

The big Cumberian shook himself, leaped from the pentagram to catch Red Lori the witchwoman as she swayed oddly, overcome by the reaction to her terror. She sagged against him, let him lift her up and hold her close.

"You did what you planned to do," he growled.

"But not—this way," she breathed.

She stared at the huge stone hands, gruesomely stained and soiled, as they withdrew out of the openings in the walls through which they had come. Behind them, Flarion was lifting Cybala from the floor. Phordog Fale was pushing away from the wall where he had been so close to fainting. Nemidomes was still sobbing fitfully, the aftermath of his fright making him shiver like pale jelly.

"Are we truly—saved?" whimpered Cybala.

"If the gods so will," growled Flarion.

Kothar carried Red Lori, whose legs were so shaky she did not trust her weight to them, across the room toward a narrow window. They stared out at the city of Zoane in the fading sunlight of a late afternoon, seeing its streets clogged with men and women staring upward, silent before the awe that held them.

"Look," whispered the witchwoman.

The barbarian saw a stone statue—the eidolon of Afgorkon—grown to an immense height. Its shadow, cast by the setting sun, appeared to dance across the rooftops of the city. It towered high, titanic, an incredible monster from the worlds of magic. Blood and ichor dripped from its stone fingers. It had no face. This was its awfulness, its cantraipal horror.

It turned on a heel and walked away to the west. Toward ancient Radimore, Kothar thought. Its stone feet made muted thumpings on the ground, that came upward to the flagstone floor of this town house chamber; it had been these he had felt as he stood within the pentagram with Antor Nemillus.

"We must follow," breathed Red Lori.

"But why? Your task is done."

She stirred against him. "Have you forgotten the sacrifice? He must be offered a living maiden. Otherwise, he may choose to stay within our world—like that."

"Flarion won't like it," Kothar growled.

The witchwoman smiled cruelly. "It doesn't matter what he likes. Or the girl, either. Their destiny is linked with mine, they must obey."

She stirred against him. "Have you forgotten..." She paused, then called, "Phordog Fale! Nemidomes!"

The magicians came hurrying across the floor to her. They seemed to have recovered a bit of their normal color, and something of their old bravery.

"We must return to Radimore at once," the woman told them. "We have one last task to perform. Flarion! Cybala! Come you with us."

They went down the stone steps away from the shattered chamber and out onto the cobbles of the courtyard, where there were horses waiting. Kothar swung Red Lori into the high-peaked saddle of her bay mare, then mounted up on Greyling. At a canter, he led the way into the crowded streets of the city. And as he did so, he urged the gray warhorse nearer the mare.

"Stay you close to my stirrup, Lori," he muttered.

The men and women of Zoane were in holiday mood, as if some enormous weight had been lifted from their shoulders. They were drunk, reeling about with wineskins in their hands, their garments half torn from their bodies. An air of saturnalia was everywhere, a forgetfulness of daily living, a need for merrymaking.

"They may prove dangerous, they may seek to drag us from our saddles to join their revels. I'll break a few heads, if need be, to get us through."

The people ignored them, they were too concerned with their drinking and their wenching to bother about six strangers. Toward nightfall, their mood might turn ugly. The barbarian knew it was the way of drinkers at feasting time. He touched the gray warhorse with a toe, urged it to a faster canter.

He could hear words occasionally from the mob.

"—gone, we can live again!"

"Aye, no need to fear the taking of our wives and daughters for the use of Antor Nemillus and the king!"

"It might be a good thing if Midor died, as well!"

"To the palace, then. Kill the old goat."

They came to a few streets where town houses stood fence by railing with one another, away from the throngs and the merrymakers. It was quiet here, Kothar sensed a frightened face or two peering out from behind draperies and shutters. From here he could see a little park ahead, and beyond that the start of the caravan road to distant Romm and Memphor.

Once on that highway, they would make good time.

All that night they went at a gallop along the hard-packed dirt of the trade road, until they were well within the boundaries of Tharia. Then Kothar turned from that highway eastward toward Radimore.

They came into the ancient ruins at midday, weary with long riding. Red Lori swayed oddly in her saddle; she was near her limits of endurance, the big barbarian realized. He leaped from the saddle, caught her as she lifted a leg over the kak, lowered her to the ground.

"I'm weary. Weary," she murmured.

"Then sleep," he nodded.

He caught her up in his massively muscled arms, walked with her to the inner court where he had fought the mist beings of Omorphon, and laid her down upon the pile of soft grasses that had been her pallet.

"I will make sacrifice later, Kothar," she murmured, smiling and letting him drape her in his fur cloak.

He waited until she was sleeping before he turned and went in search of Flarion. He found the youth with his arms about Cybala in a darkened corner of the quadrangle, whispering to her.

"Mount and ride," he told him. "Travel toward Ebboxor, where I will meet you—when I can."

Cybala pushed her black hair back from her eyes. "Does danger threaten us here?"

"It threatens you, girl. Red Lori plans to offer you to Afgorkon as a sacrifice."

The belly dancer gasped, shrank closer to Flarion. "Is this why she chose me to accompany you? That she might slay me—when Afgorkon did her will?"

"Mount and ride, stop asking questions I answered onboard the ship!"

Flarion smiled faintly, "We travel at once. And, Kothar—my thanks!"

They ran lightly toward their horses. Their mounts were weary with the long night galloping, but Flarion would walk them, with the girl beside him, until fresh strength came back into their legs. Then he would mount and gallop toward Ebboxor to the north. It was imperative they leave Radimore, be far away when Red Lori awoke.

Kothar turned toward Phordog Fale and Nemidomes where the two magicians sat crouched about a little fire the plump man had made.

"Go you also away from here," he growled.

Nemidomes protested, "My backside is sore, and my legs are jelly. I shall wait and eat, and decide with the witchwoman what we shall do."

Kothar grinned coldly. "The witchwoman is about to sacrifice a girl who won't be here," he rasped, waving a hand after Cybala and Flarion who moving down the cobbled street toward the broken gate. "What do you think Afgorkon will do, being deprived of his sacrifice?"

Phordog Fale frowned worriedly. "It's a thought to worry one," he admitted. "I for one, would not choose to stay and face Afgorkon's wrath—having seen what his eidolon did to Antor Nemillus."

"Nor I," the plump mage murmured.

They rose to their feet and walked toward their horses, with the big barbarian treading on their heels. The morning sun was high—it was almost midday—and a soft breeze was blowing through the dead city.

"Why not use a magic spell to leave?" wondered Kothar.

Phordog Fale turned and stared at the barbarian, nodding. "Aye, a spell. I have been so busy riding horseback lately, I've forgotten I'm a necromancer."

Nemidomes beamed his delight. "Ah, to be back in Vandacia once again, not forced out of fear to hide in that charnel house. I owe you much, Kothar!"

"And I," nodded Phordog Fale.

The shook hands solemnly. Nemidomes wrapped himself in his cloak, closed his eyes and whispered a word. His outline shimmered. Kothar could see the stone wall behind that mistiness for an instant, then the plump man was gone.

Phordog Fale snorted, "A clumsy spell, that one. It does not drain the body energies, true. Yet it is slow. Too slow for me. Observe!"

The tall, lean man chanted words in a language unknown to Kothar. Instantly, he was gone. The Cumberian grinned, shaking his head. "I would rather know that little song than the word Nemidomes used," he thought, "if I had to leave a place in a hurry." He laughed and moved toward Red Lori.

It was warm in this midday, and there was an ache in his body, now that the need for action was at an end. He sank down beside the witchwoman and closed his eyelids. Almost at the same moment, he fell asleep.

* * * *

A hand on his arm shook him awake to the sight of stars in the sky. The lovely face of his companion was bent above him. "Where are the others? Cybala? Where has she gone?"

"I sent her away with Flarion. Go back to sleep."

He heard a gasp, felt fingernails sink into his bare forearm. "Wake up, you! You—thing! I promised her life to Afgorkon. You knew that!"

"Afgorkon takes no sacrifices."

"He does. He will. Oh, get up!"

The barbarian rose to his feet. The city ruins were silent, lost and lovely, having forgotten the lives they sheltered once, long ago. The starlight was weak and pale, but Kothar could make out the eidolon standing where he had left it when he had taken its simulacra to Zoane. His eyes pierced its stone hands, folded now against its sides. Those rock fingers were stained and befouled with the blood of Antor Nemillus and with the ichor squashed from the servitors of dread Omorphon.

"What are you going to do with it?"

Red Lori stared from the barbarian to the eidolon. "I must summon its spirit, as I promised. But—without Cybala to offer it…"

She drew closer to the Cumberian. Kothar scowled, staring at the image. Was he mistaken, was it a trick of the light—or had the statue moved? No, by Dwallka! It was moving, turning its rock head toward them.

"Aye, Red Lori. I am here. Where is this life you offered me?"

The eidolon grew a little. It was not the titanic monster that had slain Antor Nemillus, it rose upward only until it was the height of a tall man. Yet now it turned more fully toward the barbarian and the witchwoman, and though it had no face, the Cumberian sensed the awful life imprisoned in that thing of rock.

"I wait, Red Lori! Where is the sacrifice?"

She swallowed twice before she could reply. "I have—none! The girl fled away with Flarion."

A chuckle was its answer. "I saw the barbarian send them away. I have no quarrel with him for his action. Yet where shall I find my payment?"

The girl beside Kothar shuddered. A whiteness came to her cheeks, and her eyes seemed to grow as she stared at the eidolon.

"I know—not, Afgorkon."

"Then I shall take other life in its place. Your life, witchwoman!" The eidolon stirred, turned and moved toward Red Lori.

"By Dwallka—no!" roared Kothar.

His arm tightened about the girl, thrust her behind him. His hand he put on the hilt of Frostfire, half drawing it from the scabbard. Red Lori was shaking fitfully, convulsed with terror.

"What would you, Kothar?" asked the statue.

"Her—life!"

"And what price have you, a pauper, to offer me in exchange for that life? You own—nothing. It was not your doing, this summoning up of my spirit from where I lay in the fifty worlds of my own creation! I have no argument with you, so—step aside."

Kothar drew his sword. His eyes ran down the blued steel blade, slid over the golden crosspiece, the braided hilt, the red jewel affixed to its pommel. He sighed softly. There was a sorrow in him, a wretchedness of spirit, yet he did not hesitate.

"Take—back—Frostfire," he growled.

He flung the blade across the courtyard so that it clanged on the cobblestones before the eidolon. It lay there, mute and beautiful, gathering sunbeams along its blade.

There was a silence.

"You would give up Frostfire?"

His mouth was dry, his tongue stuck to the roof of his mouth, but the barbarian nodded. When he could speak, he almost snarled.

"Aye—I would! Let Red Lori be. Take the sword."

The witchwoman gasped beside him, she pressed closer as if to assure him that by choosing her, he chose well. His nostrils caught the scent of her perfume, his flesh knew the smoothness of her own where her arm brushed his side. She was still afraid, he sensed from the hurried rise and fall of her breasts, but she was so curious as to what Afgorkon would do, she no longer quivered.

The faceless thing considered them as they stood side by side with the barbarian's heavily muscled arm about Red Lori's slim body. The sun beat down, and somewhere in the ruins a bird chattered. Otherwise, there was only the brooding silence.

Then: "Take up Frostfire, barbarian! It is too lovely a thing to lie hidden in my death chamber. And besides, it comes to me that you will make good use of it in the days and years to come.

"No, I seek not Frostfire. Nor the life of the redheaded wench you seem to love. Yet there is something I must do to her.

"Red Lori—come you forward!"

The woman stirred within the clasp of Kothar's arm. He caught the moan of fear in her throat. He would have moved to thrust himself between her and the eidolon except that his own body seemed turned to the same stone as that from which the statue had been carved. His arm fell away as the redhead moved forward.

His eyes watched her walk slowly, gracefully, toward the statue. In her Mongrol garb, she seemed only a pretty girl. The blouse was torn, shredded from long usage, so he could see the pale skin of her back. Under the leather kilt, her legs were curving columns. He wanted to reach out, catch and hold her.

The statue waited as she neared it. Then lifted its stone arms and put its hands on Red Lori's shoulders, gripping her gently. Where those stone fingers touch, a faint miasma rose upward like steam. The girl shook, but made no sound.

The stone hands lowered.

Red Lori crumpled and lay on the courtyard cobblestones. Over her motionless body, the eidolon stared at the barbarian. It spoke no word but turned and clumped away, its stone feet making those same thumping sounds. Kothar watched it move between the shattered columns of an ancient temple and disappear from view.

He stirred, his chest lifted as he sucked in air. He ran to the girl, turned her over, sliding an arm beneath her pale neck. Her eyes were closed, but she breathed—red lips slightly parted, breasts lifting and falling. Kothar bent his head, pressed lips to that soft mouth.

She stirred, opened her eyes. Those green eyes saw him, but they knew him not. Her eyes went back and forth around the courtyard buildings.

"Where—where am I?" she whispered, shrinking slightly from his arm. *"Who* am I? And—who are you?"

Kothar sighed. Afgorkon had taken his sacrifice, after all. He had robbed Red Lori of her necromantic knowledge, even of her memory. She was indeed, little more than a lovely shepherdess or milkmaid now. The barbarian grinned. This was the way he had always wanted her.

"You belong to me," he told her. "I—bought you in a slave market in Zoane."

She frowned at him prettily. "I don't remember."

"You had an—accident. But never mind that. Your name is Lori and you belong to me. So come, wench—stir yourself. We've a long ride ahead of us."

His big hand helped her to her feet. She pushed her red hair from her face, she stared down at herself, at her worn, travel-stained garments. Her cheeks flushed faintly when she saw how much of her body was revealed through the tears and rips.

"Fetch the foodbags," he said gently.

They rode together out of Radimore just as the sun was going down in the west. They had not far to go, they would be in Ebboxor before midnight. And from Ebboxor? Where would he turn Greyling after that? He was tired of spells and incantations and magicians. There was a yearning for something more substantial than necromancy in his heart.

He rode thoughtfully beside the silent girl.

When they came to Ebboxor, there was a red fire blazing and Flarion sitting beside Cybala, who leaned against his encircling arm. They would have risen, but Kothar waved them aside. He helped Red Lori down, watched as she took out meat and bread from the saddlebags.

"What ails her?" wondered Flarion, studying the girl.

"Afgorkon took away her memory."

They ate, and when they were done, Kothar drew the girl down beside him on his fur cloak. He made her pillow her red head on his chest, so he could put an arm about her and hold her close.

"Who am I? What was my past life?" she whispered.

"Later, girl. Sleep now."

They slept as once before they had slept amid these ruins. And with the coming of morning, as once before, the barbarian woke with a sword-point at his bare throat. He stared up at a hard bronzed face along the jaw of which ran a jagged scar. The steel *camail* made tinkling sounds as the war captain lowered his head slightly.

"We meet once more, barbarian. This time, you have no bow in hand, you have no weapons of any kind."

The soldiers with Captain Oddo were few in number. There were only six that he saw, until a seventh came from between two stone pillars carrying half a dozen waterskins. One he handed to Oddo of Ottrantor, the others he passed among the six hard-bitten men who rode behind the war captain.

Flarion was on the ground beside Cybala, both of them trussed like fowls for the bake ovens. Red Lori was also tied at wrists and ankles, and she stared at him dumbly, like patient beast waiting for its master to save her.

Oddo grinned coldly. "You did me a lot of harm, barbarian. Not only on the road to Radimore, but in Zoane as well." He lifted the waterskin, putting the narrow nozzle between his lips and quaffing deep.

The back of his worn velvet sleeve worked across his lips. "We came so fast from Zoane, we had no time to fill our waterskins. It was a long, dusty ride."

Kothar growled, "What harm did I do you in Zoane?"

"Pah! You helped destroy Antor Nemillus, who was my master. Not Midor, no. That fat slug took orders from his mage. I wore his livery, but I was the mage's man. Well, now—that's all ended, thanks to you. So you shall pay."

His eyes ran up and down Red Lori. "I'll take her as part payment of the debt you owe me. The other one," his head jerked at Cybala, "my men can have. You die, barbarian—to pay the rest of the debt."

Captain Oddo grimaced putting a hand to his middle. "Father of demons—what foul poison was in that water? It eats in my belly like a snake!"

Kothar glanced beyond the war captain at the seven soldiers. They too, were making contorted faces, their hands clawing at their bellies. Captain Oddo took a step, shuddering.

"You men—come here!" he bawled.

Has men were in no position to obey. Three of them were on their knees, the others were staggering about and moaning. The barbarian waited, watching Oddo of Ottrantor, who was trying to lift his sword and strike at him. Almost gently, the Cumberian withdrew the sword from those nerveless fingers.

"The curse of Ebboxor, Oddo," he muttered. The war captain fell to sprawl out on the ground. Kothar stood above him, asking, "Saw you not the skeletons as you rode into camp? No, I suppose not. It makes no difference, now. I think Afgorkon may have put an added thirst in your throats as you rode this way, however."

He waited with the animal patience of the barbarian until Captain Oddo and his men were dead. Then he cut Lori free, and from her he went to Flarion and Cybala. When they stood beside him, he nodded his head.

"It is over, all of it. Lori and I ride west toward the lands of the robber barons. I am weary of sorcery and wizards. I would take employment with the thieves, perhaps even get to command a band of my own. It is in my mind that a smart man might unite those warring baronies and make a kingdom for himself."

"What of her?" wondered Flarion, gesturing at the redheaded woman who stood rubbing her wrists where the ropes had bitten.

"She has no memory. I'll tell her only what I think she ought to know. Then mayhap I'll marry her. Who knows?"

He walked toward the girl who smiled at him, weakly but with promise. Her green eyes met his and fell before his stare. Flarion turned and strode toward Cybala. He and the belly dancer would head north into Makkadonia beyond Sybaros. Idly he swung his head and looked behind him.

Kothar was lifting the smiling girl into the kak.